The **Summer Festival is**

MURDER

Jill M. Lyon

atmosphere press

To my much-loved husband Ralph,
who rarely reads fiction.

Prologue

Take my word for it: if you don't live in a small town now, you probably shouldn't move to one. If you've been stuck in big-city traffic for hours, or on a crowded flight for yet another seemingly pointless business trip, or in the third stupid meeting of the day devoted to something best solved with a memo, moving to that beautiful small town probably sounds quite appealing. Nice scenery, slower pace, friendly neighbors, doing something you love . . . yes, it sounds idyllic.

Resist these impulses. Trust me. Miss Marple was right: all the evil of the world can be found in the average country village. Since we don't have many of those in the U.S., "rural town" works just as well. The evil is there, sometimes not far from the surface and in surprising places.

Chapter One

It was mid-July in Sheffield, Oregon, one of thousands of American small towns with similar qualities and similar problems. The weekly exercise class was breaking up. There were only four of us besides the instructor, so goodbyes didn't take long: a wave and a "See you next week!" I threw a light sweater over my yoga pants and tank top, waved goodbye to everyone, and went out the door of the storefront into Main Street. A quick look up and down—no traffic, no surprise—and I crossed the street to my car, enjoying the cool sunshine and cooler breeze after an hour of moderately hard breathing.

The drive down Main Street was truly "down," since it headed downhill toward the river that, here, was only a few miles from the Pacific. I glanced at the late-Victorian City Hall, which showed three people going in and out its heavy wooden doors; saw one local merchant heading into his neighbor's store, probably for coffee and a chat because his own premises were empty; saw four women inside a storefront beauty salon, all talking with each other. Most of the buildings I passed, before turning left up another hill toward home, were closely spaced and two-story, built in the first half of the twentieth century: they were painted different colors, had differing roof styles. A fair number of them were empty, at least on the main floor; a local housing shortage meant all of them had people living upstairs. The strongest impression most visitors would have felt would be that of quiet.

It had been decades since Main Street was truly busy on a normal day. That quiet was one of the worrying things about Sheffield.

My name is Felice Bowes, and after a moderately successful career in Washington, D.C., my husband David Titus and I had succumbed to the small-town impulse and moved to Sheffield. We had lived in a suburb of 60,000 for more than fifteen years and dealt with commutes that seemed to become longer and surlier every year. Let's just say that the old song by The Animals, "We Gotta Get Out of This Place," had started to be the underlying hum of daily life. So, after some research and visits to various communities, we found a big old house here and made the cross-country trek.

My drive this afternoon reminded me again that this is a beautiful place to live. Tall trees, sparkling water, all the fresh fish and blackberries—ripe at this time of year—one could want. Okay, the blackberry vines are considered unkillable weeds, and most of the fish gets shipped to the East Coast for people who are willing to pay three times as much for a nice piece of salmon on a plate with some grilled veggies. But—it isn't truly cold in the winter or hot in the summer. We actually take blankets and jackets to summer picnics. The pace is slow, especially during the long rainy se-ason when everyone hunkers down and tries to avoid SAD, that seasonal disorder for people who don't get enough sun.

Oh, yes, the stereotype is correct—it rains a *lot*. We

measure it in feet. The local paint store tries hard by announcing its "color of the month," but you really can't fight the creep of green during the rainy season. Algae, moss, mold, mildew . . . but I digress.

I come by my pragmatism honestly. When you have lived a few decades and in more than a few places, and worked around a lot of characters, you see things differently from those whose focus is limited to family and friends within a thirty-mile radius. Like, say, most of the people living in a small town in an isolated bit of Oregon coast. I won't be rude and say anything about inbreeding; that probably ended when the highway came through in the '30s.

Over a course of years, David and I—we had met when I first moved to D.C.—had found that we could make good friends in Sheffield, but mostly among people who had been somewhere else. We had been asked and had served on some City committees as well as volunteering elsewhere. Some longtime locals might give us funny looks, but we kept on trying to participate, even if we couldn't blend in.

And we couldn't. This place is *different.* The drive down Sheffield's uber-quiet Main Street confirmed each time what I had learned about our home, that there are tradeoffs for the beauty of the place. Fewer people live in all of Norfolk County, which totals about 500 square miles, than in our former D.C. suburb. Towns are small. Roads are twisting, narrow, conifer-lined canyons, and shopping centers—the way most Americans think of shopping centers—are nearly nonexistent. One tries hard to "buy local," but it isn't always possible. I had developed close relationships with various websites to take care of almost any need outside the basics. And for some goods and services, there simply isn't anything available, at least publicly. David and I had learned, bemusedly, that the proper procedure was to ask around until you found that someone's brother-in-law Ted "does that on the side" and will come to your house if the right person asks him.

And did I mention that it rains? Around the end of September, outdoor life pretty much comes to an end, except for the hunters and fishers who don layers of waterproofs and enjoy the various fall seasons—such as duck season, elk season, deer season, or salmon season. The rest of us head inside and wait for April. Or May. Sometimes June or July. We look outside to note whether it is currently misting, drizzling, raining, or blowing sideways in sheets.

Thus, during the months when it is *not* raining, we celebrate the fight against moss by holding festivals. Lots of them. There isn't a weekend between late May and early September without a choice of festivals along, and near, the coast. It's by far the busiest time of year.

We have a festival designed to let everyone show off all the stuff they made during the long months they were stuck inside. There is a festival to celebrate starting plants in our gardens that might even have tomatoes by September. And in five thousand-soul-strong Sheffield, among the eight or so events that take place during the dry season (aka, "summer"), the biggest one of them all is . . . the Summer Festival.

Really, that's its name.

The Summer Festival has been held for decades. This is a longtime logging town, with a lot of hard-working people still engaged in timber, fishing, and other natural resource jobs, along with those who commute (although this is one area in which David and I must scoff a bit—thirty minutes does not a *real* commuter make) to government and other jobs in the region. The Summer Festival is an opportunity for everyone to show up along the river, enjoy the midway, see a traditional logging show, and watch great fireworks. Sheffield gets about twenty thousand visitors for the weekend, especially for the fireworks. It's a great show, and we take a lot of pride in it. There was no other event all year that would bring more people, or that was more important to those living here.

The Festival was just a week away now, but I didn't expect to be discussing it when I ran to answer the phone as I came into the house, dodging the dog on our wood kitchen floor.

"Felice, you won't believe what happened during the Festival meeting this morning!" Friend and City Councilor Kate Dennis was on the other end. "The Festival Committee met with some of the Council to finalize some details, and I was lucky to get out of there without bruises!"

"What happened?"

"It's the mayor. She came into the meeting with the city manager, and suddenly, the two of them are talking about wanting a piece of the gate proceeds for the City. This year. With the Festival only a week away. I thought the Festival Committee members' heads would explode."

"Greta said that?" My jaw dropped. "Has she completely lost it?"

Greta Sutton, Sheffield's current mayor, is a retired public school social studies teacher with delusions of intelligence. Having served with her on a couple of committees, I admit freely that I don't like the woman. Short and round, her face is surrounded by salt-and-pepper hair and black cat eyeglasses (honestly, what decade is this?). More annoyingly for those having to deal with her, she is convinced that she knows more than anyone else, refuses to listen to any opinion other than her own, and, quite illegally in Oregon, follows up the force of her convictions by using behind-the-scenes conversations to strong-arm other councilors into voting with her.

It also had been noticed that she has problems with math. Making sure the budget included the actual funds to pay for her ideas was never high on her list of priorities; she generally just waved her arms and murmured something like, "We'll get a grant." If she had glommed on to the idea of demanding a piece of the action of the Summer Festival now, you had to wonder what havoc she had already wreaked on the City budget that would make her stop and think about finding some real money.

I started wondering about this myself and frowned into the phone.

"She said she was bringing up the issue for this year in hopes that the Committee would help the City 'voluntarily,'" continued Kate.

Uh-oh.

"But she says she's going to bring a resolution to the Council after the Festival and require it before the City signs the contract for the Festival to use the waterfront park next year."

"Well, you're a councilor—did you know about this?"

"Not a word, I swear! I can't believe she would come to a meeting with an idea like this without talking to at least some of us."

"She does know that you aren't her biggest fan, Kate."

Kate Dennis was in her first term as a Council member, a surprise choice by the voters over Greta's handpicked candidate. She was smart, knew about money from her years working in finance, and wasn't afraid to voice her questions and opinions during meetings—all of which made her dangerous to the mayor. Kate would not have been one of those approached as a likely ally. Now, I pictured tall Kate pacing with her hand clenched in her short, dark hair, as she did when she was frustrated or upset. There would be a frown in her big brown eyes.

"That woman makes me crazy, Felice," Kate said into my ear. "She's been here about twenty years, and I think she's messed up just about everything she's touched. Yeah, she taught social studies at the high school, but then she tried to get all the County school board members kicked out so she could run that. The school district budget was a mess when she was finished."

"You mean she's done this kind of thing before?" I couldn't help blurting out. "And was elected mayor anyway?"

"She has fans among the parents who don't pay attention," Kate groused. "You know how it is. They got sweet smiles and 'don't you have a lovely child' during parent-teacher conferences and then weren't reading the paper when she started carrying on later. I wish I could think she's trying to act in the community's best interests, but somehow, everything she does is designed to benefit herself and a few friends.

"You know," Kate continued, "I think she actually believes that local government is supposed to be about doing yourself favors."

"I wonder where she picked that up," I mused. "And given her history, you have to wonder what's she's up to now."

"I don't know," said Kate. "But I think I need to start asking more questions. Something doesn't smell right. In the meantime, she has a bunch of pissed-off Festival Committee members wondering about the future of their event. I was really glad the Draper family didn't bring axes to the meeting."

The Drapers were one of the two or three longtime logging families who made the Festival work. They had been in Sheffield for nearly a century, and the Summer Festival was their event. They and the other logging family members who made up the Festival Committee worked on it all year and raised quite respectable amounts of money to put on the midway, contests, and fireworks, among other aspects of the weekend. They also organized all the logistics, including the nonprofit groups, which themselves benefited by helping with food service and parking, and the bands that played to the thousands who showed up. No one messed with the Festival without encountering the Drapers. It was another secret about Sheffield that only emerged when you asked the wrong questions.

Kate and I talked about some personal stuff and then signed off. I made some much-needed exercise-recovery coffee and then went to work on email, one of our two cats "helping" me by sitting on the desk while I worked.

I didn't think much more about the conversation for the rest of the week. I did read in the local paper that the Festival was hurting for volunteers; groups offering pancake breakfasts, handling parking, and the like were said to be begging for help. I stay away from this stuff. I like to help, but inefficiency bugs me, and I've found that people who have run things for a long time get offended easily, even if I just ask to help and keep my mouth shut. There seem to be lots of exceedingly small ponds out there that are fiercely defended by their fish, and they're easily scared by outsiders. So, my efforts are confined to government committees, where there are rules to follow and, usually, people reading from the same hymnal, so to speak.

David had learned this the hard way. Unlike me, he had eagerly jumped into community organizations around Sheffield, going to meetings and volunteering on projects. With more than thirty years' experience in both local government and community groups, he often had some ideas on how projects might raise more than a hundred bucks. This had led to several instances of his coming home saying, "I can't believe they're doing it this way!" Although he was careful not to say this in front of the group members, my mostly mild-mannered husband had spoken up, offered ideas, and even defended them, often with frank remarks. This had served to earn him a reputation as a rabble-rouser. Which was sort of funny, even if it did make me want to shout his praises from the steps of City Hall occasionally.

Since this is one of the few parts of the country where you can count on needing blankets and jackets to watch July fireworks, everyone was surprised when, just before the beginning of the Festival, the weather turned hot. Not our usual definition of "Wow, it's hot today," which is heard any time the mercury climbs above seventy degrees. This was truly sweltering, with a forecast of ninety or better, just as midway equipment was pulling into town, the fixtures for the logging show were being dragged out of storage, and community groups were setting up for whatever they were doing to raise money for the year's activities.

"Big deal, it's summer, it's hot," say people from those parts of the country with real summers. They don't understand. Here on the Oregon coast, we only stop wearing our flannel shirts for about four months a year, and you *always* take a jacket to the beach. A hot summer day is beautifully clear and seventy-five whopping degrees.

Our houses don't have air conditioning—no, really, they don't—because it's rarely an issue. My husband and I installed a whole-house fan in our attic for the few hot days a year, but that only works when it cools down in the evening. Most people don't even have that. They don't usually need it. If it gets to ninety around here and stays that way, people are likely to start dropping like flies.

My good friend Becky Stevenson was showing her worry when we met for coffee on Thursday. Becky, a licensed paramedic who works for the local ambulance company, was already anticipating a nasty weekend.

She was turned out today in a crisp, pale blue shirt with the ambulance company logo to go with her dark nylon pants. This was toward the formal end of her wardrobe. Becky is somewhat short in inches and quite short in hair; at a similar age to my own, her hair color varies based on what attracts her when she goes to the local equivalent of a superstore. She just can't be bothered with appearances much and is perfectly happy in ambulance-appropriate gear nearly all the time. The biggest girly-fit I ever saw her throw was when she bought a new pair of black work boots. Rounding out the picture are her bright blue eyes and a brightly focused mind. Like me, she had lived in bigger places and had a different career before moving to Sheffield and becoming a paramedic—in her case, in engineering, at a technical level I had little chance of understanding. We had been friends for some years: different personalities, different skills, but a lot of trust and respect.

Becky's mood today was somber.

"There aren't enough ambulances or enough shelters to take care of that many people at this temperature," she said seriously as we discussed the upcoming event. "I think we're going to have a lot of heat exhaustion. Not to mention the fights you get when people are hot and uncomfortable."

"Is any community group going to be handing out water?" I asked. "For once, that sounds like a better idea than beer."

She laughed, then turned serious again.

"The fire guys will do what they can, and our buses will be there as needed," she said. "But the City says it can't afford to make pallets of bottled water available, and there isn't much time for anyone else to arrange it." She mused for a moment. "Police, fire, sheriff's deputies, ambulances, not enough water to drink and twenty thousand hot, angry people—this Summer Festival is going to be murder."

Chapter Two

Finally, the big Festival weekend arrived. The heat was just as bad as predicted: heavy and blazing. Our normally deep blue summer sky had a silvery haze, and the tall, water- and chill-loving cedars and Douglas firs looked tired. For our time down at the waterfront and the rest of the Festival area, I threw on a breezy white shirt and lightweight cotton pants: protected from most sunburn while able to catch any breeze and stay cool. Elizabeth Peters's redoubtable heroine Amelia Peabody would have approved, even if I didn't carry a steel-tipped parasol.

I checked myself in the mirror before leaving and saw the usual: a tallish, square-shouldered and square-hipped woman with a mane of silver hair and green eyes. I am blessed with good health and good teeth; the strong chin comes from my mother, the poster child for "stubborn and determined."

The woman in the mirror is also distressingly candid (with a few exceptions for purposes of civility) and is a grammar nerd. I try not to be annoying about it, but I do shout verb-tense agreement corrections at the television and have been known to carry a marker for the occasional sign fix. *Someone* has to. Such idiotic mistakes come under the heading of avoidable incompetence, for which I don't have much sympathy. Having had multiple careers exposing me to a lot of people, I figure I'm entitled. Before drinking the small-town Kool-Aid and moving to Sheffield, I spent thirty years first interviewing people in all walks of life as a journalist, then working among a vastly different set as a lawyer/lobbyist in D.C. Our nation's capital is a lovely place that every American should visit, but don't live and work there unless you are ready to lose all your illusions. But that would be a different story. I grabbed my big shoulder bag and headed out to join David.

Today, the atmosphere in Sheffield was far from quiet, as the usual population was swelled by thousands of visitors. Sheffield is just inland from the actual beach, with an estuarial river flowing through it—meaning the water is brackish and very tidal. We can just see the Pacific Ocean from one part of town, but due to the vicissitudes of rivers, tides, and a big bluff, there isn't any actual beachfront. The town has always been about the same size. It's always had some of the same last names among its families as well, which may sound quaint, but probably hasn't done it much good.

From the hill where we parked before walking down to the Festival grounds, we could see the main road running through Sheffield. It used to be a state highway before the State straightened the route. Now the big road bypasses the town, with most of the traffic whizzing by in a tearing hurry to get to the beach a couple of miles away. If you know anything about the Oregon coast, this will make you wonder, since the beach is rainy and freezing most of the year. You see more wetsuits than bikinis.

With most drivers not noticing the exits to Sheffield, the

town has become more isolated in the past few decades, which hasn't helped the economy or the attitude. Most businesses here have been hit by the trend toward internet shopping just like the rest of America, and we don't get enough tourist traffic to keep a T-shirt and tchotchke shop open. Businesses turn over or just hang on. A small arts community has enough talent to sell outside the city.

Among Sheffielders (I know, it sounds like a strange position in baseball), you have the usual division between those who go to work, come home again, and don't pay much attention to anything beyond their block, and those who volunteer and get involved in local government and civic groups. Which means that, once you're active, you do often seem to run into the same forty or so people at gatherings. This may explain the dearth of parties and other get-togethers at people's homes: when you see the same people at most meetings and gatherings, throwing a party is really just an expensive way to see them again. We bucked the trend by holding the odd dinner party, and also inviting everyone we knew to a Christmas open house each year, because *someone* should have a Christmas party and our big old house was a great venue. This crazy notion probably was among the reasons we were viewed with suspicion.

This weekend, the Festival made full use of a nicely developed waterfront park that ran along the river, with paths and a pavilion, the logging show grounds, and a fenced area holding the midway. The noise from live music in one direction and the screams and electronic whooping from the midway in the other made for a major decibel level, along with all the excitement of the contests. That was also the reason we didn't bring our Scottish deerhound, Angus; while a calm soul, he just didn't need the noise and the crowds.

"Where do you want to start?" I asked David as we neared the waterfront park.

"The show's about to start," he answered, pointing to the bleachers toward the back of the Festival grounds, and we headed that way.

At David's and my age, midways and the accompanying greasy food don't really make our list of fun things to do. We don't care about the rides, either. But we do like to see the logging show, a fixture and the original purpose of the Festival. It always brings out a lot of big guys testing their abilities to saw large logs in pairs, climb up wood poles in spiked boots, and handle an axe without causing serious injury. This year, the high temperatures were making themselves felt, without the usual ocean breeze that keeps things pleasant. Not surprisingly, the contestants had eschewed the usual plaid shirts for T-shirts, and some even had made the concession of work shorts rather than heavy jeans.

Thankfully in some cases—maybe not so much in others— there apparently was a rule against going completely shirtless. The sweat was flowing freely, and I was glad to see most of them chugging bottles of water. The beer would likely come later.

As usual, the performances were impressive, and the overall champion was a local guy, which caused a lot of cheering. Given the noise and the heat, by the time the axes were down and the logging show grounds were littered with sawn-off rounds of wood, I was developing a headache, even sitting in bleachers under cover. David headed off to talk with some friends he spotted down by the river, and I found myself seeking the shade of the large waterfront park pavilion and something cool to drink.

Suzanne Dryer, who served on the City Council along with Kate, was serving food for a community group she headed. Suzanne is a lifelong Sheffielder and small business owner: besides the City Council, she participated in a lot of groups that upheld what she considered important local traditions. Suzanne was slightly built but wiry, and I knew she had worked hard to prepare for this weekend. Now, dressed in a striped top and jeans with an apron wrapped around her, she was selling food and drink from the brick shelter in the park near the midway. There were several other people hanging out in the shade, including a young woman whom I knew worked for the local paper—I had seen her covering events before but didn't know her name—and had a camera hanging around her neck.

I was about to beg that Councilor Dryer hand over some of her lemonade when I saw Mayor Sutton stalk up to the counter, a vision (I'm not sure of what) in head-to-toe turquoise: cotton shirt, pants, and some sort of loose, sleeveless jacket with flowers embroidered on it. I think even her usual sensible, black shoes had been replaced by turquoise sneakers. If the woman wanted to stand out in a crowd, she was certainly dressed for it.

The mayor leaned over the counter to speak with Suzanne. Given what I had heard from Kate the week before, and anxious to learn more, I turned my back to feign inattention and listened hard.

"Suzanne, I know you've heard about our meeting with the Festival Committee," she said in a voice that carried quite clearly. "I think we're perfectly right in asking for part of the proceeds, and I'm planning to make that a condition of their using the space from now on. I'm assuming you agree with me?"

"Greta, I've told you before and you know it yourself, you're not supposed to ask for Council votes outside of meetings. I don't want to talk with you about this."

"I'm the mayor," replied the woman, staring through her black cat glasses. "I can talk to you anytime I want, and I want to know that you'll vote the right way on this. Our city needs the money."

"You mean *you* need the money to pay back what you've been grabbing from the budget for your pet projects," said Suzanne. "I've been voting with you, you know that—but I'm not sure we'll have another Festival if you get your way on this."

"I need your promise on this vote, right now," insisted the mayor in a hiss. "I got you elected, and I can throw you off the Council just as easily."

"You did *not* get me elected, Greta," Suzanne hissed back. "I'm not going to talk with you now, and if you keep threatening people to get your own way, you could get tossed out of office yourself, or worse."

My goodness, I thought. *Something is rotten in the state of Sheffield!* I looked around quickly to see if the reporter had heard anything and saw her writing furiously in a notebook.

I'm not sure why I felt the need to talk with her. Worry about the city's image? Desire to cause trouble? Anyway, it seemed important, so I ambled over.

"What did you get from that?" I asked her. After watching her notetaking, there didn't seem much of a point in being subtle.

"It sounds to me like the mayor is pressuring people to vote with her, and there was something about questionable finances," she replied. She knew I had taken part in some City activities. "Can you add to that?"

"I don't have definite information, but you should ask some members of the Summer Festival Committee," I suggested. "I've heard they're pretty upset about a proposal from the mayor and city manager. Some of us have become very suspicious about the state of City finances since Greta became mayor, and he seems to be hand in glove with her. And I can tell you that you're right about the pressure. She has a habit of ignoring the Ethics and Open Meetings laws, and it looks like I'm not the only one who's getting tired of it."

"It's hard to get readers interested in ethics rules," she said with a grimace.

"Well, there are the next steps," I mused, looking out over the crowd. "A complaint to the State means an investigation of City officials. That's a pretty nasty scandal, and it could be followed up by a lawsuit or charges, not to mention fines. If the City faces liability, that could really hurt its future. And, if people finally wake up and get ticked off, you might even have all the fun of a recall election."

"Really!" She stared at me. "Maybe I can make a story from this."

I tried not to roll my eyes as she walked off. I hadn't even gone into the other consequences: City liability would affect its insurance premiums, which could affect its bond ratings, which could make it more difficult and a lot more expensive to borrow the money needed for vital infrastructure improvements. But that wasn't very sexy, either, compared with public scandal and a political campaign.

I looked around for David to tell him that I was stirring up trouble (he would just say, "*Again?*") and couldn't find him.

But the band was playing a song he likes, so I walked away from the screaming midway and toward the bandstand to see if he was listening, wishing I had remembered to wear a big, floppy hat to keep off the blazing sun.

Apparently, my exchange with the reporter had been noted and was the subject of some discontent.

"Felice," said an imperious voice behind me, and I turned to look down at the round face and cat glasses. "I don't appreciate being talked about to the press."

Greta and I had disagreed enough in public meetings that she knew better than to try on a sweet smile and high-pitched persuasion with me. And since we weren't in a public meeting, I didn't have to be professionally civil to her. *This could be fun.*

"Gee, Greta," I drawled in the most arrogant voice I could produce. "I know you prefer to be the only person reporters talk to, but some of us like to make sure they get the truth occasionally."

She bristled. "How dare you! I make sure the paper has the right information about what's going on in our city."

"You make sure they have what you want them to write and what makes you look good, but it doesn't bear a lot of resemblance to the truth. You shouldn't have been talking with Suzanne the way you did, the way you do all the time with Council members. She knew it, you knew it—I just made sure the reporter did, too."

I wasn't keeping my voice down—there may have been some finger-pointing as well, I was too upset to notice—and I saw a few people looking our way. *Good. It may not add to my popularity among the St. Greta contingent, but maybe a few others will wake up.*

"You can't talk to me that way," she spluttered. "You don't

24

know who you're talking to."

That was a challenge I just couldn't ignore, and my lifelong habit of civility simply evaporated. I felt myself drawing taller and my eyes hardening.

"It looks like a short, unpleasant woman who thinks she has a lot more authority than she actually does, and who is driving Sheffield toward bankruptcy nearly single-handedly. Did I get something wrong?"

"You have no idea what I'm trying to do. I'm going to be the most admired and remembered mayor ever by the time I'm finished. And I have more power than you think. I can make sure you're never appointed to another City committee ever again."

"Ooooh. Be still, my heart," I answered. "Until you're out of the way, and I don't really care how it's done, no one with any intelligence is going to want to have anything to do with City government. You are a disaster, and Sheffield would be a lot better off without you."

I think she said something else, but I was finished listening. The emanations from the woman felt poisonous, and suddenly, I couldn't stand to be in the same zip code with her. I turned and walked off, not really paying attention to my direction. I hate confrontations, but I certainly didn't want her seeing my hands and knees shaking, so I resisted the need to sit down. It took a few seconds for my vision to clear enough to notice that I had been heading toward the midway and the music stage once again.

When I got close to the band, I recognized two of the musicians—a husband-and-wife duo who often played at local events. George Russell was a big guy who had let his muscle go, sporting the flowing locks, full mustache, and uncontrolled beard combo often found among creatives on the coast. I thought there might be a decent-looking fifty-year-old under there somewhere and he certainly spoke well, at least on topics that interested him. He had recently been appointed to the City Council, a choice of the mayor, and tended to be one of her supporters.

He lost more credibility with me when he spoke as though he were on the razor's edge of environmental issues and was the only person in town who could speak with authority on the subject. He seemed to think himself the self-appointed protector of our small piece of the planet, with a mandate To Accomplish Change; although realistically, the City didn't have much authority to do anything on that front. Despite Oregon's well-earned reputation for forcing Green (I'm not talking about the moss this time), I don't think the Sheffield City Council had any way to demand that every homeowner buy a wind turbine or stop using plastic wrap, even if the voters would stand for it. As a result, my cynical little brain had a hard time taking George at face value.

His wife Rita had the dark complexion and features of her mixed Hispanic and Native American heritage, also with long, flowing hair and a heavy build. She was a one-time friend who had abruptly told me one day that I was too much of a capitalist to associate with and now studiously avoided me. I had been stunned at the time. This is a reason to end a friendship? I don't think we had even discussed economics.

Even stranger, she and her husband had started some unpleasant, and frankly ludicrous, rumors about David and me; we couldn't figure out why. They both seemed too intelligent to be afraid of two people who had done nothing except move to Sheffield from somewhere else. We never did

26

discover what their motivations were and just decided it was one of the vagaries of living in a small town with its share of eccentrics. But just to be contrary this afternoon (I blame the headache), I could stand among the crowd and enjoy the music—and maybe annoy her if she saw me—so I did.

With one ear on the heavy beat, I kept looking around, watching the crowd. Thankfully (Becky would be pleased), most had cold drinks in their hands, and most had been smart enough to wear some sort of hat. I wished someone had sent me the memo. When the outdoor environment is gray most of the year, you forget that the big bright ball in the sky is capable of hurting you when it finally shows itself, and I was feeling it in spite of my care in dressing. I always get sunburned on the first sunny day of summer, and my hats collect dust on the closet shelf unless David reminds me to grab one. Now, I pulled a brochure for some other festival out of my purse and waved it in front of my face, trying to create a bit of breeze.

Back near the pavilion, two people had approached Greta, and the round face broke into a big, fake smile while her hands fluttered in response. I couldn't hear the conversation—good, I had no desire to lose my lunch—but I did see her hand over a bright turquoise flyer that read "Chat with the Mayor." This was a favorite shtick of hers: she harangued local businesses into letting her come and sit in their stores for a few hours once a week for a month, and residents supposedly could come and talk with her about their concerns. The whole idea always gave me a flash image of Lucy van Pelt behind her psychiatrist stall, charging Charlie Brown a nickel—and it was about as effective.

Greta refused to admit that she had no authority to resolve any of the issues that people brought her. The best advice she could give them was to call City staff, because, under Oregon law and the City charter, she wasn't even supposed to contact staff members directly other than the city manager. But she held up these so-called "chats" as evidence that she was in touch with Sheffield residents. Who knows? Maybe she had an ugly house and preferred sitting somewhere else.

I looked around at the other people listening to the music. I didn't recognize most of them, but a tall figure about twenty yards away looked familiar. Carl Roetgen waved at me and walked over, then indicated that we should walk away from the stage a bit. I immediately wondered what he wanted.

"Hey, Felice—enjoying the Festival?" Carl had a light, somewhat gravelly voice that somehow, nevertheless, always struck me as oily.

"Hi, Carl. Everything is looking good, although I hope we don't have any problems from the heat."

"Yeah, it's pretty hot. I hope everyone sticks around for the events this afternoon."

Carl was one of the most successful local business owners, a dealer in heavy equipment and fittings for the timber and maritime industries, and a substantial sponsor of the Festival. He also seemed to dabble in various projects that, somehow, always needed some special favor from City government. While I appreciated Carl's contributions to the local economy, I disliked his assumption that he could push to the head of any agenda when he needed a favor. But then, as a woman, I had obvious reasons for disliking any old boy network.

Now, I looked up at his short, fair hair, blue eyes, and chiseled features—he kept himself fit, too, it really was too bad about the oiliness—and waited for him to come to his point.

"David around? I didn't see him with you."

Not surprisingly, I immediately thought he actually

wanted to talk with my husband. Then I remembered the standard Sheffield misunderstanding: people assumed that couples were joined at the hip, always agreed on issues, and always knew where each other might be. Carl might be just asking a throwaway question.

"I think he's down at the waterfront. Did you need him for something?"

"No, no, that's fine. Listen, have you heard anything about the next Planning Commission meeting?"

Aha. NOW we're getting to it. I had been on the Planning Commission at one point but had not re-upped when my term was over. It was a good way to stay in touch with changes to the local environment, but it brought in a lot of people who hadn't given much thought to how they were going to carry out their projects, or how their house addition that crossed the property line might not work for their neighbors. I had wanted to help but had become too frustrated to stay on the board.

"I haven't seen the latest agenda. Do you have something pending?"

"Well, you know I have that property outside town that I'd like to develop."

I had heard about this. Sheffield had a real housing shortage, as did the rest of Norfolk County, but there weren't many individuals with the wherewithal to build enough housing units to ease the situation. Having a subdivision of any size would be a real improvement, and while I didn't trust Carl's way of doing business, I appreciated his proposed contribution. I nodded to show that I was with him.

"Greta Sutton said something about wanting to annex the property and make it part of Sheffield. I had heard she was putting it on the Planning Commission agenda."

This was another surprise, and I think my face showed it. Beyond the problem of the mayor setting out a committee agenda—improper, but par for her course—Carl was one of Greta's cohort. Her backing was one of the reasons his projects shot to the top of agendas while others had been waiting months for approvals, and she would usually smile at him whenever he showed at a meeting, then assure everyone that "we really should do anything we can to help someone who is helping our city." Never mind how much money one of his favors would take out of the tight City budget. Yuck.

"Adding your property to the city would mean City services to your housing units—is that what you're seeking?"

"No, not at all. I'd really like to avoid City taxes, and you know, there are those SDCs. I don't want the property annexed, but Greta seems pretty determined."

Without going into the boring details, systems development charges, or SDCs, are the fees municipalities charge for new development, usually in the areas of water, sewer, streets, and the like. New housing units, commercial buildings, and industry add demand to systems that may not have enough capacity to handle them; SDCs contribute to the cost of extending or upgrading. Sheffield didn't have much development, but the City had passed some sizeable SDCs some years before. If Carl's property was inside the city limits, each building in his development would get hit with several thousand dollars in additional costs.

"Ah." I didn't know how to react to this, but I certainly didn't want to get in the middle of a dispute between Carl and his mayor buddy. "No, I hadn't heard anything. Hope it works out for you; I think your subdivision would be a great thing for the area."

"Thanks," Carl said, already moving his attention elsewhere. "Well, enjoy the Festival."

"You, too," I countered as he headed off. I thought he might be moving in the mayor's direction but didn't pay attention, turning back to the music instead.

Chapter Three

The Russells clearly were in their element, but after twenty more minutes, the bluesy R&B they were playing was losing its appeal. It's perfect for a dark club somewhere but didn't really fit a hot summer day in the sun. I turned away from the music stage and continued my wander through the Festival grounds, avoiding the midway to see if I could find David toward the parking lot. There was a line of vendors at the edge of the property, with their booths under marquee tents and selling everything from pottery to glass jewelry to storm windows (too bad we don't have festivals in January, when you might really *need* storm windows, but hopefully, some people think ahead). I am easily distracted by sparkly stuff, so I tried to keep my eyes fixed firmly ahead. Which is probably why I saw the round, scurrying figure in turquoise as she rounded the end of the row, looking in both directions before she ducked behind the end tent. Greta again, but why was she looking like she didn't want anyone to see where she was going?

Felice, you're being both paranoid and nosy, said my better self. *This could be personal and none of your business.* I told my better self to shut up. *If the mayor is doing something*

sneaky like meeting people on the quiet during the Festival,
someone needs to be paying attention. I ducked into the
marquee at the end of the row and took the few steps to the
back of the tent, smiling at a distracted vendor as I went by.

Sure enough, there were voices coming through the
canvas.

"Greta, are you sure this is a good idea?" said a male voice.
I couldn't identify the speaker immediately.

"What could be wrong about the two of us meeting?" the
mayor replied. "We have lots of things to talk about, and we're
in charge of the city."

"Actually, Greta, *I'm* supposed to manage the city," said
the man. *Aha!* I thought. *It's the city manager.* No flies on this
girl.

City Manager Dwight Orkman hadn't been in town that
long. He had been hired in a rush less than a year before when
the former city manager left for a new job. I was one of a few
people active in government who had wondered about the
hurry—usually, city councils at least try to have an open,
competitive hiring process—and didn't know much about his
history, other than that he had worked for another city for
several years before showing up on the coast. However, he
seemed ready to put down roots in Sheffield; I had heard he
had just bought a house some-where in town. He was fairly tall
with light hair and a red complexion; he was also fit, I
understood, due to a lot of swimming.

"We already meet every week to talk about City business,"
he continued now. "I don't think it looks good for us to meet
at a public event, especially to talk about Council matters."

"You said you were going to meet with the Festival
Committee on your own," Greta urged. "I need to know how

it went."

"Not good, to tell you the truth," Dwight replied.

'WELL,' Dwight. Not 'good,' 'well.' My inner grammar nerd automatically rebelled. *You want to run a city, use decent English.*

"The Committee members are pretty upset. Right now, they say that if you and the Council go forward with a demand for a percentage, they'll cancel next year's Festival."

"Oh, they can't be serious," chirped Greta. "The Festival has been the biggest event in Sheffield for years, and the fireworks are famous all up and down the Oregon coast! They're not going to cancel over a little money, and you and I both know we need it."

"You weren't at the meeting. It was mentioned that both you and I are newcomers to Sheffield compared with them and their families and that we're trying to mess with something that's bigger than we are. You know more about them than I do—could they raise enough of a stink to really cause trouble?"

"I don't know," mused Greta. "But we can't let them stop this plan. This money is just the beginning of what we'll need to build that building!"

Building? What building?

"You know better than I do whether you'll have the votes to make this happen," Dwight went on. "And you know that I've been backing you on a lot of issues, making recommendations to the Council that the staff doesn't always like and that aren't included in the City budget. But I'm not sure I can recommend the change to the Festival contract that you're looking for here."

"Oh, yes, you can, Dwight," hissed the mayor. She was doing a lot of hissing today; I couldn't help but notice. "We need this money. I'm rounding up votes from councilors, and you'll bring the recommendation forward. I brought you here because of this, I got you hired because of your promises, and I think you need to do some thinking about the investment you've already made here. I'd hate for you to lose it—it can't be easy for someone like you to find another job with your connections."

Connections? What connections? I was feeling very ignorant.

The two of them apparently dispersed after that—I suppose there wasn't much more that Dwight could say. I was left standing in the back corner of a vendor tent, wondering into what sort of a minor snake pit I had wandered. So, the mayor wants to get money from the Festival to help pay for a building? The councilors, at least some of them (Kate was apparently being left out of the party), knew about the plan to squeeze money out of the Festival organizers. But what did they know about a building? I was familiar enough with the City budget to know there wasn't anything in it about constructing a building, nor any money in the conceivable future that could build anything bigger than an equipment shed. Prefab. Did I mention that this is a small city?

Previous City governments had worked hard to keep Sheffield solvent and functioning through bad economic times, but it was a close thing. The City staff had been reduced to the point that everyone was stretched to the limit, many working less than full-time hours and several with multiple job titles. Budgets remained extremely tight. Other Oregon cities had eliminated libraries and swimming pools, their police and fire departments—some had even declared bankruptcy. We had not, and it was a matter of pride, although it couldn't realistically last as costs rose and revenue remained flat. If Greta, Dwight & Co. were threatening that stability, a lot of people were going to be angry. And what was that about Dwight's background? He had been hired in a hurry; hadn't the councilors seen his résumé and checked it?

I tried to put the politics out of mind and enjoy the Festival. As expected, I found David down at the dock on the river, talking with a small boat owner about engine volumes, tidal currents, and the exact point at which the river stopped being an estuary. I love the man dearly, but I don't always need to be present during his conversations.

My main squeeze and sweetie is a nice-looking man. Just over six feet, wide shoulders, silver hair, and a neat beard—but then, facial hair is almost an imperative in Oregon. His blue eyes twinkle when he smiles, and we get along probably because each of us figures we're the lucky one of the pair. Plus, he makes me laugh. Not when he's standing around exchanging interminable stories, but sometimes. Other times.

I nudged his elbow, deciding to play wife, since the discussion appeared to be about over. "David, are you ready to get something to eat?" I smiled at the boat owner at the same time.

"What?" said my husband, looking at me absentmindedly. He does get involved in his work. I gave him a moment, since I wasn't asking about estuaries. "Oh, right, sure." He exchanged a few more sentences with the boat owner, and they waved each other off.

As we headed back up the hill toward the midway, I filled him in on what I'd heard during my various eavesdropping and watched his face cloud over.

"Had you heard anything about this building plan?"

"No, I haven't, and it's ridiculous. Sheffield doesn't have the money to build a building. Greta may be hoping for a miracle grant, as usual, but I don't know what kind of building she thinks she's planning."

"What's also interesting is how many people she's pissing off, demanding all this support," I responded. "It would be nice to think that some people in town are finally waking up to what's happening in their government."

"Oh, well," sighed David, trying hard not to get upset. He hates bad government even more than I do. "Not my circus, not my monkeys." This was one of his recent phrases. I didn't want to tell him it was already passé.

"Yeah, well, tell that to our City utility bill when it gets raised through the roof to pay for their next crazy project."

Intra-couple communication complete, we headed out to enjoy the Festival for the rest of the day. We talked with vendors, chatted with friends, and I noticed several of the people I had already seen at various points throughout the day, including the reporter taking photos.

It was a fun day, not spoiled by the sight of the bright turquoise figure moving through the crowd. At various points, I saw Mayor Greta talking with Carl, with a couple of former City councilors and mayors, and even with a County commissioner who had shown up for the festivities. I had to frown at that, hoping that a County official would know enough about Sheffield to withstand the blandishments. Lots of smiling, lots of arm-waving, a few heads-together moments with those whom she might want to show closeness. And of course, more handing out of flyers.

I really was trying not to notice, although that might not be clear from what I'm recounting. But the woman was conspicuous, and now I had reason to be suspicious of her. So, I couldn't help seeing at one point late in the afternoon when Greta met her husband Patrick about fifty feet away from us. They exchanged some conversation before Patrick, a figure somewhat taller than his wife, leaned in and seemed to become a bit more intense. Greta responded angrily, gesticulating with both hands before putting them on her wide hips and glaring at him. Patrick turned and walked off, no doubt feeling the burn on his back.

Okay, that's one conversation I'm glad not to have heard.

I often wonder about couples, although I would never be so rude as to ask. What makes someone live with, and seem relatively content with, another someone who is so difficult to be around? What could their home life be like? Of course, I must consider that others probably wonder the same about David and me: we are quite different from each other and both very independent people. There have been a few who have suggested we're really different-gender versions of the same person, but that's just rude. I would never spend a half hour standing around talking to someone about estuaries. Elizabethan fashion trends, maybe. Classic English mysteries. Something completely different and much more interesting.

I guess it's all in how you look at it.

Chapter Four

In any case, we went home for the rest of the afternoon and ate dinner, sticking to ordinary topics and staying away from local politics. As it headed toward sunset, it was time to get things together for the trek back down the hill for the weekend's highlight—the fireworks! As usual, as soon as we had shoes on and opened the hall closet door, deerhound Angus assumed it was time for him to join us in what would obviously be lots of fun. He may have looked like he was sound asleep on the couch, but you can't fool Angus. I always marvel at how a ninety-pound dog can dance around in delight through a room full of furniture without knocking anything over.

"Angus," I told him, "you are doomed to disappointment tonight." The outing would not be much fun for him once the flashes and booms started; up on our hill, he'd barely hear them and be fine. We pacified him with a treat and headed out, making our way down to the waterfront to wait for the famous show.

Amazingly enough, given the blasting heat of the day, it was already cooling off fast now that the sun was setting and the crowds were gathering. It was better to get there early: twenty thousand people quickly fill up all the available space on the grass of the park, nearby hillsides, sidewalks, and pretty much everywhere else with a view. We like to find a place near the water, where the shells will explode mostly overhead.

We had equipped ourselves with expandable chairs, blankets, and windbreakers over long pants and sweaters. Ninety degrees with no air conditioning during the day, now 50 with a stiff oceanward breeze for the evening—only on the Oregon coast in July. Although you do save money on clothes, buying all long-sleeved shirts. And the trees are tall and impressively dark green against the deep blue of a coastal sky, not to mention the sparkle of the water. Like I said, tradeoffs.

Now, the sunset was beyond beautiful: a long, slow slide from golden light to pink, then violet, into that amazing rich blue before full night. The tall trees were black silhouettes against bands of color. It always looks like the perfect camera shot, but the image never comes close to reality; I had finally learned to leave the camera turned off and just enjoy it.

Up around the 45th parallel, dawn and sunset take longer than they do in the tropics. Even with the sun disappearing, we had about an hour before full dark, and it was a good opportunity for people-watching, if you're into that. Most of the crowd was from out of town, and there were a lot of large family gatherings. We did wave to various friends while glancing around. Suzanne was still working near the food counter in her apron. I didn't see Becky but knew that she was likely stationed at her ambulance, in the parking area on the other side of the midway. Since most people were sitting down, you couldn't help noticing those still standing and walking around. At least one of them looked familiar.

I nudged David. "Isn't that Patrick Sutton?"

"Looks like him. He looks like he's looking for something."

"Or someone, maybe. I don't see Greta with him." The mayor's husband was standing close to the water and looking over the crowd, hands on hips and an annoyed look on his face. Just in case he was looking for his wife, I cast an eye around myself, I guess thinking I could shout to him and point if I saw her. However, despite the brilliance of her attire, there was no sign. After my gaze returned to Patrick, he headed up a slight knoll, I assume for a better vantage point, and turned in a full circle himself. He then turned toward the midway and logging show area and walked through the crowd and out of our view.

In watching him, my attention was caught by the music stage. It looked like George and Rita Russell were on again, although their playing was mostly drowned out by the continued noise from the midway. *Long day for them,* I thought, *I hope they're getting a decent wage for this gig.* The neon lights were coming on, giving the carnival that air of cheap excitement that looks like such fun from a distance. I wanted deeper dark to enjoy the fireworks, however, so I put all the lights to my back. I checked my watch in the dimming light—nearly ten o'clock.

Finally, the first shell heralded the beginning of the much-awaited show, and everyone left off talking to switch to "oohs" and "aahs." A few small boats on the river contributed with air horns to show their approval. It was another great fireworks event, with showers of color, good timing, and great combinations.

Fireworks are among my favorite things, being about the biggest shows of sparkly stuff in existence, so I tend to concentrate overhead. But I did see the city manager at one point, leaning against a pillar of the waterfront park pavilion. He was illuminated by a bright explosion of shells and was within my normal field of vision. My brain noted momentarily that he hadn't been there a few moments before, but my attention went quickly back to the reds, greens, blues, and golds exploding above the crowd.

After twenty amazingly quick minutes, the finale erupted in an intense series of shells that made me laugh with their exuberance. Then came the ringing silence that always marks the end of fireworks. We all waited in case there were any forgotten shells still to be launched . . . and then heard the collective exhale, and the noises of thousands moving around and preparing to go. The Sheffield, Oregon, Summer Festival fireworks show was over for another year, barring the discussions of how good it was that would take place over the next few days.

David and I made the well-deserved "wow, that was really great" comments to each other as we folded up the chairs, put them back in their carrier bags, then shook out and folded up the heavy wool Navy blanket we had put on the ground. We shared out the load, then started walking toward the end of Main Street that marked the hill going home, thanking our luck that we didn't have to join the huge queue of cars trying to find their ways out of town.

The hill is a pretty steep incline, not easy even unburdened. With the weight we were carrying, a stop near the top to catch our breaths was warranted. We turned back to enjoy the ocean breeze, the half-moon now well to the west, and the view toward the Festival, some of which was still going strong even though the fireworks were finished and most people were leaving.

The right side of our view—the midway and music stage—

was lit up "like an aureole full of glowworms," as David likes to put it (don't ask me where he gets these things). There would be music until midnight as well as the die-hard teenagers determined to ride all the midway rides until they went dark. As my vision scanned the grounds, I noticed the contrasts among the neon and movement of the midway, the lesser colored light of the music stage, and the deep darkness farther to the left, where I knew the bleachers stood and where the logging show had taken place that afternoon. With the smoke from the fireworks dispersed by the easterly wind, it was a cool and beautiful night, if slightly more adrenaline-tinged than most Sheffield late nights.

I didn't know, then. From where I stood, high on a hillside five hundred yards away, I couldn't tell that, with the carnival noise in the deep background, everything in the bleachers area was empty and cool and eerily quiet. The trees that surrounded the logging show area and bordered the river looked down on where people had been showing off their skills just a few hours before. They were swaying and rustling slightly in the wind heading toward the Pacific. Newly cut rounds of logs were still lying around the area, showing pale, round shapes in what small light filtered in from the midway area and the half-moon.

I wasn't there, thankfully, to see that one of the rounds was slightly misshapen and appeared to have a frame of some kind on it. Close up, the faint light would have shown it to be a face; and the frame was a pair of dark, old-fashioned. cat-style glasses, although the open eyes were no longer making use of them. The round, open mouth below the eyes had finally fallen silent. The rest of the mayor's body, strident turquoise against the dark field, was laid straight out on the ground, and she was very dead. But I didn't know, then. Almost no one knew.

Chapter Five

Sunday arrived, thankfully cooler, although just as bright. We left the windows open instead of closing them against midday heat as we had for the last three days, and I repaid Angus for his forbearance in staying home the night before with a long walk through the neighborhood. His long nose gathered information about everything that had occurred along the route in the approximately sixteen hours since we had last been this way. He had a good run in the neighborhood dog park, and we returned home, both of us exercised and content.

The contentment, at least for me, didn't last long. The phone rang within a few minutes of our return, and Becky announced darkly, "I don't even know how to tell you this, Felice."

"Tell me what?" I had a sinking sensation as my mind raced through horrible scenarios. "You sound serious. Did someone get hurt in the heat yesterday?"

"You might want to sit down. Someone killed the mayor."

"What?" came out louder than expected. "*Greta's* dead? You're kidding, right?"

"No. I got called out first thing this morning to the Festival grounds. It's Greta Sutton. She's definitely gone."

"Oh, my God," I said, sinking into a kitchen chair. "How did she die? Who found her?" I couldn't help grimace at how crass my questions sounded, but somehow, I needed the information.

"Well, they don't know yet how she died; there'll have to be an autopsy."

"Oh, of course."

"Somebody from out of town found her; I think it was someone camping out near the Festival grounds who was going for a run at dawn. Don't know his name."

"At least it wasn't someone who knew her. How awful!"

"And you didn't hear it from me, but it looked like someone hit her on the head pretty hard."

"Okay, well, there are a lot of people who have wanted to do that for quite a while." And then I thought about my friend who, despite the medical training that gave her some detachment, had had to respond to the death of someone she knew. "Are you okay?"

I heard her sigh through the phone. "It wasn't my best early morning. There was a choker near the body with some nasty stains on it. We didn't get near any of that, of course; the police got there pretty much when we did, and they were still there when our bus left."

"Oh, Becky, I'm so sorry you had to deal with all of that." I knew a tiny amount about logging, mostly from watching the shows at the Festival and elsewhere. A choker is a large chain with a heavy hook at one end: it's used around felled logs to attach them to an overhead pulley line so they can be hauled away from the felling site. At the show, contestants had run choker races, running across obstacles to hook up a choker, then running away to clear the site. There had been several chokers left in the grounds after the show, awaiting Sunday's cleanup. They wouldn't take monumental strength to swing, but the heavyweight hook on the end of one would be a lethal weapon.

She was quiet for a moment. "Felice, don't take this wrong, but I have to ask. You're one of the people who really didn't like Greta Sutton; do you know who might have done this?"

I knew better than to take Becky's question at face value, or I would have been appalled. She had seen something horrible that morning and was naturally upset. But I did take a moment, moving the phone from my ear to stare at it before replacing it to answer her.

"I know you're not really asking if I killed the mayor. Jeez, Becky, I certainly didn't like the woman, but I'm hardly likely to resort to swinging a chain at her or suggest that anyone else do so. That's just . . . gross."

"I didn't think so, but she was a controversial woman who caused some strong emotions on both sides. There are going to be a lot of questions asked of a lot of people before this is cleared up."

There wasn't a lot more to say at that point, so after telling Becky that I hoped she could get some rest, we hung up. I stood in the living room, watching the dog sleeping across most of the couch (as usual), and wondering about the death of a most unpleasant woman.

The more I thought about it, the more I realized that my sarcastic comment wasn't far off the mark. There *had* been a lot of people who had reason to swing a heavy object at Greta Sutton; I had seen several examples just the day before. And

Becky was right, in a way: the police had a reason to question me, as Greta's and my mutual dislike was common knowledge. I thought back to our brief exchange at the Festival the afternoon before. I didn't remember everything that had been said—hadn't I said something about being rid of her? *Oops.* I wondered whether that would be enough to bring the local police to my door for an interview.

My logical little brain started wondering about alibis. We didn't know yet when she had died; I hadn't even asked Becky about that, as it would have to be established by a coroner. I was probably in the clear, since I had been around other people for most of the day, including thousands during the fireworks. Afterward? What if she'd been killed in the middle of the night? *Oh, well—no sense worrying about that just now. I'll think about that when the time comes.*

"All right, Scarlett," I said out loud. "This is going to be a bitch of a mess. I have a feeling Greta Sutton is going to still be causing trouble even though she's dead."

Not a difficult prophecy but certainly an accurate one. Although we mostly stayed in on Sunday, you could feel the buzz in the air following the discovery of the mayor's body. The Summer Festival went through its final day, with midway noise, music on the stage, and local contests, but I knew that a lot of Sheffielders were just going through the motions, volunteers who had pledged to show up. The news of Greta's violent death would have spread everywhere and overhung everything.

Meanwhile, the police were trying their best to figure out what had happened, I assume before trails went cold and visitors who might know something useful disappeared. If I was wondering whether I would be the subject of an interview, I didn't have long to wait. Sheffield's police chief, Thomas Abhay, showed up at our door himself late Sunday afternoon.

"Felice, I need to talk with you about yesterday," he said in his polite-cop voice.

"Sure," I said, knowing that we both knew I didn't have to do so. Chief Abhay wasn't a close friend, but we had a relationship of mutual like and respect after serving together on a local Public Safety Committee. He looked the part of dignified law enforcement: about six feet, but he held himself taller, with broad shoulders and strong arms emerging from the short sleeves of his dark blue uniform. Dark hair speckled with gray, especially at the temples, in a military cut; a look to his features and skin tone that told of his ancestry from the Indian subcontinent; and the requisite facial hair held to a brush mustache. I love my sweetie dearly, but I could have fantasized about Tom Abhay if I let myself. Hey, we all need pastimes, and small towns don't give you that many options when it comes to fantasizing.

His looks aside, Sheffield was lucky to have Tom Abhay. He had a distinguished military career, was still fairly young, and could have been somewhere a lot more interesting than tiny Sheffield. But Abhay had strong loyalties. He had risen through the ranks and took a lot of pride in his small force, which he ensured had unusually good training for the size of the community. And if he was off-duty, he might very well show up somewhere on a big motorcycle, a wild-guy quirk that made me smile in an otherwise quiet, straight-arrow man.

Neither of us was smiling now, however. I walked him into our breakfast room, where he could face me across the table, and we both sat down.

"I understand you saw the mayor yesterday afternoon," the chief began calmly. "Can you tell me about that?"

Then I did smile slightly, if only at all the unspoken information carried in his question. "I wish I hadn't seen her," I answered. "That's a very understated way of asking me about my argument with her, right?" I had to assume that someone had told him of our encounter; it had taken place in front of dozens of people.

His mouth tilted slightly. "Okay."

I quickly tried to remember whether Chief Abhay was one of Greta's adherents. As a City department head, he would be expected to show neutrality, but personally, he might not care to hear criticism. After a moment, I realized I just didn't know how he felt about her and decided not to pull any punches.

"I actually saw Greta Sutton several times over the course of yesterday afternoon," I started, "and I think she must have argued with half the City government within a few hours. My short exchange with her was the least of it."

I explained about hearing her bully Suzanne Dryer, the reporter hearing it and my interview with her, and the mayor's subsequent attempt to bully me.

"We've been told that you threatened her during that conversation," Abhay said.

"I admit that I called her a disaster for the City, and I did say that no intelligent person would want to have anything to do with local government while she was in office. But I certainly didn't threaten her physically. That would be stupid. I wanted to stay far away from Greta Sutton and her poison, not get anywhere near her."

"Okay," he said again, although I could tell he wasn't completely ruling me out. "You said you saw her several times during the day?"

"Yes." I shifted in my seat. "This feels a little weird, like I'm tattling during recess or something, but you need to know." I took a breath, trying to organize my statements to stay neutral and factual.

"I overheard a private conversation between the mayor and the city manager about a half hour later—they met behind the vendor tents. And I also saw, although I didn't hear, an argument between Greta and her husband late in the afternoon." I laid out the details of Greta's threats to Dwight Orkman, including the mention of a building and his background. I watched Tom's face carefully to see any hint of whether he knew about either topic, but he gave nothing away. *I'll bet he plays a mean game of poker,* I thought. *Wouldn't a City department head have heard about a proposal of this size? How am I going to find out more about this?*

The sketch of the disagreement between Greta and Patrick was quick, since I had no idea of the subject matter. The chief nodded during that bit; he apparently had heard about that from another source. Not surprising, since it had taken place in the middle of the Festival.

"And I don't know if it matters, but there was one time that I *didn't* see her, when I might have expected to," I continued. I told him about Patrick Sutton's apparent search for someone shortly before the fireworks show. "I don't know that he was looking for Greta, of course, but she wasn't with him, and he could have been."

"Did you see her?" Abhay asked.

"No, and I looked. She was wearing a distinctive outfit, so I looked around, thinking I could point her out to him if I saw her. But I didn't see her anywhere among the crowd."

"Did you see where he went?"

"Yes. He turned in a complete circle while standing at the top of that knoll in the middle of the park and then headed toward the midway and the logging show grounds. But he still looked like he was searching, not as though he had seen what he was looking for."

The implications of Patrick Sutton's direction suddenly hit me. Greta's body had been found on the logging show grounds, and from Becky's information, she likely had been killed there.

"Do you know yet when she died?" I couldn't help a slight sharpening of my voice.

He looked at me with no expression. "Not yet. But the preliminary exam seems to indicate it was late in the evening, not in the few hours before she was found in the morning."

"Oh. So maybe actually *during* the fireworks?"

The chief nodded slightly. I winced, thinking of what may have been going on while we were all "oohing" and "aahing."

"Well, in that case, I think David and I should be off your list; we were sitting in front and surrounded by other people. Someone certainly saw us there."

Then I thought of my quick sighting of Dwight Orkman during the show and gasped a little. Where he had been standing, leaning against the waterfront pavilion, he could easily have come from the dark logging show grounds, probably without anyone noticing during the noise and distraction of the shells going off overhead.

"What?" asked the chief quickly. I told him what I had noticed, albeit briefly. "I wouldn't have considered Dwight likely; he and the mayor have been hand in glove since he was hired, and he seemed a pretty loyal supporter. But, given what

I heard during the afternoon, I don't know. She pretty much threatened him with the loss of his job, and I know he's sold his house in his former city to make an investment here.

"Wow. This feels weird and rather unpleasant," I said slowly a moment later. "I'm informing on people, and all but one of them, or even all of them, are completely innocent."

"This was a murder, and you're helping the police work out who committed it," shrugged Abhay. "All the bits of information we get help us to build up a picture of what happened. I wouldn't worry about it."

I reflected on the fact that one of the possible suspects I had just implicated was Tom's boss, since all the City department heads reported to the city manager. But that was just too complicated to deal with just then, and I had too many other questions to ask.

"Well, you guys are obviously working flat out," I changed tack. "I assume you're talking with everyone who is relevant, but that could be a lot of people, and those from out of town are either about to leave or have gone already. How are you going to manage it?"

"We get a lot of help when something like this happens, at least for a while," the chief assured me. He reminded me of Norfolk County's Major Crime Team, which assembled local, county, and even state law enforcement resources for a few days after a serious crime. The team worked under the direction of the local detective in the relevant jurisdiction—we had one in Sheffield—and received priority status at Oregon law enforcement labs in Portland for tests like DNA matches. Lesser tests, like fingerprints, could be done locally due to the spread of electronic databases and newer collection techniques.

But this wasn't a television show, where all the magic test results came in just five minutes so that the crime could be solved inside a 48-minute program without the actors needing a costume change. Postmortem results would take days to receive, and DNA testing could be a month or more, even with priority status. In a state with a lot of geography but not that many people and only one large city, resources are not what they probably should be.

I appreciated Tom's coming to talk with us rather than sending the detective, although I didn't want to make a big deal of it by mentioning it. The chief probably had a fairly long list of people to get through, and since he knew us, he might be able to gauge our truthfulness better than a stranger would, anyway.

"This isn't the usual type of serious crime," he continued. "We get the occasional murder, but the mayor being a public official, and the way the crime was committed—this is a much more complicated situation. I don't know that we'll catch who did it before we have more information, like an exact cause and time of death. But we'll get him eventually."

I didn't doubt him then. But as I left to get David for his own interview, I couldn't help wondering what the reaction to her death would be throughout the community, and how that would play out between now and whenever her murder was solved.

Chapter Six

Thirty years ago, people might go to the grocery store or a coffee shop to cluster around and talk about a major event: starting rumors, exaggerating facts, and just generally being energized by discussing an unusual happening. Now, of course, we have social media, which means that vastly more people can start rumors, exaggerate facts, and give uneducated opinions, from anywhere, faster. Usually, I try to limit my exposure to social media—there are just so many images of rainbows, grandchildren I'll never meet in person, and uplifting quotes I can stand on a given day—but on that Sunday and in the following days, those sites were a good way to check whether anyone had any additional, real information and to get a feel for the overall reaction.

In the case of Greta's death, a lot of the postings were predictable. There were the usual saccharine accolades during the day following her killing: "She was just the BEST person, and the most WONDERFUL mayor!"; "Sheffield will be just lost without Greta Sutton!"; "That woman was just a *saint*, all the wonderful things she did for this town!" I didn't respond to those, and it was only momentarily tempting; after all, my version of the Truth About Greta Sutton was only another opinion in Social Media Land.

I wish people would be more accurate in their statements as a general rule, and this applies equally when mentioning the recently deceased. Frankly, postmortem comments seem to convert the most ordinary people into minor idols once they're dead. What's wrong with portraying them accurately? "He was a decent husband, if not the most affectionate; he tried to hold a steady job and he loved his children. He enjoyed hobbies that might have seemed strange but was never arrested. And that gambling problem was just a rumor." You know: not critical, but truthful—appreciating someone for who they truly had been. Do we turn dead people into something they weren't to exaggerate our own loss and justify our sorrow? Or assuage our relief, and accompanying sense of guilt, that it wasn't us who died? Or maybe just to continue the habit, in the hope that others will gloss over our own faults once we're gone? But I'm digressing again.

For Greta Sutton, the commentary quickly started dividing into two highly differing camps: those who wanted to beatify her and immediately name a park/street/ballfield after her (Ballfield? For a nearly elderly woman who couldn't have run ten steps without wheezing?), and those—fewer, because of that strange superstition about not speaking ill of the dead—who acknowledged their sighs of relief, their hopes for a more responsible leader and an end to the prospect of a nasty scandal, City financial hardship, or outright ruin. Most of these were polite, at least, although the odd "Ding, dong, the bitch is dead" did creep in. I had a feeling those people might be getting a visit from someone on the Major Crime Team.

Not that her murder—that it had been murder was

understood immediately, as the word went out about her likely being hit on the head, and hardly anyone does that to oneself—wasn't scandal enough. I didn't realize at the time what that dichotomy of opinion might do.

And of course, the phone calls were flying thick and fast, as well. Kate Dennis called me first thing Monday morning.

"Hey, Kate," I answered, not really knowing how to start. "How's it going?"

"I'm still feeling a little light-headed over this," she answered. "I mean, a lot of people really disliked the mayor, but who knocks a stupid old woman over the head in the middle of a festival?"

I gathered she had heard about the choker chain found at the scene, but I wondered if Council members had been privy to any other information.

"Kate, are Council members hearing anything the rest of us haven't?"

"Nah—I think Greta's friends and supporters are all commiserating with each other, but the cops aren't telling us anything. I know the Major Crime Team has taken over the case, but I don't think we'll hear anything for a while."

In an area with a small population and tight resources, sharing and collaboration were absolute necessities. The MCT was the only way a lot of resources could be devoted to solving a difficult crime, at least for a short time. The concept had worked well before—I was aware of at least one drug ring that had been broken up—but given the nature of Greta's murder, I wasn't sure the five days allotted for intense work by the Team would be enough.

"Is Chief Abhay being asked to provide some kind of report at the next Council meeting?"

Kate was the Council president, which normally didn't mean much, but it did call on her to assume the duties of the position in the event the mayor was unable to perform them, so to speak. She did not become mayor now but would preside over meetings until the Council appointed someone to fill the mayor's term. That person would serve only for the rest of the year; the mayor and half the Council were up for election in November.

"I thought of asking for some kind of briefing, but I don't know what the chief will be able to say," Kate said thoughtfully. "It's worth asking, though. I'll ask the city manager to talk with him about it."

This already marked a change for the better. The late Mayor Sutton would not have hesitated to contact the chief, any of the officers, or even the dispatchers directly to ask for whatever she wanted.

"I didn't see you down there on Saturday," I added. "Were you at the Festival? Did you see Greta then?"

"We had a family event in Salem in the afternoon," she replied, "but we came back before the fireworks. I think I saw Greta milling around in her turquoise getup, but I didn't talk to her. I mean, why ruin a perfectly nice day? That 'sweet old lady' smile of hers made me want to upchuck."

"Well, we won't have to see that again," I mused.

"Felice, do you know anything about who might have done this?"

"Do I know who might have bashed the mayor over the head? And did I, for some reason, decide not to give that person up to the police? That's absurd. Why are people asking me this?"

"Well, if you must know," Kate said slowly, "I've already

heard from a couple of people about an argument you had with her on Saturday afternoon. They'd like to think you're the prime suspect."

"Wow, that's really sweet of them." I shook my head. "As if I were the only person who couldn't stand the woman. I wasn't even the only person she argued with.

"I certainly did not bash the mayor over the head or hear of anyone else who planned to do so. If I had been stupid enough to consider killing her, I would have been much more subtle."

"True. This was nasty. You're very . . . candid in your statements. But you don't make personal insults, and I've never seen you lose your temper, even over Greta Sutton." Now she was joking back.

"And we don't know yet whether it was someone who did just lose his temper and pick up something handy," I responded, "or part of something more premeditated." Kate's statement made me realize how much the rumor mill was already churning. I wondered just how many people were talking about me as a potential killer, but I had to put that aside.

"We aren't going to know that for a while," Kate added. "My understanding of how the police work in a case like this is that most information comes from labs in Portland. We probably won't know exactly how she died for some days yet."

"And meanwhile, the rumors will circulate, and the factions will keep crystallizing." I bemoaned the truth of small-town life. "I wish we could just put everyone in stasis or close a lot of mouths with duct tape until the results are known and we can deal with facts."

"Like the facts will make a difference," she scoffed. "You really haven't lived in Sheffield very long, have you?"

She was right. Even during our few years in the community, we'd heard some amazingly outlandish rumors based on few to no facts. Which made me consider again how many people would start hearing things and getting upset, and what they might do as a result.

"Are you going to have trouble leading the Council, Kate?" I asked, wondering if public meetings were about to get controversial. "You definitely weren't one of those backing the mayor."

"I'm going to try for solidarity, at least. We'll have to conduct some kind of ceremony, maybe leave her center chair vacant for a meeting. I think that's appropriate," she said. "I think we'll be able to go forward after that, but it's going to take a while to work through all the pending issues she had started, and I do plan to try to turn some of her work around. The big question is whether I'll have Dwight's support."

We both fell silent at that. I thought about telling Kate of the conversation I overheard between the dead woman and the city manager, but it was too early to get into that kind of intrigue and too much of a confidence. Plus, it didn't really say much about Dwight's preferences. He had sided with the mayor over staff objections, but would he now back Kate in overturning some of those decisions? Or would he stick with Greta's former faction of the Council and keep pushing her agenda, even knowing it was bad for the budget? Kate had a relationship of her own with the city manager through her position on the Council, but she would have to work with him more closely now.

"Kate, you know all this better than I do, but you might want to sound him out a bit on some of the issues that concern you," was about all I felt comfortable saying. "He may not have

62

been as supportive of Greta as he seemed, but you won't know until you've talked with him whether you'll be able to trust him."

Which reminded me of the big question. "Um, speaking of rumors, Kate, have you heard anything about the mayor and Dwight proposing a new building for the City?"

"What, you mean *building* a new building? No way—we don't have an extra dime for something like that, especially given the way Greta has been siphoning off the budget for her pet projects." I knew that Kate and at least one other Council member had been especially angry about a measure diverting a full fifty thousand dollars from an already-passed budget to support a recreation program offered by a local nonprofit—one where Greta volunteered. It was a lot of money for a small city on a tight budget, and the largest improper siphoning in dollars that I had heard about, but councilors had been pressured several times since Greta's taking office. This was a murky area, since Oregon law requires balanced budgets and spending procedure is followed.

"That's what I thought, but I heard her mention something about a building in a conversation Saturday that I wasn't supposed to hear. I would recommend you try to track that one down—that could be behind a lot of the strange stuff that has been brought up at Council meetings recently, including this Festival gate percentage mess."

"Wow—thanks for the tip. Something else to bring up with Dwight."

"And I should probably mention that I also had a conversation with Carl Roetgen on Saturday. He was pretty upset about Greta's plans to annex the property he wants to develop. Is the Council moving forward on that?" Our conversation was beginning to sound more like an interrogation, but I thought I should bring up anything that Kate might be facing.

"God, I have a lot of work ahead of me," she groaned.

"You have to do something to justify that fat salary, my friend." Which was a laugh—City councilor was a volunteer position and no one, including the mayor, was paid. It always made me wonder why people were willing to spend a fair amount of money on signs, flyers, and advertising to get themselves elected. Is that a true sign of ego, or what?

"Kate, I am so glad you are there to take this over," I said more seriously. "I think you're the best person the City could have to work through what needs to be done."

We hung up a few minutes later, with me feeling that at least I had given some useful information to someone who would know how to use it properly. Kate was well-liked, even by those councilors whom she opposed on issues; the tall, former finance manager had a way of voicing her concerns and objections in a thoughtful, even kind way that I could never have managed. If anyone could bring factions together while improving the quality of local government, she was my choice. My head hurt just thinking about the impulses I would have had to suppress—to shoot laser death-glances at some of those people at the very least. Democracy is great, but I really would have made a much better absolute monarch. *Benevolent, fair, but don't screw with me.* And I would wear a really big tiara. It was a good thought.

Chapter Seven

Unfortunately, the rest of the world didn't recognize my right to benign leadership, so the next few days included the usual round of un-queenlike tasks without a tiara in sight. God, I hate making beds; was there ever a chore more subject to persistent failure? Although getting into an unmade bed is just *uncivilized*, somehow. And don't even talk to me about dusting.

Just to be clear, though—I am not howling in a domestic wilderness. David is an honest believer in "our house, our work," and he does more around our house than I do. And I bear no grudge toward the nonhuman members of the household. I'm sure the dog would help if he could figure out how and if there were peanut butter in it for him—Angus is a calm, intelligent and social soul with a devout wish for a happy pack. He will do pretty much anything you can devise for peanut butter. The cats—smart, gray Alexander and affectionate but absent-minded, gray-and-white Roxana— assume that all of this is being done for them and are happy as long as they don't have to point out that you're doing something incorrectly.

I gave many thoughts to the investigation into Greta's death during the next few days but could only hope that the various authorities were moving forward. Inquiries on social media into what was happening were met with ignorance, as far as I could tell, although I heard that various Festival vendors and visitors were being tracked down for interviews.

In the back of my mind, there was a growing conflict. I hadn't liked Greta Sutton; in fact, I had been convinced she was a completely negative influence on Sheffield. But I continued to wonder about, and be upset by, her death. I couldn't shed tears for the victim, but I was angry about the crime. Who had the utter gall to think they could carry out and get away with killing her? The idea cast a sort of dark spot in the middle of the community environment, like a blight in a green lawn, and I couldn't help thinking that the spot would grow if not tracked down and eliminated.

The next City Council meeting was on Wednesday evening, and I decided to attend, to lend visible support to Kate and possibly hear whatever Chief Abhay could impart, if nothing else. That evening, City Hall's parking lot was full, as were parking spaces on both sides of the street nearby; but I found a spot about a block away. Not surprisingly, nearly all the audience chairs in the Council chambers were filling up as I went in, with knots of people conversing around the room. The atmosphere was not funereal, and it didn't seem as though the conversation centered solely on the mayor's death, but I couldn't think what else would have drawn this many people to the normally sparsely attended meeting.

The Sheffield City Council chambers aren't particularly impressive. Spending a lot of money on "fancy decor" would have caused grumbling among the citizens. The room had two entrances, one from City Hall proper and another from the parking lot. There was a nice dais at one end with a long, wooden desk paneled and trimmed out in a dark stain and sitting about a foot higher than the rest of the room, the City seal on the center panel. It was in a semicircle so that councilors could see each other for the substantive discussions that normally would take place during meetings. These had not been heard much under the late mayor. Behind the desk was a mounted bronze sculpture of water and trees with a painted mural around it. The dais was lit up by a row of track lighting. The rest of the room accommodated several rows of hard chairs, which didn't make sitting through a meeting any easier. Come to think of it, that may have been another reason why few people usually bothered to attend; those chairs were butt-killers.

I waved hello to Kate on the dais—she was conferring in low tones with Suzanne Dryer but waved back—and noticed the distinctly empty seat in the center, as Kate had predicted. Someone had draped a piece of black fabric over the back of the chair, and there was a bouquet of flowers sitting on the desk.

I sat in an empty seat toward the back, said hello to some acquaintances, and looked around to get a better idea of who was here and, maybe, why. At least some were people I knew were Greta supporters, always present to be seen at whatever official ceremony might take place. My jaded self was reminded that there really isn't much going on in Sheffield on the average evening; this way, they could tell all their friends that they had been here for the governmental mourning. Strangely, Patrick Sutton was not present; I could only guess he didn't need the reminders of his wife's absence.

Attending in force was the Draper family: four people including an older man I assumed to be the patriarch Ron, two younger men who looked like brothers, and a young woman. I had a feeling that expressing sorrow over Greta's death wasn't on their agenda—quite the opposite, probably. I hadn't checked the agenda after deciding to come to the meeting, so I didn't know whether that controversial "grab a piece of the Festival gate" measure was still up for discussion.

There were still a few minutes until the proceedings started, and I was just trying to identify others of my audience neighbors when a tall shape materialized in front of me.

"Hello, Felice," came Abhay's deep voice.

I looked up. "Hi, Chief. I'd ask how you're doing, but I don't imagine the last few days have been too enjoyable."

"You got that right," said Abhay, dropping into the empty chair beside me. I turned to look more closely at him and saw the dark circles under his dark brown eyes, although he still radiated his usual air of calm command.

"Kate Dennis said you might be able to give a short report on the investigation tonight," I continued, torn between staying professional and making a sympathetic noise. The man didn't need people telling him he looked worn out. "Is that possible?"

"Yeah. I can't say much, but we know people are curious, and maybe we can stop some of the rumors."

"That's helpful. There are only a couple more days of the Major Crime Team focus, right? Has that worked well?" This was the closest I felt comfortable to asking, *"Do you know who did it yet?"*—an inquiry I figured he'd had to respond to much too often since Sunday morning.

"One more day. We've done a lot of work, but there's a lot

left."

I nodded, repressing my desire to ask a lot of questions he wouldn't, or couldn't, answer.

"That's why I came over here. Can I come talk with you again tomorrow?"

I looked bemused, which pretty much reflected how I felt. "Sure. Is there something else you think I can tell you?"

"I'd like to go over the events of Saturday with you again— you seemed to have seen more than most people. And I have a few other reports I'd like to fit with your story."

"Wow. Okay. I'll help however I can."

He nodded, got up, and went back to the staff table as I pondered what he had said, wondering whether I was, indeed, a suspect in the murder. But I didn't have much time to think about it, because Kate was bringing down the gavel to start the Council meeting.

There are good reasons why most people don't go to their local City Council meetings. Let's face it, they're boring. Most people have little interest in what takes place there. Unless you have a paranoid streak and are convinced that councilors are stealing your tax dollars to take jaunts to Jamaica (okay, a few do, but it's unusual), it's difficult to sit through all the reports, staff recommendations, check registers, and whatever else is an integral, daily part of government without your eyes glazing over. There's just so much discussion most people can stand about whether it's time to replace a thirty-year-old piece of equipment or whether a street project will include curbs and gutters. Unless it's your street, of course.

Across the curved desk were three seats on either side of the mayor's vacant place. From left to right were George Russell, the musician and environmentalist; Anne Perez, another former schoolteacher about the same age as Greta and her staunchest sidekick; and Kate, sitting for tonight in the chair closest to the center. On the other side of the black-draped place were Dennis Waitly, a fiftyish man I liked for his candid comments; Suzanne Dryer, whom I'd last seen serving food at the Festival; and Pete Ichikawa, a local charter fishing boat owner who had also been a Sutton mouthpiece.

Usually, the only time there were lots of people at a Sheffield City Council meeting was when there was something controversial going on, or perhaps, like tonight, something ceremonial in which people would feel a need to participate.

Kate's job, as I saw it, was to make this one boring, too, by getting through the potentially emotional or controversial bits as methodically as possible. She did a good job, starting with the announcement of the mayor's death from her seat next to the empty center chair.

"We are all saddened by the tragic death of Mayor Greta Sutton last weekend," she began, her dark head bent over the desk before her eyes came up to range across the audience. "Mayor Sutton was well-liked by many in the community, and while her actions were sometimes controversial"—angry rumbling from some seats in the audience, head-nodding from others—"there is no doubt that she cared deeply about Sheffield. This is a tragedy, not only for her family but for the city as a whole—we don't like to think of Sheffield as a place where this sort of thing happens.

"We will hear from Chief Abhay later in this meeting about the status of the investigation into her death, and I'm sure he will tell us all he can, so I would appreciate everyone refraining from questions or speculation about that.

"We'll now take a few minutes to allow public comment on this or other subjects not on the agenda. Please limit your comments to five minutes, and if someone else has already stated what you wish to say, please consider whether you also need to speak, as this is meant to be an opportunity to bring matters before the Council for our consideration. I know there will be other ceremonies or services designed to remember the mayor."

It was cleverly done and succeeded in preventing the meeting from turning into a wake or fomenting an increasing level of hostile questions about the murder investigation. There were only four speakers who felt the call to express their love for their lost leader when it came down to it, and they mostly did it with honest emotion and without any demands to law enforcement other than stating a hope that the person responsible was caught soon. Luckily, no one felt the urge to step up and say anything negative about the victim, or perhaps those who might have were stymied by the measured gaze of the police chief, whom I noticed kept scanning the audience. I could tell Kate's relief when the last speaker finished and no one else came forward, but that's only because I know her well.

The agenda portion of the meeting proceeded without incident. I began to wonder whether Greta had planned to add the Festival issue to the agenda without prior notice. She had done that in the past to prevent any prepared opposition to something she knew would be questioned. It's permissible if the Council votes to add it, but not strictly kosher if you're running a transparent government. In Mayor Sutton's case, agreement to the amendment generally was set up in advance through her contacting other councilors. That activity was less ambiguous and definitely wrong.

Note to self: when you go to a meeting, check the agenda first. I wasn't quite dozing off, but my head came up quickly when Kate said, "We have another item tonight," in a tone that showed her discomfort. I looked over to the Drapers, and they had stiffened too, like retrievers going on point.

"There has been some discussion in another forum about possible changes to the operation of the Summer Festival," she hedged. Turning to the Draper contingent, she continued, "First, I'd like to congratulate the Festival Committee and other organizers for another successful event. Yes, we had a tragedy, but I hope everyone in Sheffield appreciates all the hard work that went into the event. Many local groups will benefit from the Festival, as always, and the fireworks show continues to improve every year."

There were nods and mumbles of assent; it was impossible, of course, to pass around unmitigated congratulations.

"You will see on the agenda a discussion item about revenue from the Summer Festival," Kate continued straight-forwardly. "We'll certainly entertain discussion about this, should a majority of councilors wish to do so, but this item is one that is new to several of us. Given the events of this weekend, I'd like to recommend that this item be tabled for the time being. Without some significant discussion, I can't imagine that we are ready to take this forward tonight. What does everyone think?"

I leaned forward to take in as much as I could from the councilors' expressions. How far would Greta's influence go now that she wasn't here? And what sort of other, interesting reactions might there be, especially from City Manager Dwight?

As usual when in front of an audience, councilors looked

at each other, down at the table, and back toward the meeting chair—anywhere other than at the spectators. Anne Perez and Pete Ichikawa, Greta's most reliable sidekicks, looked at each other and seemed to be ready to say something in protest. Given the conversation between Greta and Suzanne Dryer that I had overheard, I was not surprised to see Suzanne nodding in agreement. Among other reactions was George Russell's silence; he was among the "looking down at the desk" contingent.

Overall, Kate's solution seemed to be carrying the day. The two sidekicks saw the lay of the land and suppressed whatever comment they may have been planning. After about ten seconds and a couple of looks in each direction, Kate spoke up again.

"Okay, I will take that as assent. City Manager, I don't believe we need a motion to table a discussion item, do we?"

"Uh, no," said Dwight, looking at his notebook. I doubted the Rules of Order were in front of him, so I guessed this was more to give him some time than anything else. "No, you certainly can table this for this meeting. Do you know when you'd like to add it to another agenda?"

"Why don't we just leave it for the moment," said Kate with a quick glance around. "I think all of us have some adjusting to do, and we have a vacancy to fill. The Summer Festival is a major Sheffield tradition; perhaps it's only fair that our new councilor has a chance to participate in something that might prove controversial."

This seemed to be the acceptable way out of the dilemma, as there were nods and mumbles all around, including Dwight's. Few people will protest a delay in a controversial issue; it's a lot easier than fighting it openly, and you can always hope it will just go away. The Drapers exhaled and relaxed, then got up to leave, along with several other attendees, although the room was still more than half full.

I checked the agenda, belatedly looking for other items. The proposed annexation of Carl Roetgen's property wasn't listed, so that probably was further down in the pipeline. Work through the listed items continued, and it was close to the end when Kate asked for City department reports. She began with Chief Abhay, addressing him as he sat in the audience.

"Chief, I know it's early days yet, and I know your department has been working flat out along with others from around the area. On behalf of the Council and the rest of Sheffield, I want to thank you for all your hard work and ask you what you can tell us about the investigation into the mayor's death."

Abhay walked to the speaker's table, the light glinting off bits of his uniform. He looked solid, responsible, and tired as he sat and turned to address the dais.

"As you mentioned, Councilor Dennis, we've been working with a lot of other agencies since early Sunday morning. We assembled the Major Crime Team, which gives us access to resources we don't usually have—it's being led by our detective Jim Paget. That effort will go on for a while longer.

"We've talked with a lot of people, and we have more to talk with. We've also collected some evidence that's gone to Portland for lab analysis. We're waiting for results from a postmortem—that report should be here tomorrow, and we'll know more then.

"I can't say a lot more than that right now. Obviously, this is an important case for the Department and the City, and we'll be carrying on the investigation along with our regular work and getting good help from other departments like the Norfolk County Sheriff and the State Police."

Looking up, he glanced into the audience and continued. "I'd like to ask anybody who may have seen anything unusual last Saturday, especially during the evening, to call the Sheffield Police Department or come talk with us. You might not think it's important, but your information may fit with other pieces we've collected and could help us."

Abhay looked down at his notes and then back up again, his eyes scanning the room before coming back to rest on the city manager and the councilors on their dais.

"That's about all I have for now. Personally, I'd like to echo that this is a tragedy for the City and that citizens can be sure that we will work on it until it's solved. Thanks for the opportunity to come talk with you, and we hope to have more information for you soon."

Chapter Eight

Thursday brought another bright, dry morning of deep blue skies and enough warmth for short sleeves. I carried my daytime coffee quotient—one big mug of dark roast is all I allow myself, at least for the first several hours—into our sunroom to look at the landscape outside.

The room was one of the reasons David and I had fallen for our big old house. Walls of large, square panes of glass set into a wooden framework made up the windows on three sides with a view down the hill to the river. The sunroom certainly had won the votes of the family livestock, especially in summer when there was actually sun to give the room its name. Today, cats Alexander and Roxana and deerhound Angus had laid claim to their patches of developing sunshine and were lounging, the cats at each end of an old white cotton sofa and the big dog stretched out on the pastel Chinese rug in front of it. They didn't move much when I walked in.

"Good morning, lady and gentlemen," I addressed the room in my best hostess voice. "Welcome to the resort—can I offer you sunglasses? Perhaps a towel or a drink from the bar?"

Angus was too deeply into doggie paradise to respond at

all. One cat opened an eye long enough to glare at me, then closed it again with a long-suffering sigh. Cats just have no sense of humor.

True to his word, Chief Abhay knocked on the front door a few minutes after ten. David had already left for a round of errands, so it was just Tom and me walking back to the kitchen and its breakfast room table after I let him in.

I would never say this to him, but it was weird having a large man in uniform walking through my house. Not so much the uniform itself, but all the accoutrements: lots of black attachments, like the leather belt and square of the radio mic on his shoulder. And then there was the big, black gun in its black holster on his right hip. It was a bit like having an alien world suddenly connecting with mine, even though I knew and liked the man. I understand why cops don't like armchairs when they're in uniform—everything they're wearing makes them a lot bigger than usual, and they just don't fit well. And obviously, a bigger, more intimidating presence is a good idea when they're dealing with their usual clientele.

Luckily, my momma raised me right, and I didn't have anything to worry about in Abhay's presence.

"Can I get you some coffee, Chief?" I asked as I walked to the counter for a refill. Yes, it would be a second cup: it's my quotient and I'll break it if I want to.

"Smells good, but no, thanks, Felice. I've been drinking way too much coffee over the last few days."

"I can imagine. Anything else?"

He opted for a glass of ice water, and we both settled down at the round, dark oak table. I decided to let him sit for a bit without starting a conversation; regardless of all his training and experience, the man clearly had had a tough few days, and our house can be a pleasant haven.

He sat for a minute, looking through the casement windows at the street beyond, his eyes focusing briefly on a couple of twentysomething guys walking by with backpacks. *I guess a police officer never stops being a police officer. Good to remember.* He took a deep breath, then exhaled, and the salt-and-pepper head turned to me. I tried to look friendly without being inquisitive.

"So. Today is the last day that we get the full attention of the Major Crime Team," Abhay started. "And right now, we have a lot more questions than answers about the mayor's murder."

"Is that a surprise? From the circumstances, it didn't look easy, unless you found something that pointed to someone immediately."

"Nah, we didn't. What forensic evidence we did find is up in Portland, and it could be weeks before we hear anything. Frankly, I don't think it's going to be all that helpful."

He put his elbows on the table, clasped his hands together, and looked at me. "The evidence around the crime itself probably isn't going to solve it—at least, not anytime soon. There were just too many people in town and too much going on. We need to figure out *why* she was killed. I think it has something to do with her activities, either privately or as mayor. That's why I'm here.

"But first, I need to go over what you saw on Saturday again. Tell me about all the times you encountered the mayor and the other people you noticed during the afternoon and through the fireworks."

After the passage of days and many times going through it for myself, I felt a lot less squirmy than I had on Sunday. I sat for a moment to get my thoughts together, staring up at our breakfast room ceiling with one hand on my coffee mug, then looked down at the table and started a calm recitation.

"I saw Greta around the waterfront pavilion, talking with Suzanne Dryer and asking for her vote on getting a piece of the Festival gate," I started. "That's when I noticed the *Chronicle* reporter, who was obviously listening and taking notes. I talked with her for a moment to find out what her angle was and see if I could put her straight, then Greta chased after me to tell me not to talk with the press. I had sort of had it with her by then, so I blew up a bit and told her off." I winced and glanced at him, but he just kept his expert noncommittal look and nodded.

"Let's see. I noticed her around the grounds for a while longer—she was passing out those stupid 'Chat with the Mayor' flyers and talking with people. I went over to the music stage for about a half hour, talked with Carl Roetgen—I told you that he was worried about Greta trying to annex the property he wants to develop—then headed for the vendor tents. When I saw her disappearing behind a tent, I wondered whether she was meeting someone and what she might be up to. It isn't the noblest thing I've ever done, but I went into the tent and overheard her conversation with Dwight when they discussed the Festival issue. He was not enthusiastic about following it up, and she basically threatened his job, and they mentioned something about a new building."

I went through my other observations from the day, including the very public disagreement between Greta and her husband and my later sighting of him just before the fireworks started.

"And you're sure that the mayor was not with him then?"

"Definitely not, because he was looking annoyed and I assumed at the time that he was searching for her. And I looked around, too, and didn't see her anywhere."

"And he headed away from the waterfront park and toward the midway and show grounds." The chief was already familiar with my statement.

"Ye-es," I confirmed, realizing that Patrick had been heading to the apparent scene of Greta's murder, although I didn't know at what time that had happened.

"Did you see him again that night?"

"No, but there were so many people milling around at the end of the show. We were just concentrating on packing up and heading up the hill. I really wasn't paying attention."

"And you also saw Dwight Orkman that evening," Abhay prompted.

"Yes, in the middle of the fireworks show. The shells lit up the grounds enough that I noticed him leaning against one of the pillars of the pavilion. I know he hadn't been there a few minutes earlier, but I didn't see how he got there or from what direction."

"Do you remember seeing anyone else acting strangely or someone you know being somewhere you wouldn't expect them? How about the other City councilors?"

"I saw Carl walking around the park at various times and remember wondering what he was doing; his business was a big sponsor, but I don't think he had any actual responsibilities for the Festival. I think I saw Suzanne selling food most of the day, and again that evening, but not once it started getting dark. I didn't see Kate Dennis at all—she's since told me that she and her husband were in Salem most of the day."

"Yes, we've confirmed that."

"Oh, good," I said with a sigh, relieved that I didn't have to worry about a good friend lying to me or the police, although since Kate had been back in town for the fireworks, she still could be a suspect. "I don't remember seeing any of the other councilors. Except George and Rita Russell were playing on the music stage, it seemed, every time I looked over there."

"During the fireworks?"

"I think I heard them then, although the stage was too far away to see clearly. And of course, you couldn't hear much of anything else once the show started."

I couldn't think of anything else despite his additional questions. The chief sat in thought after I stopped talking, looking conflicted, which was not like him.

"So-oo," I ventured, "what's going on?"

He put his elbows on the table and looked straight into my eyes.

"You know about the concept of community policing, Felice, right?"

The question caught me off guard.

"Not entirely. I know it means more involvement with individuals on a day-to-day basis—more of gearing your work to emphasize that police are members of the community and not just people in uniform who look at everyone with suspicion. But that's about it."

He gave me that one-sided smile again. "Yeah, that's the basic idea. But it also means that we sometimes ask for help from the community, and that's why I'm here."

My eyebrows went up, but I kept still while he continued.

"You aren't a sworn officer and you don't have police training. But in this case, I don't think police interviews are going to get us much further. Also, I haven't got the resources to devote to this without leaving Sheffield lacking everyday protection.

"You're levelheaded, you have a legal background, and you're active around the city. You know the other people who are." He took a deep breath before continuing. "I'd like to ask you to talk to folks—carefully—and pass back to me what you hear."

I was stunned, my brain running through scenarios until I realized I needed to respond. "I have to tell you . . . I have been increasingly worried about what this could do to Sheffield if it isn't solved," I began. "But do you really think I can help? You know there are people here, especially the old-timers, who don't like David and me."

"That's actually one reason for choosing you. I don't think you'll play favorites. I know you're upset by possible ethics violations, just as an example—that points to someone who will be honest about what she finds, whatever it might be."

"Okay. Thanks. So—I talk casually to people about what's going on in the city that might have led to the murder. I have the excuse of hearing Greta mention things on Saturday and can work for more information on those. Obviously, I don't tell anyone I'm working for you"— I looked over at Abhay and he nodded —"and I can keep some notes, maybe get some ideas on how things fit together, and pass what fragments I get on to you."

"That's pretty much what I was thinking. I can tell you some of what we've learned on our side—that's mostly to make sure you don't walk into anything dangerous. I'm giving you a real warning there – I don't want you in a risky situation.

"I've thought about this a lot, and I wouldn't ask the average civilian to get involved in a murder investigation. But

I just don't know how else we'll get to the bottom of this case."

"So—no meetings with big, hairy suspects at night without taking David and the dog," I smiled at him.

"No meetings with anyone who seems like a real suspect," he glared at me. "You leave that to us. This is someone who has already killed a woman for some personal reason in a pretty nasty way. Don't ever forget that."

"Not likely. I certainly don't want to get bashed in the head by a choker chain, if that's what it was."

"That's what we thought," Abhay said after a hesitation. "But we got the postmortem report back first thing this morning, and this is probably some information that I should pass on to you. I'd appreciate it if you didn't say this to anyone else, at least until we make it public, and I'm not sure yet if and when we're going to do that.

"We did find a choker chain at the scene, and it did show signs of having been used to hit someone. We're fairly sure it was used on the mayor, but the lab results aren't back yet, so I can't confirm that for sure."

He continued to stare right at me. "But one other thing we noticed when we examined the body at the scene was that her hair and neck in back were wet. There wasn't any water on her face, so we just assumed it was dew from her lying in the grass overnight. But the autopsy shows that this was an even nastier crime than we thought.

"Greta Sutton wasn't just hit in the head because she made the wrong person lose his temper. Greta Sutton was hit over the head to keep her quiet, taken to a specific place, and then her head was put into a plastic bag of water and held there. Greta Sutton was very deliberately drowned."

Chapter Nine

"Holy crap." It came out before I could put a brake on my mouth. I suppose I had assumed that Greta had just driven the wrong person to momentary rage on Saturday night. Lord knows she had been good at it. But Tom was right; this was different.

"They're sure about this? She was deliberately drowned?"

The chief nodded, watching me closely.

I stared out the breakfast room window without seeing, trying to let the whirling in my head subside to something coherent. The fact raised so many questions and had so many implications.

"Why? Why would someone go to that much trouble?" I said slowly. "She was an old lady; well, not elderly, but no match for any young or strong person. If you want to kill her, why not just bash her over the head and be done with it?" I stared back at Abhay.

"That's what I've been wondering ever since I saw the report this morning," he replied. "This is mean; it's deliberate. Maybe more importantly, it took planning and it took time to carry out. It almost certainly means that she was a target because of something she had done."

"Could it be a serial method? Do you know whether anything like this has happened before? We haven't lived here long enough to know."

He shook his head. "I haven't looked at the records, but I don't need to—for Norfolk County, at least. I've been in law enforcement around here for more than twenty years. We've had some killings, of course, but nothing that involved a blow to the head and drowning, especially on dry land with a plastic bag full of water. There's nothing at all that's similar."

"So, this was definitely about Greta, and someone hated her enough to plan a complicated scenario and carry it out. He had a lot of nerve, too—there were twenty thousand people in Sheffield that night! Anyone could have been wandering around and seen him."

"I'm still hoping that someone did, but it's looking less and less likely. The autopsy report says she died between 9:00 p.m. and midnight. We're thinking it had to have been during the fireworks when nearly everyone was concentrating on the show. In areas away from the waterfront park, it was pretty dark and deserted."

"Have you been able to talk with the midway operators?" I assumed that those people were used to noise and lights and might have been more aware of something out of the ordinary happening near them.

"Yes, the sheriff's deputies and state police caught up with the midway, both before it was broken down and taken away, and at its next stop," Abhay answered. "Those who weren't operating equipment were either looking at the fireworks or watching for the usual trouble on the midway—kids, or someone who had one too many. None of them saw anything suspicious."

"Like an unidentified someone carrying an unconscious woman over his shoulder. Yeah, that would have been too easy," I grimaced. "I guess the next question is: how about people in Sheffield with a criminal history? Anyone this nasty who might have carried out a murder?"

Abhay bent his head to one side and pursed his lips before answering. "We have our share of bad guys, but we're pretty familiar with all of them. One or two might take a heavy object to someone, but it probably would have been about drugs, someone would have been drunk or high, and it would have been simple. The guys we know about wouldn't have the brains to carry out a crime this deliberate."

I realized I was going over ground that the police had thoroughly traversed during the past several days. "I'm sorry; you've asked and answered all these questions for yourself already. I didn't mean to interrogate you."

"Never hurts to have another brain thinking about a problem," he responded with a small smile. "But you can see what I mean about having to be careful if you're going to talk with people. This guy is . . ."

"Devious? Clever?"

"Yeah. I didn't want to say smart, because someone really smart would have found another solution to his problem besides killing the mayor."

I hadn't thought about it that way, but he was right. "Which means the biggest question we need to answer is— what was the problem? Wow, this is just like Hercule Poirot. Find the *why*, and you'll know the *who*."

"Just remember, Felice, this is real life. Do *not* try to solve this and confront anyone. If you do think you've discovered a lead, don't tell anyone but me."

"Or David. I have to keep him in the loop, and I might look less suspiciously nosy if he comes with me sometimes."

"Okay. He isn't a cop, either, but at least he's bigger than you and might give someone second thoughts about hurting you. Talk with people as casually as you can and let me know what they say. We have statements from most people associated with the mayor, so we're looking for inconsistencies as much as new information."

We spent another several minutes listing the people he wanted me to approach. There weren't a lot of surprises: City councilors, business owners, even Patrick Sutton, Greta's husband—all of them people I already knew, at least a bit. Approaching some of them was going to take some prior thought, as some were among the cadre of Sheffield long-timers who thought David and I had hidden horns and tails. Abhay issued another warning, I made additional promises to be careful (without rolling my eyes; I did understand how difficult this was for him as well as potentially serious for me), and he finally left.

David was less than jubilant about the idea when he returned home that afternoon and I had a chance to talk with him about my meeting with the police chief. As often happens when we discuss something, we were both in the kitchen, leaning on counters on opposite ends of the large space. Or at least I was leaning, trying to look nonchalant. David's initial posture was a lot more rigid.

"He wants you to do *what*?"

"Just talk with people. Be casual and careful, and let him know what's said."

"Talk with potential murderers. You're not a cop. What's

to keep someone from coming after you?"

"For asking them about the last time they saw Greta? With a sympathetic look over the loss of their friend? Chances are I won't get anywhere close to the killer, David—it's more about filling in gaps about what was going on around her, what she may have said to someone, or done, with her usual lack of thought."

His blue gaze was challenging. "No one is going to believe that you're grieving with them."

"Well, duh. I'm not going to pretend that I liked her. But I can give the impression that I'm worried about what happens next for the city, and that isn't an act. I *am* concerned about the community, especially once it gets out just how nastily she was killed."

"I can understand that." The level of his voice had come down a bit, so I knew he was past "initial negative reaction" and into thoughtful mode. Once David gets thinking about a problem, he generally has particularly good, helpful ideas, and I wanted that help. I walked over to the other side of his counter while he thought.

"You're going to have a hard time getting in front of some of these people; maybe it would be better if I came with you for those meetings." His head came up and the blue eyes snared me again. "And I definitely want to be with you if there is even a remote chance you might be in danger."

"That's good, sure. I haven't had a long time to think about this yet, but there might be social occasions where we could meet some of them. Isn't there a fundraiser coming up for that community theatre we don't like?"

"I think so. I'll look into it." But he wasn't finished yet. "Felice, if you're going to do this, I'm not going to get in your way. But I am going to be watching to make sure you're careful." I nodded. "And while we're casually meeting with people, I'm going to be doing some observing of my own."

This was a good thing. David tends to stand on the sidelines at social occasions unless he gets into a one-on-one conversation, like the one he had with the boat owner the previous Saturday. Then I usually have to pry him away with a verbal and nonverbal crowbar, up to and including, "We have to go now, dear" while smiling and tugging on his arm.

But when he's in observation mode, he comes up with telling insights. He once spent an evening during a conference with some work colleagues of mine, one of whom I just couldn't stomach, without knowing exactly why I felt that way. We went back to the hotel room at the end of the dinner, and he announced simply, "That guy is an idiot." He then offered two pithy sentences to explain his conclusion, and I realized he was spot on. It didn't help my relationship with the colleague, but I never had to wonder again why I didn't like him.

As it turned out, I didn't have to manufacture a reason to talk with new widower Patrick Sutton, which was good, because I had been completely unsuccessful in dreaming up something. The very next morning, I was out for a morning walk with my first-half-of-the-day mug of coffee and an enthusiastic Angus when we found Patrick at the neighborhood dog park just five blocks from the house.

I had known that Patrick was another retired school-teacher, and that he and Greta were not each other's first spouses, but hadn't known that they had a dog: this was a smallish, black-and-white miniature collie sort of animal. Patrick himself was midsize, of medium height, with short sandy hair. I usually saw him in a dress shirt and khakis, but today he was wearing shorts and a T-shirt for his outing with the dog. Both were inside the fenced enclosure, the dog running around doing doggy exploration while the man watched. Like most dog parks, this one has a double-gate entrance so that dogs and owners can come and go without other dogs rushing out or in case there was some canine excitement between those coming and already there. Both Patrick and his dog turned as we entered the first gate and walked across the small space to the second, the dog running to its owner as we waved to each other.

I hadn't met Patrick that many times, but my conversations with him had been more civil than those with his late wife. He was a mostly pleasant man whose students had liked him and who seemed interested in the facts of the world around him, a major contrast to his wife. My brain did some rapid calculations on how best to use the opportunity; I didn't know when I would get another. *Stay civilly friendly, stay open. He's probably been fawned over by Greta's friends; you can be a neutral, adult person to communicate with.*

Angus, bless him, started my work for me. He greeted both Patrick and the dog with his usual smiling dignity, trotting over, his wiry flag of a tail waving. After doing the mandatory, mutual back-end greeting (with the dog), Angus, as usual, focused on the person, using his height to wedge his head under Patrick's hand and coax some head-stroking—which, in Angus' optimistic world, could very well lead to ear scritches, the absolute best.

Patrick had been looking somber, but it's hard to withstand an Angus onslaught without smiling, if not laughing out loud. His face softened as he stroked the wiry head and looked up.

"Wow, he's big, but he's really nice. What's his name?"

"That's Angus. Tall and mostly calm, but he does love meeting people."

I hesitated, looking for the right opening. "I'm sorry for your loss, Patrick."

"Thank you." The standard condolence received the standard answer. His face remained carefully blank, although I looked hard for signs of grief. "It's hard to believe she's gone; I keep waiting for her to sweep through the door, talking a mile a minute."

"I can imagine." *Careful, Felice. Jeez, this is hard.* I did feel genuine sympathy for the man's loss but also had to concentrate on saying the right thing to get him to talk with me, all while suppressing the impulse for a truthful comment and staying believable. It was a tall order on short notice.

"I guess the last several days have been pretty awful. I hope the police have been keeping you up to date."

"A bit. But I seem to be a suspect. It's always the husband, right?" he said with some bitterness.

"Well, given the usual sort of thing they see, I suppose it's natural they start there," I said carefully. "But I think Chief Abhay and the other agencies are probably smart enough to move past that. All the confusion of the Festival certainly doesn't make their job any easier."

He shook his head, eyes to the ground. "I keep asking myself—who would want to kill Greta? How did she even get to the show grounds instead of watching the fireworks? What the hell was going on?" He seemed angry as he met my eyes, which to me was a good sign. Wouldn't a guilty person concentrate on looking bereft?

"David and I noticed you shortly before the fireworks started. You looked like you might be looking for her."

He looked at me with some suspicion (*oh, wow, I hope I haven't overdone it*), but I kept a look of friendly concern on my face. I breathed a silent sigh of relief when he continued.

"Yeah, I was looking for her. Looked all over the damn park; we were supposed to meet no later than nine thirty. But I couldn't find her. She'd been talking to people all day, although she wouldn't tell me what it was about. 'City business,' was all she would say. 'Today's a chance for me to get what I want.'"

"Mmm." *What did she want? WHAT DID SHE WANT? Damn, can't ask that.* "I saw her several times that day, in different places. She did seem to be busy."

"Yeah. She promised me that we would have some time together to enjoy the Festival, but I hardly saw her. I was pretty mad by the end of the afternoon. Had an argument with her right in the middle of everything."

"Oh."

"People must have noticed, because the cops asked me about it."

Okay, we don't need to tell him about one person who saw it. Is that really what that exchange meant? "I hope you finally had some time together."

"I think she finally ran out of people to talk with. But then again, I go back to how she ended up on the logging field," he responded. "We had dinner together at that food tent on the midway, listened to some music, but then she said she had to go see someone and I lost her in the crowd." He stared at the ground. "I didn't see her again," he finished.

"I'm so sorry," was all I could think to say.

Patrick's head came up and he glared at me. "Why should I believe that? You hated Greta."

"No, I didn't hate her," I said gently. "I didn't like her, that's true, but that was mostly because of differences over what I thought she was doing to the city."

I stopped for a moment; it was important that he trust what I was saying. "It's horrible that something like this should happen to anyone, Patrick. I am terribly sorry that you've lost your wife, regardless of my relationship with her. And I'm worried about what this might do to Sheffield. It was a horrible, violent crime, and it's going to be difficult for people to deal with it."

Okay, Patrick—how hard is it for you to deal with it? I kept looking at his face for some sign. His features showed tension, but was there loss?

He started speaking slowly. "Greta wasn't the easiest person to get along with, I know that. She could be pushy, and she didn't always listen. I warned her about what she was doing outside Council sessions. I got irritated with her, sure; a lot of people did. But that wasn't a reason to kill her."

"So, who might have thought there was a reason?" I asked carefully. "Was she working on something that might have made her some enemies?"

He stared off, across the river toward the nearby tree-covered ridge that was in full light from the late-morning sun.

"She definitely had some project going, but she wouldn't tell me anything about it. Frankly, that was the cause of some of our arguments lately. I didn't like her thinking that she couldn't share ideas with me, and it made me wonder whether she knew there was something wrong about it. I asked, but her eyes would just light up and she would say something about 'being remembered forever.'"

"That sounds like some kind of City project," I pondered.

"Who do you think might know more about it?"

"Oh, Dwight Orkman is definitely in the middle of it. You know she brought him to town and pushed through his being hired as city manager?"

Internally, my jaw was dropping. I knew that Dwight's hiring had been sudden; I don't think many of the City councilors had even seen his résumé before the vote. But I hadn't heard the reason and had probably been over-trusting in thinking he had been discovered through networking or organizations involving public officials, or had called when he heard about the vacancy. I should have known better.

I could only make a noncommittal noise while my anger with the dead woman rose up again.

"Oh, yes," Patrick said. "Dwight approached her with some deal he had going, some development or other. His price for bringing it here was to be city manager. With him in that position and her as mayor, they could make it happen regardless of any opposition. She was thrilled about it, but she kept saying she wasn't ready to make it public yet. But I know it included a building that Greta said would have her name on it.

"That's why she had a lot of meetings with Dwight, more than their usual weekly briefings. If anyone knows the details of what my wife was up to," Patrick said bitterly, "it would be him."

The revelations filled in a lot of the immediate blanks in my mental "Greta/building" file, but this wasn't the time to tell Patrick about my own knowledge of meetings and discussions between Dwight and Greta. The conversation hadn't told me much about Patrick's possible motives, but it had underscored my need to learn more. I expressed David's and my condolences again, collected my now-bored deerhound, and went on with our walk. I clearly had to talk with Dwight Orkman about several issues. The immediate problem was how to go about it.

Chapter Ten

I spent more time that afternoon on social media than is generally good for my mental health, but I figured it was the best way to get a read across a broad range of people on the continuing reactions to Greta's death. What I read wasn't good.

It wasn't so much an argument between those who had been the mayor's friends and those who hadn't. I had expected some of that, although I never understand why people waste energy arguing with others on social media. You aren't going to change any minds, and everyone else reading it is annoyed. On the other hand, I suppose it feels safe, since there's much less chance of an escalation to physical force between two people on computers or smartphones—assuming they don't know where each other lives, which isn't a given in a small community like Sheffield.

There were, yes—and I tried not to make faces at my own laptop—those who lamented that we had "lost the best mayor we ever had" and "a lovely, caring woman." There were continued calls to remember Greta by naming something for her: a park, a street, even the Festival ground bleacher field where she had been killed, although that didn't seem in the best of taste. Thankfully, those wanting City Hall renamed or calling for a bronze statue seemed to be outliers.

Whether I agreed with them or not, those were the most positive comments. A lot of what I saw was depressing: unfunny jokes about this being the best way of getting rid of everyone in City Hall; statements assuming she had been corrupt; and most frequently, comments about Sheffield being "always" doomed to have bad things happen here. A lot of it was, of course, badly spelled, punctuated, and stated. There was a lot of negativism, gloom, and knee-jerk paranoia.

What was not present was, to my dismay, any sense of outrage. Think about it: in a healthy community, where people expect overall good developments and good services, where they are planning for a better future, a crime as horrific as the murder of a mayor would be . . . an outrage. There would be demands for round-the-clock police work, requests for help from outside the city, and an overall sense that this was something that had no place in our community, something we had to solve so we could move on. Yet, among those who were technology-savvy enough to be active on social media, those who cared enough to comment on the biggest tragedy that had happened in Sheffield in some time, there was none of that. There seemed to be a complete absence of any sense of a community that needed to work together—absolutely no comments about "this shouldn't happen here."

This made me even more concerned about solving Greta's murder. If we were to have any chance of instilling a positive community spirit—and I don't mean to sound like a cheerleader—citizens of Sheffield would have to be shown dedication, commitment, and efficiency. We had to find out who killed the mayor and why, then show people that the community could recover and be stronger.

The more I thought about it, the more the questions came back to City Manager Dwight Orkman. I hadn't liked the way he was hired and had said so at the time (although I'd had no knowledge of how improper it actually was), but our conversations since had been civil, and I thought—I hoped— he understood that my concerns were procedural and not personal. It would be hard enough to introduce all the issues that might have some bearing on Greta's death without him clamming up and glaring at me because of some old misunderstanding. Not being a police officer, I hardly had the credentials to interview a hostile subject. And have I mentioned that I'm not fond of confrontation?

As usual, I went to my go-to guy for ideas: David. And once again, we were talking where these discussions generally take place: leaning against opposite kitchen counters.

"David, how on earth do I justify going into Dwight's office to interview him about the murder? I can't tell him I'm doing it for the police investigation, and I don't want to tell him that I saw him suddenly appear from somewhere else in the middle of the fireworks. What do I do, make a fake blackmail claim to get him to talk about this mystery building? 'I know what you were doing with the mayor,'" waggling my fingers and growling in my best Snidely Whiplash imitation (which is, I admit, not good).

David looked at me as if a large and interesting bug were doing the merengue and warranted scientific study. After all our years together, he should know better; this behavior was not that unusual.

"Uh, no, Felice, I don't think blackmail is the answer. Can

you come up with some reason why you need to go see him? And why are you focusing on meeting him in his office, anyway?"

"Ah, that is one of my long-standing interpersonal communications secrets," I said, putting up an index finger and trying to look wise. "It especially works with men. *They* think they're more powerful behind their own desks. They don't realize they're just as vulnerable to someone who isn't intimidated, and it throws them. If I see him in what he thinks is his safe place, knowing Dwight, he'll put on a condescending, 'I'm in charge, little lady' attitude and probably let out more than he would somewhere else."

"You don't think he'll feel safer shutting up and not saying anything? It's City business, in his City Hall, while he's behind his big, important city manager desk." David countered.

I deflated a bit. "Okay, maybe. But maybe he'd also be more open to flattery while sitting in his power chair. If I can word it right. And say it with any degree of sincerity."

Hmmm. What's my angle? I stood and mused, eyes narrowed and staring at the floor.

David watched, trying to hide his smile. I had learned, over the years, that he was not being patronizing at these times, so I didn't have to walk over and knock his block off. He was honestly enjoying "watching your brain at work," as he put it.

"What if I got an appointment to check in and see if there is anything I can help with?" I started off slowly. "The City government is in disarray; people will be moving around on the Council and from City committees. I think that might give me a reason to ask a lot of questions about the effects of Greta's death on City business, maybe even what will be coming before the Council.

"It's a bit lame, David, but I think that might work." I turned and looked at him directly. "I can sound helpful, and I think the fact that I disagreed with Greta's agenda gives me a reason to ask him whether it's likely to change. I'm being polite by going in and asking rather than challenging him at a public meeting—that's worth mentioning and may get him to open up. I think that might be a good angle."

"It might work, but you know you're only going to get one shot at him. And what if he finds out you're working for the police?"

I thought for a moment.

"If he didn't kill her, that shouldn't bother him; the chief reports to him and it's a good use of scarce resources. If he did kill her, then I have more problems than how to interview him in his office."

David scowled. "I don't suppose you're going to let me go with you."

"What—you think he's going to reach across the desk and bash me with a stapler? David, if Dwight did it, we know he was smart enough to get Greta away from other people and somewhere that wouldn't be associated with him. If there's one place I'm safe from him, it's in his office."

"True. But do me a favor and don't accept any requests from him to meet you anywhere else."

"Done. Definitely."

"And while you're in City Hall," David added, putting on his own wise look, "you might want to talk with Pat Gregorio."

"The finance director? Why?"

Pat Gregorio had worked for the City for more than twenty years and lived here longer than that, and what she didn't know about its history and finances could fit into a really tiny Dixie cup. She won awards for her small-town budgets, auditors loved her, and she constantly looked for ways to stretch every dime of City funds without burdening taxpayers. I liked her open smile and frank manner and respected her work even more than that of most of those mysterious numbers people.

"I told you I was going to do some asking around myself," David said smugly. "I can't tell you who told me this."

This was good for an internal laugh—David spends a fair amount of time hanging out with a group of men at the boatyard who work on small craft, and any married woman can tell you that a group of guys exchanges more gossip than any lingerie party.

He continued, "But Greta was telling a few people that Pat wasn't completely trustworthy."

"What? How so?"

"Apparently there were hints of extramarital activity that Greta indicated might compromise Pat's integrity."

"What? Yuck!" I made a face. I hate this stuff. In these days of both public and private cameras everywhere, having an affair is pretty dumb from a logistical perspective. I can never understand why members of Congress are idiotic enough to think that somehow, as well-known public figures, they won't be seen heading into some tryst location. More importantly, I think people who engage in sex outside their marriages probably should find another solution to their problems. But I *hate* sneering and gossip about such things, the smirking and righteous whispering, usually by people who have their own secrets. My friends and acquaintances know it, which is probably why I don't hear much about what often is the favorite topic of conversation in small towns.

"Wait. You said the information was that *Greta* was

passing this around. Did your source think it was true, or was he just pointing out what Greta was doing?"

"Does it matter?"

"Yeah, it matters if I have to go talk with Pat. I'd much rather get her take on what Greta was saying than have to ask her about her private life."

"Well, my source wasn't sure. The overall feeling was that Greta wasn't acting very mayoral, regardless."

I sighed. "No kidding. Okay, I'll spend some time in Pat's office. I just hope she'll still speak to me afterward."

A call to City Hall got me an appointment with Dwight the following afternoon, which was interesting in itself; I assumed he would be more booked up with everything going on. I debated with myself the appropriate costume for the occasion, ranging from big-city power suit to Sheffield casual—what kind of impression did I want to make?

I didn't want to antagonize the guy by being too author-itative—especially if the goal was to get him to feel comfortable and start talking—so the suit was out. At the same time, no one would believe me in Sheffield's usual ultra-casual, including myself. I settled on good linen slacks with a striped shirt and a lightweight jacket, a sort of "I'm coming from another meeting and running a bunch of errands and thought I'd drop in" ensemble. I also stopped to realize that I was putting a lot more thought into this than it needed.

The city manager's office at City Hall was in the older part of the building, separate from the wing with the Council chambers: it wasn't impressively large but was high-ceilinged, with heavy wood frames around windows and doors and a background odor of old paper, old polish and old business. Some predecessor had thought to soften the atmosphere by installing commercial-grade carpet in the space, but the upgrade hadn't extended to any color on the walls beyond the ubiquitous off-white.

I had been in Dwight's office before but took another look around with new eyes when I arrived to get a better sense of his personality, or at least that part of his personality he wanted to make public. I saw a couple of framed education certificates; an old map of the city in multiple colors marking zoning boundaries; and a copy of a photo of him with the mayor, planting a tree during Arbor Day, that had appeared in the local paper. On a bookcase under a window stood a bronze metal figurine of a logger; it looked dusty, as if it had been in the same place through several occupants of the office, as it probably had. Bookshelves held the usual collection of old binders, volumes of State agency regulations, and rarely used reference books. I didn't see any family photos or other personal mementos: perhaps not that unusual, since Dwight hadn't been in Sheffield that long, but there was still an impersonal, somewhat cold air to the office.

The man himself, thankfully, was staring at his computer screen and didn't notice me peering around. I was able to see the cowlick in his short blonde hair and the slight sunburn of his neck above the collar of his dress shirt. He did, after about thirty seconds, deign to look up and notice me standing, at which point he gestured me to a chair, his hand smoothing over his tie.

Okay, it's Mr. Big in his office, after all, I thought while hiding a smile. *Let's see how this goes.* I decided to let him break the silence, so I sat down, put a polite smile on my face, and waited.

Dwight put his elbows on his desk and clasped his hands

together under his narrow face, where the sunburn continued. My smile was not returned, although the tone was civil enough. "So, Felice, what can I do for you?"

"Dwight, I appreciate your taking the time to see me; I know how very busy you must be."

He issued a rueful chuckle. "Uh—yes. As you can imagine, there's a lot going on."

"Yes, the ripples from Greta's death are certainly making themselves felt. Are you keeping close tabs on how the investigation is going?"

"Chief Abhay is keeping me in the loop, of course, but I don't usually get personally involved in criminal investigations, even though he reports to me." He glanced down as if to divorce himself from the police department's work.

Nice statement of the obvious, Dwight. I will ignore the insult to my intelligence.

"No, I understand that. And meanwhile, you have to deal with the aftermath of losing the mayor. Dwight, that's why I'm here. Kate Dennis and I are friends, and I personally think the Council is in very good hands with her"—I searched his face and saw a noncommittal nod—"but I've been hearing a lot of talk out in the community that worries me."

He grimaced. "I wouldn't expect you to be the kind of person to pay attention to gossip."

"Thank you. But I'm not talking about gossip. There seems to be a lot of negativity in Sheffield over the mayor's murder, and I'm a bit concerned about where the city might be headed."

"Like what?"

Here goes. "Well, I've heard that Greta was working toward a legacy of some kind, that she had an agenda she hadn't disclosed to other councilors or the public. It's distasteful to repeat this, but you should know that the rumors are going around. Do you know anything about it?"

He hesitated. "If she hadn't told the rest of the Council, why do you think she would have mentioned anything to me?"

"Dwight, come on. If she wanted something from the City, she'd have to work with you to get it. I know there isn't any unusual expenditure in the budget, but I also know that Greta felt she was entitled to go after anything she thought was important. And there are rumors that she was working with you on a large project of some kind."

Poor Dwight. That fair skin of his offered no concealment at all, and now his whole face was redder than any summer sun had made it. Was I going to get some facts from him, or would I have to admit that I heard his conversation that Festival afternoon, not to mention the additional details Patrick Sutton had provided? Or would he potentially incriminate himself by denying everything, in which case I'd better say nothing at all about what I'd heard?

He remained silent, so I changed subjects and pushed a bit more. "It's public knowledge that you and the mayor were trying to change the Summer Festival contract to get a piece of the gate for the City," I reminded him. "That wasn't in the budget; it hadn't even been discussed in a Council meeting. What was that all about?"

We seemed to have hit on something Dwight was more comfortable answering. One side of his mouth went up in a condescending smile, and I could pretty much predict what was coming next.

"Felice, you've been active in the City, but you aren't on the Budget Committee," he began. "Sheffield is solvent, and we've managed to balance the budget, but we have to look for new sources of revenue. Getting more money for the use of our facilities is low-hanging fruit that we just can't ignore. I know it's a controversial idea, but it was one we thought we had to pursue."

"'We' being you and the mayor?" I responded. "Don't you think that's something that the Council as a whole should have discussed?"

"That wasn't necessary—fees are my responsibility, so I don't need Council approval," he returned.

I wasn't sure I agreed with that assessment—the Council had authority over most charges and would want to approve anything considered a new fee—but I set it aside. I did notice that he hadn't explained why, in that case, the mayor was involved at all. And I certainly remembered that he had been very reluctant to pursue it, although he didn't know that I knew.

I knew he wasn't the author of that plan. Dwight was lying, but why? And how did I find out more about that damned *building*? It was time to try yet another tack.

"Dwight, I really came here to find out if there is anything I can do, since I know the City is in something of an uproar. I'm not suggesting the staff needs any help, but there are some factions forming in Sheffield and there could some controversy coming. How much of Greta's agenda do you think is going to move forward?"

"Well, we spend according to the approved budget, as you know," Orkman replied with narrowed eyes. I bit my lower lip hard not to say anything to that; he had gone along with several Greta Sutton attacks on the budget that had robbed City departments of the funds they needed for approved projects.

"Any change to that has to be approved as a budget

amendment," he went on, "and other issues are the Council's decision. I can't predict what the councilors might want to discuss."

But you do decide what staff recommendations go before them, I thought, but it was time to back off the subject and see if I could glean some information another way.

"Right," I said with an "oh, silly me" smile that always seems to work with men. "Well, we'll have to see how things progress."

There was a beat of silence.

"In spite of the turmoil, how are you settling in?" This seemed impossibly lame, but Orkman seemed pleased, perhaps just to change the subject.

"My wife and I have bought a house here in Sheffield," he said, mentioning the neighborhood, "and she's now working for a local developer. I think we're close to being unpacked, and we're starting to get out and see the area when we have time."

I caught the offhand "local developer" comment but tried not to react to it. Was this part of the "big deal development in exchange for city manager job" package? It was too complicated to think about right now while I was trying to probe his alibi.

"Oh, good! Did you enjoy the Summer Festival, at least on Saturday? I thought I saw you there, during the afternoon, and then I think later, during the fireworks."

"Uh—yeah, Saturday was good. We walked around and looked at everything, ate on the midway, and stayed for the fireworks."

"Didn't I see you walking around during the show?"

His glance sharpened. "Yeah. We sat down, but I couldn't get comfortable, so I walked around. Good show."

"Yes, I'm always impressed by how good the show is."

I had the distinct feeling that my welcome had worn thin, and I couldn't think of how to circle back around to the Mystery Building. I offered again to help if needed, received a thin-lipped nod and dismissal in return, thanked him for his time, and left the office. I walked out of City Hall into bright sunlight and the cool breeze from the Pacific. Had I learned anything of use from the meeting?

"Yes. Dwight Orkman is lying about what he did on Saturday," I said aloud to the thankfully empty street. "He's lying about what he and Greta were planning. And I have to start going to more Council meetings to find out what will happen next."

Chapter Eleven

I hadn't talked with Becky for a while and missed her company, along with her insights into current events. Not to mention the local emergency responder gossip, which always included great stories even if they weren't always true. Public safety personnel were a gossipy bunch and a great source of wild rumors, although I wouldn't mention that to Tom Abhay or the fire chief.

It being summer, Becky and her ambulance had been busy, mostly due to the antics of the tourists in town. Why do people staying away from home do truly stupid things they would never attempt in their own neighborhoods? Another question for a future ponder.

We met for lunch before her shift began the next afternoon. After catching up on family issues—Becky has interesting grown children from an earlier marriage—the conversation veered over to the ongoing investigation into Greta Sutton's death.

"The scuttlebutt at the firehouse is centering on Dwight Orkman," Becky said before taking a forkful of a tasty-looking southwestern salad. "But that could be because no one likes him, anyway. Personally, I'm still wondering about the husband. He seems pretty harmless, but sometimes those still ponds have scary stuff going on in the depths."

"Hmmm," I responded—about the only response I could make through a mouthful of salmon in blueberry vinaigrette. I had come to appreciate this awesome combination; it isn't just something glommed together because we have a lot of both. When I had recovered from my mouthful of wonderful flavors, I wanted more detail about her statement.

"Why are they centering on the city manager? Personally, I have a hard time finding a real motive for him. Just not liking the guy isn't enough to think he's guilty of murder."

She lowered her voice and leaned across the table toward me. "I don't know that I agree with the suspicion, but the guy isn't helping his cause with law enforcement. Orkman came to the Public Safety Center a few weeks ago. He was there to look around and talk about the need for more equipment next year, but some of the guys asked questions about the budget. They're worried that the money isn't there because of all the special projects the Council's been approving. Apparently, Orkman said that Greta was a pain in his backside and that he was tired of having her riding him."

"He really said that?"

"Either that or something like it. He made it sound like he thought he could run the City a lot better if he didn't have to deal with her."

"That was really stupid. Even if it were true, you don't say something like that about one of your employers to subordinates; didn't he know that would run like wildfire around the department?"

Becky nodded. "It certainly has. When you add that to

what you heard about her threatening his job . . ." she shrugged, "maybe it was enough to make him do something drastic."

I sat back to take this in. I had a hard time believing that an experienced, professional city manager would find murder the best remedy for getting hassled by one councilor, however insistent. When it came down to it, Greta was one vote out of seven. Even if she had controlled a majority on most issues, Suzanne's comment at the Summer Festival indicated there were some cracks in the bloc. I would think some smart appeals to some of the other councilors might have solved Orkman's problems without his resorting to violence.

On the other hand, I had heard her threaten him professionally, and it hadn't sounded like her first use of that ploy. They each had dirt on the other, given the behind-the-scenes manipulations surrounding his hiring and the development he supposedly brought in exchange. Maybe the only way to keep his job and his reputation had been to get rid of the person who could bring him down.

And what was the deal with those other councilors who voted with her when she demanded it: Anne Perez, Pete Ichikawa, and Suzanne? I had never understood that. What might she have had on other councilors that guaranteed their submission? Plus, I realized that I was thinking from my own perspective, which did not include resorting to bashing people over the head as a means of problem-solving—outside my imagination on a particularly bad day, at least.

It slid my thoughts once again to what an unpleasant woman she had been, and the insistent wonder that someone would have chosen to live with her.

I added, "I wouldn't completely rule out Patrick Sutton,

either; he seemed upset but not heartbroken when I talked with him a few days ago." I told Becky about my meeting with Patrick at the dog park, then decided to plunge in with the background of my work for Chief Abhay. Someone other than David probably should know, and Becky was good at keeping secrets. Plus, she knew a lot of law enforcement people and might be able to get me rescued in a hurry . . .

"Felice, is this a good idea?" she asked when I had filled her in. "Yes, you're good at asking questions, but some people are certainly going to wonder why you're sticking your nose in, and not everyone likes you."

"Oh, thanks a lot. I *know* that. But that's one reason the Chief asked me to do this. Most of those who might be responsible are connected to local government or business, he thinks, and I know those people. And if someone doesn't like me, I'm not losing anything if I ask them potentially tough questions." I grinned at her.

"Who else have you talked with?"

"So far, just a longish conversation with Dwight. He was patronizing—big surprise—and he was lying."

"Given what I've heard, no surprise there. But that still doesn't make him a murderer."

"Of course not. But there is something going on at City Hall, Becky. There's a project the mayor and Dwight were working on without telling most of the Council. I have several more people I need to sound out about that—I think it's important. It doesn't take a genius to figure that Greta was killed because of her actions as mayor."

"Unless it was her husband."

"Unless it was her husband. But then, who could really blame him?"

We shared grimaces. *Sorry, Greta—what a legacy you've left.*

"You know who else you need to talk with," Becky added after a long sip of her iced tea. "Ron Draper."

"Does he still run the Summer Festival Committee?" Ron was one of several Draper logging family members, part of the group of original Sheffield families who had started the Summer Festival as a logging show at least four decades before. I had seen him and some other family members when I attended the City Council meeting right after Greta's death. "I knew I needed to talk with someone about that 'percentage of the gate' debacle, but I wasn't sure of the best person."

"That would be Ron. The word is that he was furious when Greta and Dwight brought up the idea. He said something about threatening to move the Festival out of Sheffield if it went forward. I think the phrase that was quoted was something like, 'know-nothing newcomers,' although perhaps not that clean."

"That has some nice alliteration, but I get your drift." I thought for a moment. "Since I'm a know-nothing newcomer myself, how on earth do I interview him? The 'I want to help during troubling times' routine isn't going to work with him."

"Maybe you could tell him you're thinking of running for Council," Becky suggested. "Then it would make sense for you to know about his family's dealings with Greta and Dwight."

I put down my lemonade and stared at her, the light dawning.

"Becky, I think that may be the best way. It's an approach that could work with other people, too. I'll feel bad when they find out it wasn't true, but if it helps smoke out a killer, so be it. Thanks a lot."

We were righteous enough to refuse dessert—well, it was only lunch—and walked out into the parking lot together.

"You know more of the police and firefighter end of town than I do," I said before we parted at our respective cars. "Please don't tell anybody what I'm doing, but if you hear something I should know or think of someone I should talk with, please tell me."

"I can't believe David is really happy about this," she grumbled, but agreed. And I felt a lot better for having some backup.

But Chief Abhay told me not to bother with the Drapers. "We've talked with them at some length," he told me when I called in with a status report. "They didn't like the mayor and they really didn't like her idea of taking money off the top of Festival proceeds, but they talked with some of the other councilors and figured there was a good chance they could keep it from passing. They've been around Sheffield for a really long time."

"Do they know that it's likely to come up again at a Council meeting?" I asked. "Dwight Orkman told me that the Festival percentage was low-hanging fruit in the quest for new City money. Of course, he was trying to shine me on at the time, so I don't know how serious he was."

"I haven't seen the agenda for the next meeting, but you can be sure that they'll show up with a lot of supporters if it does come up."

"It doesn't sound like that issue was the motive for Greta's murder then, unless someone else's ox was being gored by the idea, and I can't think of anyone. Do you want me to go to the Council meeting?"

"I'd appreciate it if you did," he responded. "I need you to take a close look at the Council. What you've told me about the city manager is interesting, but the fact that we know he's lying doesn't mean he's covering up a murder. I'm going to look into Mr. Orkman a bit more, although I'll have to call the County if we want to bring him in for questioning, since he's my supervisor."

"And what about this—"

"Building, yes, I know, Felice," he said with a smile in his voice. "Talk with more of the councilors and I'll see what I can find out on this end."

He mentioned a couple of councilors he especially wanted me to interview. Thankfully, the list didn't include Pete Ichikawa or Anne Perez; Greta's and my known clashing would have made them difficult to approach, given their inexplicable devotion to her. But they had solid alibis far away from the Festival. He did want me to talk with Suzanne Dryer and George Russell, who both had been there Saturday night and had alibis, but who might have seen something. *Oh, goody. How will the "I'm thinking of running for Council" angle work with them?*

I was going to have to be creative.

Since I had seen Suzanne during the Festival, it made sense to talk with her next. And after all, I had seen her arguing with the mayor, so perhaps she had a foot in both the Saint Greta and not-so-saintly camps.

Suzanne was Sheffield-born and at least the third generation to run her family's business, so I suppose she had to be considered local gentry. The nobility idea might have worked better if she'd had a decent education or ever spent some time away from Sheffield, but she did volunteer a lot. And she knew everyone in town. I didn't respect her much as a City councilor—when I had worked in a group with her in the past, I could tell that she hadn't done her homework—and her views tended to harken back to Sheffield's 1970s heyday rather than facing forward. But we got along okay on the basic issues in projects where we had worked together, and she was devoted to the community. As a formerly loyal Sutton follower, I was hoping she could give me the skinny on what was brewing within City government.

I tracked her down at her family's drug store. Suzanne, her thin form dressed in a plaid shirt and leggings, was sending her adult son to the back to collect merchandise for a cleared area in the "Seasonal" row of the store. Time to put away the pails and shovels and beach balls—even though we didn't have a local beach—and get out what looked like packages of "harvest" decorations. Three generations worked at the store, since her dad was the pharmacist while Suzanne managed the operation. I waited until she was free, then followed her back to where her office was located.

"Hey, Suzanne," I started, "Do you have a minute?"

She looked around. "I guess so. Do you need something?"

"I've been doing a lot of thinking since the mayor was killed. I'm worried that the town seems sort of disturbed; have you noticed?"

"It seems like I've been spending a lot of time talking about it," she said, shooting me a glance. "I wouldn't think you were too upset—you couldn't stand Greta. I heard you telling her off on Saturday."

Yes! An opening.

"That's right, you had just been talking with her when she came after me. You must have put in a long day that day."

"Yup. I got there at seven in the morning to set up, and a

couple of people didn't show, so I had to serve most of the day."

"I think I saw you there just before the fireworks. Wow, were you there all that time?"

"No, I got a few hours off later in the afternoon, then came back to close up—that must have been when you saw me. I don't like to miss the fireworks; they're always so good. I sat with my family for that, then I went home and crashed."

So, an alibi with witnesses. Not to mention that I don't think you had the strength to swing the chain, wiry or not.

Suzanne stared at me. "So why are you asking about Greta, anyway? I thought you didn't like her."

"Oh, no question: she really rubbed me the wrong way. But I heard you on Saturday—it sounded like she was asking for your vote one too many times."

Suzanne's thin mouth worked, finally pursing before she answered. "I told her I didn't want to talk with her outside Council meetings. She just wouldn't listen. That plan to charge the Festival Committee—that was just crazy. She would have ruined the Festival!"

"So, she was calling you about other issues, too?"

"All the time. I didn't think much of it at first—she always acted like she wasn't talking with anyone else—but then I found out she was calling other councilors, too, to make sure she had a majority on any issue she cared about. That's just wrong!"

Nice of someone to notice. I kept my face carefully neutral.

"What were the issues she cared about?"

"Some of it was weird. You know that neighborhood out on Woodyard Road?"

I nodded; it was a small enclave of twenty-year-old houses about ten minutes east of us.

"Well, those people have been asking to have their street widened and repaired for just years. It's a mess, full of potholes, and they don't even have sidewalks. Some of them have come in here complaining about it, and I even talked with the last city manager about it. That project was finally on the Public Works list this year, and Greta suddenly decided she wanted to use the money for something else!"

"For what?"

"For *flower baskets,* if you can believe it. Greta said that flower baskets on all the streetlight poles down Main Street would be better for the town than a new street off in one corner of it. She was trying to talk everyone into changing the budget allocation."

"Which probably led to some pretty angry people." *Good grief.* Only Greta Sutton would be sugar-brained enough to prefer flower baskets to a decent street for residents, but I could just hear her saying it.

"It sure did. That's when I'd really had enough; I told her I couldn't go along with that and I didn't want her calling me anymore. But she just wouldn't let me alone. And that," she said, leaning closer, her shoulder-length brown hair swinging forward, "wasn't the craziest thing."

Oh, yes, yes, yes! I prayed silently. But I didn't trust myself to say anything, so I just raised my eyebrows and looked accommodating.

"You know the City owns property down by the river, west of downtown?" I nodded. The parcel was several acres with plenty of power and near transportation. It was seemingly a good investment for someone, but since the last recession, there hadn't been any interest from anyone equipped with the several million dollars it would take to develop it properly. The

City Council had discussed various uses for it, including warehouses, but had adopted a policy statement seeking to ensure that the eventual owner would create jobs, but not the noise, smell, or emissions a major industrial process might mean. It was a nice goal but meaningless, given the lack of development candidates so far.

"Well, Greta came to me a while ago, all excited. She said someone wants to buy the property and build something on it. She called it 'her legacy' and acted all super-secret about it."

"Did she tell you what whoever it was wanted to build? Or who they were?"

"No, she said no one could know yet. That kind of made me mad, you know? Why mention it if she wasn't going to tell me anything? But she said we all needed to be ready to make it happen."

"So, she was asking for your support on what should have been public City business, that most of the Council hadn't even heard about yet, without telling you any of the details."

"Yeah." Suzanne stopped, jerking her head back and looking into the distance for a moment. Then her eyes came back to my face. "I guess she really took me for granted, didn't she?"

"She didn't seem to care that she was having improper conversations with you, and frankly, she didn't seem to think that you would make independent decisions."

"Well, I kind of wish she were around now so I could tell her off!"

I waited for a moment—not much to say to that—then came back around.

"Suzanne, do you know if anyone else knows about this developer and the project?"

She thought for a moment. "I think Dwight must know something. I don't think the company came to Greta by herself; I got the feeling that they had come to the City. Dwight must have talked to them first."

Uh-huh. You bet he did. So not even Suzanne knew why Dwight was being foisted on the City and she had been expected to vote to hire him. The level of "bad" at City Hall just seemed to get deeper.

"I would guess that Kate probably doesn't know?"

Suzanne shook her head.

"So maybe, this is something that should be put on a Council agenda," I added carefully, "or that someone should ask Dwight about in a public meeting? So that it can get out into the open? It does involve City property."

"Yeah. I think I'll call Kate and tell her what I know, then maybe the Council can ask some questions."

And my work here is done, I thought. Mentally, I rubbed my palms together. The next Council meeting should be fun to watch, and maybe something would come to light that could move the murder investigation forward.

In the meantime, I had to find a way to talk with George Russell, the other councilor Chief Abhay had mentioned. This was going to be tougher: the Russells didn't have a business anywhere I could visit. Add to that the fact that George and Rita openly disliked David and me, and both a location and an approach became difficult.

Miss Marple would have picked up her tin of pennies for the church steeple fund and gone knocking on their door. *Nice camouflage, Jane.* I didn't have that option. Sheffield norms included some sort of companion animal in nearly every home, quite often large and canine in nature. If I sauntered up to the Russells' front door, I stood a good chance of having said animal released and told "Sic 'em" or the like. Another approach was needed. When could I semi-naturally run across George Russell when I would have a chance to ask him some semi-natural questions? I didn't want to wait until the next Council meeting.

A small light bulb went on overhead. The best option would be an environmentalist meeting, as I was confident that George was active in every group with "eco," "resource," or any reference to some element of nature in its title. I called Joy Bauer, who ran the County economic development organization, of which we were members. She could be counted on to know meeting dates for most of what went on, as she spent a decent percentage of her time attending all kinds of organization meetings all over the county.

Joy sounded cheerful when she picked up. "Felice, how are you?" she said. "I haven't talked with you in weeks."

"Yes, sorry about that. It doesn't seem that I've been out much since the Summer Festival."

"And the murder of the mayor! That was just horrible. Do the police know who did it yet?" Joy lived in a larger town about thirty miles down the coast. She certainly would have heard about Greta Sutton's murder from countywide media, although she wouldn't be following it as closely as those of us in Sheffield.

"No, not yet. There were thousands of people around at the time and, frankly, a lot of locals with motives."

"Yes, I know you didn't like her," Joy said with a touch of censure.

"I wasn't the only one." *Obviously.* "But the police are

working hard and the rest of us are trying to move forward. It doesn't help the town to have this unsolved.

"Joy, I wonder if you can help me," I continued, changing the subject. "Are there any meetings of environmental groups in the area coming up within the next few days?"

"I didn't know you were interested in environmentalism," she responded, not surprising as I had never shown much interest before. As the rest of the country knows, Oregon has enough tree-hugging activists to populate most of the small countries of the world. I've always figured that area of interest could get along without me, so I've devoted my time to other issues.

Now, I needed to have a reason handy to want to go to a meeting.

"I've been hearing some talk about the state of the river," I began vaguely. "You know how it is—a lot of what you hear is rumor, and I've been wondering if anyone is working with real data. Do you know of any groups that are discussing this?"

While I stood some chance of striking out with this approach, it wasn't completely stupid. There usually was some sort of discussion going on about the state of the river (estuary, really, as it was close enough to the ocean to be affected by tides); plus, George and Rita's house was near it. He likely would be involved in anything having to do with local waterways.

"Actually, you're in luck," Joy said slowly, the clicking noises coming through the phone telling me she was checking the calendar on her screen. "There's a meeting of the regional Water Resource Council tomorrow night."

Bingo! I had heard of the group, which was using up State-supplied consultant money to discuss potential water shortages caused by climate change. Water shortages. On the Oregon coast. Yes, our area receives about nine feet of rain a year, and yes, that amount has been going *up* since people started noticing climate change. And no, we don't have a lot of population growth. Never mind. Just about the time the money ran out, the consultants would produce a nice, thick report, a copy of which every Council member would receive. Those who took the time to read it would realize there wasn't much in there they didn't already know, like the fact that cities would use water resources more efficiently if they built extremely expensive and completely out-of-reach regional distribution systems. After a news release and some minor press, the report would end up on office shelves in several locations and gradually gather dust—although having it would be required if any member community on the Council wanted State funding for a water project in the future. Not that I'm cynical or anything.

"That sounds promising. Can you tell me more about it?"

She gave me the place and time. We promised to go to lunch soon—it really had been a while since I had been face-to-face with her—and we rang off. Now, all I had to do was sit through a meeting that was liable to make me a little crazy and find a chance to take George off in a corner to tease out what he knew.

Chapter Twelve

The details of the Water Resource Council meeting the following night escape me, even if somewhat might be interested. If the printed agenda wasn't overly long, the discussions were, and without an apparent destination.

My natural inclination in meetings is to try to find solutions so everyone can get their tasks and head on out to do real work, but it was obvious early on that this was not the reason why most attendees had shown up for this get-together. In this case, it was about a dozen people around some small tables in a local library meeting room. Some were there to vent about an issue concerning their water service; some just showed up to indicate their "concern." I'm as much a believer in discussion for its own sake as the next person—okay, maybe not—but since I had arrived too late to buttonhole George Russell before the meeting (of course he was there), I sat off to one side, identified myself as "an interested observer" when asked, and mostly tuned out about twelve minutes into the proceedings. I waited for a break when I could sidle up to George.

It came after nearly an hour. Tom Abhay owed me.

My head came back up from the book I had quietly been reading inside my notebook as chairs shuffled and people started moving. Luckily, George, in a chamois cloth shirt and jeans with his long, graying hair tied back, was hanging near his seat, while most participants bolted toward the bathrooms or ambled toward a side table with water and a tray of cookies.

"Hi, George," seemed like the best opening; I didn't know how he would react to my presence.

"Felice," came back gruffly but not uncivilly. "What brings you to the meeting?"

"Well, this isn't an area where I know very much, so I thought it would do me some good to observe the discussions. With all our rain, I don't think about our need for water very much."

George pulled a cellophane-wrapped packet of what looked like dark green crackers from his pocket. I guess a natural foods market version of what—dried kale?—worked better for him than home-baked cookies. It wasn't a product I had seen before, but I didn't plan to ask where he got it.

"Most people don't, but it's vital to our health and well-being. Our whole existence is based on water." His face had become very earnest-looking and this sounded like a speech that had been launched before. George was known for his intense focus, especially on environmental issues.

"Oh, of course!" I agreed. "With fishing, maritime work, timber's use of water, along with people's need for clean drinking water and wastewater treatment—it's a huge subject." I hoped my eyes weren't unbelievably wide, as I don't do "earnestly devoted" well.

But in all honesty, it *is* a hugely important subject. Coastal Oregon is dependent on natural resources for its economy:

seafood, timber processing, maritime industries, as well as the tourism that rests on the natural beauty of the area. Small Oregon cities play a surprising role as homes to the largest charter fleets and commercial fishing fleets on the Pacific Coast (I know, you'd expect them to be in some California port, or maybe Seattle). One small city, Newport, is now a hub of serious marine science for the entire U.S. West Coast.

Digressing again. George was looking at me through his bushy eyebrows and beard with more appreciation, so that was good.

"Yes, it is," he replied. "Just because we get a lot of rain doesn't mean we don't have concerns about the future of our water supply. I keep an eagle eye on the industries around here; they'd love to pollute the river if they thought they could get away with it. I watch all the wildlife—we have a great view from our house."

"That must be wonderful!"

"It is. We have a pair of nesting ospreys in a tall fir, and a pair of otters that play in the river. We see them often. I had the power poles moved so the lines don't interrupt the view, but it would be better if we could be off the grid. I'm thinking of installing a residential wind turbine—not sure whether solar panels could work for us."

As he muttered about energy sources and I tried to keep up the conversation, George's intensity turned inward and he munched on a cracker. It seemed like a good time to change the subject.

"George, how is the City Council doing since Greta's death? I know people are concerned about where the city may be going."

"Huh? Oh." His gaze sharpened quickly as his mind moved

off trees and solar gain. He stared at me for a moment. "Well, the last meeting was more of a placeholder. You were there, right?"

"Yes. I couldn't tell whether Greta's agenda was going to move forward or what Dwight was going to recommend."

"I don't think that plan to take money from the Summer Festival is going anywhere," George said firmly.

"That does seem to be a nonstarter, although Dwight still appears to be backing it."

"Dwight works for us," George said, more firmly than I might have expected. "He needs to understand that things will be changing now that Greta's influence is gone. The Summer Festival is too important to interfere with."

"I enjoyed listening to you and Rita that Saturday. You seemed to be playing most of the day."

"Yeah, we were on and off. It's a nice opportunity to play our music for a lot of people."

"Weren't you playing even during the fireworks? I thought I heard you in the background."

He looked toward the door, where most of the meeting participants were trickling back in. "Yes. We toned it down some, but we stuck around."

"It's incredible that Greta apparently walked through all those people to the place where she was killed." I was pushing my luck but needed to talk with him about his alibi if I could swing it. "Did you or Rita see her from the stage?"

"No." He swung his head around and glared at me. "We were concentrating on playing during the noise of the fireworks. I don't know if she went past us."

Obviously, this was a question he had been asked enough times to make him testy about it. I realized that my constructive talking time with George was about over. "It looks like the meeting is about to start again, so I'll sit and watch for a while more. Nice talking with you!"

"Yeah," he threw out before heading over to a side table to pour a glass of water. No plastic water bottles for this group. They brought glasses or mugs, and someone filled a pitcher. I thought it an appropriate touch.

I stayed in my seat for another fifteen minutes of water discussions just to underline my role as interested observer, took some generic notes, then rose, smiled at everyone, and left. I hadn't had a chance to learn whether George knew about the mysterious building, but I might be able to figure that out by watching him, along with the rest of the Council, at the next meeting when Dwight dropped the bombshell.

In the meantime, I needed to take another trip to City Hall to talk with Pat Gregorio. I had been putting it off, as the whole reason for going was distasteful. I liked her, and besides not wanting to think of her as a killer—Pat just seemed way too smart for that—I wasn't sure how to preserve a good relationship with her after invading her personal life.

The next morning, I made my way to her upstairs office after waving at her staff members, who handle City Hall's front desk along with their other duties. Her door was open, but I knocked on the doorframe before sticking my head over the threshold.

"Pat, sorry to bother you, but do you have a minute?"

She gave me one of her wide smiles. Her long, salt-and-pepper hair was pulled back in a clip, and she wore her usual work outfit of casual slacks and a knit top with a silver locket on a long chain around her neck.

"Yeah, come on in." She swiveled from her computer while

I sat in one of the chairs in front of her desk.

We exchanged minor pleasantries—neither of us needs a lot of that to get to business—and then I sighed and jumped into it. There wasn't much point in prevaricating with her, so I wanted to be as candid as possible without telling her about my assignment from the chief.

"Pat, Sheffield seems pretty divided since Greta Sutton was murdered. I know how I felt about her impact on the city, but you saw her as mayor more than I did. What did you think of her?"

She seemed surprised. "Why are you asking?"

"I guess I'm just trying to understand things. She seemed to be liked by a lot of people—she was elected, after all—and then this violence happens. Now, there are some people who want to name a flipping ballfield after her"—Pat smiled again knowingly—"and some who are simply happy she's gone. I'm not trying to stir up trouble. In fact, I'm trying to find a way to resolve it. You saw her a fair amount in her role as mayor; what were your feelings about her?"

Her mouth worked for a moment. "Shut the door."

I reached around and swung her office door closed, then turned back to her with a raised eyebrow.

"I'll tell you something, Felice, that I wouldn't tell everyone. I hated that bitch."

Okay, that's candid.

One corner of my mouth turned up before I could stop it. "Any reason in particular?"

"Oh, man, how long have you got? She was screwing up the budget right, left, and center for her 'special projects'"—Pat waved air quotation marks—"she pressured the city manager to do whatever she wanted; she kept calling City staff, including *my staff,* without going through proper channels. I've been working frantically for months to shore up the budget from the damage she's done and keep Sheffield solvent, but I never knew what was coming next.

"I'll tell you, Felice—I've been through a lot of mayors and councilors and about seven city managers in this job, but I was pretty much at the end of my tether. I was thinking of retiring and just letting the whole thing go to hell."

I nodded. "That was the sort of stuff that drove me crazy about her, too—okay, besides the sweet old lady crap." Pat chuckled. "If it bothered me, I could only imagine how difficult it was for you. What were the biggest problems?"

"You knew about the library director?"

I nodded, grimacing.

"She had no business getting involved in that. She got a perfectly good person fired just to promote her own friend for a City job. I was just disgusted, although thankfully, it didn't work. But that didn't involve my own department."

"Right," I supplied, "although it must have been uncomfortable for the rest of the staff. What hit you more directly?"

"Well, as Finance Director, I'm in charge of both drafting the City budget and making sure we live by it once it's approved."

I nodded.

"You know we take *months* to come up with a balanced budget, trying to meet everyone's needs. Things are tight, and once it's approved, it isn't supposed to be a casual thing to just change it."

I nodded again. Pat's devotion to Sheffield's solvency was almost legendary.

"I kept finding out that Mayor Sutton was getting

amendments approved by the City Council; never any discussion, never any preparation. Money kept being diverted from projects we had worked really hard to fund."

"Like what?"

"Oh . . ." Pat's head tilted up, checking the ceiling as she sifted through recollections. "Just a couple of examples: a street project out at Woodyard Road. Those people had waited for *years* to get a decent street, and then I heard that the mayor wanted to divert the money to some ridiculous purpose."

"I heard flower baskets."

"Right. It's Public Works money, so it has to be a Public Works project. She was trying to claim that it qualified. I think we got out of that one; I don't think it passed before she was killed. But you heard about the loss from the General Fund?"

"Was this the nonprofit support thing?"

"Oh, that one made me *crazy,*" Pat said bitterly. "Fifty thousand dollars to support some program that wasn't even a City issue. Do you know how much we can do with fifty thousand dollars? That's a lot of money out of the budget. And there was more."

"More?" I was surprised.

"She moved money around in the Park Maintenance Fund. Parks closer to downtown—and near her house, by the way— were going to get a bunch of new equipment and more maintenance. That meant parks in other parts of Sheffield weren't going to get any maintenance at all, not even mowing the grass. She also kept calling me—directly—to ask if I would make small changes in the Funds. Outside of channels, just at her personal request! I kept telling her 'absolutely not.' I didn't even find out what they were.

"And something was going on just recently. The mayor

called one of my staff to get an extra copy of the printed budget. Lisa pointed out that she already received a copy—we're very careful about those, they're expensive to produce—and she said she wanted a separate one to make notes in because she was going to go through the whole thing."

"For what? She certainly wasn't claiming there was anything wrong with it?"

"Lisa asked her that. She made some 'chirpy noises,' Lisa said, said she was sure it was fine, but that she wanted to see where there might be some room."

Light was dawning in my brain. "Room, I'll bet, for some matching funds for a building."

Pat stared at me. "A *building*? We don't have enough money in the budget for a big box of Legos."

I started laughing; I couldn't help it. After a moment, her face relaxed and she smiled back.

"Pat, there was something going on about a developer and a building. It was some big secret Greta had." I didn't mention Dwight's involvement; Pat could handle her own relationship with her boss. "There's likely to be more coming out about it, but that's all I know so far."

"That should be interesting," she returned. "We'll have to see how the new Council deals with it. I have to say, though, I'm glad Councilor Dennis has a finance background."

I nodded again. But I had to keep going.

"Pat, were all your problems with Mayor Sutton professional ones?"

She frowned. "I didn't have a social relationship with her, if that's what you're asking."

"No." I hesitated for a moment. "Ah, jeez, this is gossip and I *hate* gossip, but it's out there and I need to ask you. Did you know that Greta was questioning your professionalism around town?"

Now Pat's own eyebrow quirked. "Questioning it how?"

"She was hinting that you were having an affair with someone." I said it as flatly as I could manage. "I don't know who or anything else about it, but she was using it to hint that you might not be trustworthy."

Pat sat for a moment, staring to the side at her office wall. "That royal bitch," she finally hissed. "I wouldn't give in to her 'little requests' to make budget changes and told her to lay off my staff, so she tried to publicly embarrass me and maybe get me fired." She turned her head to look directly at me. "That is complete crap. I don't even know who she might be hinting at. I hate even having to say it, and I sure hope my husband doesn't hear about this."

"Pat, none of my business; I really don't want to ask about your personal life. But if you knew about it, given all your other problems with Greta, you have to know that it gives you something of a motive to get rid of her."

She looked at me, aghast. "Are people saying that *I* killed her?"

"Not that I know of. I think several of our local worthies would rather it was me. But I've been asked to talk with people, and now I'm hearing all kinds of garbage I would just as soon not hear. I had to ask you."

She sat another moment. "Yeah, maybe, I can see that. But I can't think of many things dumber than killing someone. Like I said, I was close to leaving the job to get away from what she was doing. I might even have taken part in a recall effort, and staff usually stays far away from things like that."

She shook her head and grimaced. "Man, now I have even

more reason to hate that woman, and I can't do anything about it."

"I'm asking everyone what they were doing on the Saturday of the Festival. Can I ask you, too?"

"I won't ask why you're asking, but okay. My husband and I spent the day walking around, had dinner on the midway, then watched the fireworks. You can ask him whether I might have gone to the logging show grounds, because I didn't leave him during the show."

That was good enough for me, at least to relate to Abhay. I apologized for probing, hoping we were still friendly, and we talked for a short time about recovering City finances before I took my leave. If I didn't know it already, the conversation convinced me that Kate's stint as interim mayor was going to require *a lot* of work.

Chapter Thirteen

The crowd for the Council meeting the following week was smaller, with only a few residual people from the remembrance group that had attended the previous one. That happens with local government. Something unusual brings a lot of people to a meeting, and maybe a few become interested or suspicious enough to come to another one. If it's interest, you hope that maybe you'll get a new councilor applicant in the next election to contribute to the next set of leaders and move the community forward. If it's suspicion, they may show up for a while to show councilors "you're being watched" before they get completely bored and disappear again.

This was a work session rather than an official meeting, so the councilors had left the dais to sit around a large rectangular table set up in the center of the Council chambers. Dwight Orkman and the City attorney also had seats there. Given the formation, it was difficult for me to sit somewhere where I could see everyone's faces, but I found a place among the audience chairs where I could watch Dwight and about half the group, including George and Suzanne. Kate, sitting at one end of the table, had her back to me, and I had a partial view of

Dennis Waitly, Pete Ichikawa, and Anne Perez. I realized that, besides faces, I would have to watch backs and other body language if I were going to get any useful information as events unfolded.

The agenda, thankfully, was not too long, and the meeting got under way as usual. Not surprisingly, after the standard household items came a discussion of finding a replacement for the mayor. Under Sheffield's City Charter, the councilors would appoint an interim mayor from among a pool of applicants (that could include one or more of themselves) to serve until January, when winners from November's upcoming election would take their seats. I was glad to hear a couple of councilors suggest that Kate take the office: although she was new, she clearly had won people's respect as she had mine. I was also glad to hear her say that she was willing. Since we were already into August, she could serve as interim mayor for the last five months of the year, then move back to her councilor position for the rest of her four-year term, unless she wanted to run in November to keep the job. Any appointee not already on the Council would have to be elected in November in order to keep the seat, so the likelihood of a lot of other applicants was small.

The Council couldn't take official votes to make decisions at work sessions, but the members came reasonably quickly to a consensus on when to open and close an application process for the position.

Then came the issue of the Summer Festival, and I started scanning faces. It had been tabled at the last meeting, but this would be the benchmark to determine which of Greta's old followers would continue her agenda.

Dwight introduced the topic by summarizing the state of

the City's budget—solvent, but barely, although he took quite a bit longer to say so—and listing possible avenues for new revenue—limited. He brought up the issue of charging more for the use of City assets like the waterfront park.

"As you may know, Mayor Sutton and I were looking into the idea of moving from a small flat rental fee for the space to a percentage of the proceeds from the event taking place there. I did hold a meeting with the Summer Festival Committee; I can report that the idea was not well received."

There was a grumble from the councilors, but Dwight soldiered on. "The reaction isn't surprising, but I think you should discuss this as a council. The waterfront park is a significant asset, with the potential for attracting larger events like the Summer Festival. We provide public safety support for events, and our Public Works employees must support them as well by blocking off streets, providing cleanup services, and the like. The fees we charge don't recoup those expenditures."

Suzanne Dryer was quivering with the need to break in.

"You know that the Summer Festival people do their own cleanup, Dwight. The Committee has been putting on that show for years and it brings thousands of people to Sheffield. The Committee uses that money to pay for swimming lessons for elementary school kids, and the rest of the money is used for the next year's Festival. No one is getting rich from the Summer Festival. I can't believe you would try to hurt our biggest event this way!"

Kate put up her hand and Suzanne subsided, although she was clearly still angry.

"There obviously are strong feelings about this issue, which brings up my primary concern. Dwight, why was this issue not discussed with the full Council before you and the mayor decided to move forward with it? I find that the most troubling aspect of this, and one that is unacceptable."

Mine was among the heads nodding at Kate's statement, and I watched Dwight to see how he would react—and whether, knowing what I did about his conversation with the mayor, he would lie.

"At the heart of this, it's an administrative issue," he asserted, his eyes sweeping the group. "My department heads and I are responsible for decisions about fees and licenses. There wasn't any need to come to you with this."

"And yet, Greta Sutton seemed to think she should get involved," boomed a deep voice from one of the Council members I could see only partially. It came from Dennis Waitly, another long-term resident with ties to local timbering. He had held a variety of appointed posts in the City government before running for Council. Dennis was a big guy, like George Russell, and he had the requisite beard, but he kept his hair in a short brush cut, appeared more fit, and had friendly crinkles around his blue eyes. He normally stayed quiet but had been known to ask probing questions, usually what I considered good ones. He had followed Greta's lead on some issues, but I don't think she had counted him among her "safe" votes.

Dennis' statement seemed to take the lid off, and suddenly several voices were raised at once. I couldn't follow all the statements, but while there may have been a voice or two defending her, I don't think the late mayor would have been pleased if she had been there to hear how her troops had mutinied. I watched as Dwight leaned back, clearly reading the negative reaction.

Kate waited to allow the discussion to die down a bit, then

put up her hand again.

"If I'm reading what I'm hearing correctly, I think we have a general consensus against changing our policy"—she glanced over to Dwight to emphasize the Council's position—from rental fees to a percentage of event proceeds. I believe Dwight is correct in calling the overall issue an administrative one, but the Council clearly has a preference on how the City government handles this. Do I have this correct?"

Several heads nodded (I was a bit worried that Suzanne would crack a cervical vertebra, hers was going up and down so vigorously), and there were glares directed at Dwight.

Kate continued. "At the same time, Dwight has a good point about our expenses not being met. Perhaps City staff could investigate changing the fee schedule to ensure that our costs for supporting all events, or at least most of them, are recouped. Does that sound reasonable?" Some hesitation, then more nods. After a moment, Dwight nodded back and made a note on his agenda. The Great Summer Festival Revenue controversy appeared to be over.

And the outcome would not have been a big surprise, at least to some. I looked around the audience and realized that none of the Drapers had attended the meeting. Somebody had told them they didn't have to worry; I couldn't help wondering who.

Every controversy secretly circulating around the late mayor seemed to be turning up that evening. Under "Notes from Planning Commission" on the agenda was the item of Carl Roetgen's property and whether to annex it. The Commission's monthly meeting was the night before each Council work session so that issues arising there could be discussed by councilors before moving further through the process.

From the way Dwight hesitated before outlining the issue, it was clear he thought it was important.

"The Planning Commission is requesting your guidance on this matter. You'll see a map in your packet"—there was shuffling through papers as the Council members found the page—"with a large parcel just northeast of the city highlighted."

"This is Carl's property, the piece he wants to develop, isn't it?" asked Dennis Waitly.

Some councilors nodded, while others clearly hadn't heard of the proposed project.

"Yes. He's proposing to build twenty-two single-family homes on the property, although I don't have a plat map to show you," referring to the detailed map of building lots, streets, and other improvements that would have to be filed as part of a development plan.

"So—if this property is outside the City limits, is this just an informational item?" asked Kate.

"Well, no," answered Dwight. He seemed to be quivering a bit. "It's been suggested that the City of Sheffield may want to annex the property and bring the development inside the City limits. The Planning Commission wants to know whether to move forward with the annexation process."

There were a few interested noises from councilors, many of whom bent over the map again to look in more detail.

"As you can see, the property is adjacent to City boundaries in at least one place. And there is no question that Sheffield could benefit from the additional tax revenue and population once these homes are occupied."

"Let me get some clarification, Dwight," said Kate. "Is this an inquiry from the property owner?" Some property owners liked being inside City limits because of the services they could guarantee home buyers, and the City had received such requests in the past.

"Uh, no, Councilor Dennis," Dwight answered. "The idea actually came from Mayor Sutton. However, it's something I would recommend we move forward on, as there are several potential benefits."

"Another Mayor Sutton idea she apparently didn't think the rest of us needed to hear," Kate said wryly. "Do any councilors have thoughts on this?"

After a moment, Suzanne spoke up. "I know the annexation process is pretty complicated. Doesn't a lot of it depend on whether the property owner wants it? Do we know how Carl feels about it?"

"Yes, Councilor Dryer," Dwight responded. "I, um, have spoken briefly with Mr. Roetgen about it, and we don't have his agreement just yet. However, if you wish the Planning Commission to move forward without his approval, we still can do so. I think it's worth pursuing."

So at least he's admitting that Carl is opposed, I thought, remembering my conversation with the business owner during that Festival afternoon.

"I don't see this going very far if Carl fights it," said Pete Ichikawa, and there was some head-nodding from others, including Suzanne and George Russell. Carl's influence was well known around the city, whether one liked it or not.

"It may not, but there is a process to follow, and I'd like to pursue it," Dwight responded, a set look to his features. "Can I take that guidance back to the Planning Commission?"

Councilors made some noncommittal noises—this wasn't

something that would be coming back to them anytime soon—but I saw that Dwight was taking that as approval as he wrote notes in the notebook in front of him on the desk. *Yes, she's going to be with us for a long time still,* was all I could think, and I shook my head slowly as the meeting moved along. What was circling around the back of my mind was the thought that, since Carl's opposition to Greta's idea gave him a motive to kill her, he hadn't accomplished his objective—if he had been the one who had murdered her, of course.

The bombshell I'd been trying to investigate wouldn't have been immediately obvious from the agenda. It took me a minute to notice "Use of City Property" listed most of the way down the page. Clearly, Dwight had been anxious about too much attention coming to the potential development of the waterfront property.

When the meeting progressed to that point, it was clear that Suzanne had called Kate as she had told me she would—or someone had—to let Kate know at least an outline of what was going on.

"Next on the agenda is a discussion of potential use of City property," Kate began. "Dwight, I understand there has been some interest in our waterfront industrial land. This appears to be yet another issue where the Council needs to be brought up to speed. Can you tell us what this is about?"

"Yes, Councilor Dennis. This is actually some potentially exciting news for Sheffield." Dwight knew he had ground to make up from his secret deliberations with the late mayor. He clearly was trying some verbal sleight of hand to divert attention.

"We have received a proposal from an energy solutions firm about developing the ten-acre waterfront site owned by the City. As you know, the property has been zoned Light Industrial, and the Council has held past discussions about desirable businesses that could be located there. However, we have not had a lot of serious interest in the property.

"This company, AllGen Partners, contacted me some time ago. They're interested in building an energy campus on the property where employees would work to enhance alternative energy delivery systems. We don't have all the details, but the facility would include a good-sized building with about fifty employees and would use the transportation and waterfront capabilities of the property in its work."

There was much straightening of spines at the Council table as people sat up to take in the proposal. Suzanne was wide-eyed, with her mouth open; other councilors were "oohing." No one was looking as if they'd heard it all before, not even Anne Perez, which told me a bit about how closely Greta had held this tidbit to her chest. I glanced over to George Russell. Given his environmental interests, he should be ecstatic over a major alternative energy facility here in his hometown. He was nodding along with others, although his mouth was pursed and his shoulders looked tight. He probably felt, and rightly so, that he should have been consulted on the project given his environmental credentials. Dennis Waitly was looking serious.

I was pretty impressed myself—this could be a major image coup for the city, not to mention the addition of good jobs. My mind raced ahead to possible integration with the marine science going on elsewhere along the coast.

Thankfully, the Council wasn't as starry-eyed as I was. Kate started the questioning: "Dwight, what do we know about this company? I don't think it's local; do we know how serious it is and whether it has the money to carry out the project? Is it going to need concessions from the City?"

Dwight explained, haltingly, that he had met with the company (*Met with it? Dwight, shame on you; you're still lying*) and that it was backed by a venture capital company that specialized in energy. The project was still in the planning stages, but one of the issues to be decided was whether the City was willing to sell the real estate.

"I think this is a very exciting opportunity for Sheffield," he continued. "It may require some matching funds or other concessions from the City, but I think the staff would recommend that we do everything we can to ensure that this project moves forward." I checked the room: it was hard to prove or disprove that statement, since the only other staff member present was the City attorney, an independent contractor with his main practice in another town. Pat Gregorio, a staff member whose work would be hugely impacted, was not there.

"George, you're our resident environmentalist," piped up Pete Ichikawa. "What do you think?"

All eyes swung to George Russell, who blinked and nodded before answering. "Yeah, it sounds pretty exciting. Alternative energy is the future; having a development facility here in Sheffield could really put us on the map. But there's a lot of information missing. It sounds like there are still a lot of uncertainties, right?" He looked over to Dwight.

Suzanne didn't look quite as happy. "Greta Sutton knew about this project because she hinted about it to me. Why are we only hearing about this now?"

Dwight looked defensive and even angry, although he seemed to be trying to hide it. "Mayor Sutton was fairly insistent that I tell her first about any developments in City business," he stated shortly. "I felt that I had to tell her about the contact, and although I warned her that it was preliminary, she wanted to push ahead."

I couldn't lose the opportunity and I couldn't stand his lying directly to his supervisors. I stood up and looked straight at him.

"Dwight, are those really the facts? Weren't you actually in contact with these people *before* you came to Sheffield? Wasn't bringing the building here part of the deal to make you city manager? And didn't Mayor Sutton even have plans to require that the building be named after herself? I think it might have been a little more than just pushing ahead, and the Council was being kept completely in the dark."

Dwight glared at me. "I don't know where you got that information." He paused. "Yes, some of that is correct, although I don't like how you've characterized it."

Gasps from the rest of the councilors as Dwight turned to look at the group and continued. "Given developments, all of that hardly matters now. I was under instruction not to distribute the information about the contact; perhaps I should have disregarded that. Regardless, this does seem like an important development for Sheffield, even with the possible implications for our future budgets."

There were some follow-up comments, speculation, and disapproval for the way Dwight had performed; without additional information, there wasn't much more to digest. But the word was out. Before her death, Greta obviously had thought she could rush this project through the Council with a minimum of discussion and get her name on the building as a token of the developers' gratitude. Given her former hold on the Council, she might have been able to do so.

But the project wasn't as simple as Dwight had made it out to be, and it looked like he was still lying to his employers. Greta had clearly said that the City needed to raise money for "her" building when I heard her that fateful Saturday afternoon, and what I had heard from Pat Gregorio about the mayor's pending comb through the budget seemed to confirm it. There had been no clear statement of that in this discussion. Did Dwight really think he could dump that problem on councilors later without backlash? How attached to this idea were councilors going to become before they heard the real story? A mandate for serious cash from the City would doom the project, given the current financial situation.

I was becoming weighed down by the information I was gathering and the need to keep it confidential. But while the meeting was winding up, I needed to check things out with George, since we were now on speaking terms. I made my way to him in the pushing of chairs and gathering of possessions.

"George, that was some news about the City property. What a proposal!"

"Yeah, hi, Felice." He didn't look particularly pleased to see me again. "Yeah, it's quite a project."

"I couldn't help noticing you didn't look all that excited when Dwight dropped the information. Had you heard about this before?"

"No—no, I hadn't. No, I think it's a great idea. Alternative energy is certainly the future, and a center here in Sheffield could have a lot of benefits." His intense gaze centered on my face. "I was a little upset that Dwight and Greta Sutton were working on this without letting the rest of us know, that's all. We're all getting tired of hearing about Greta's secret projects."

"Well, this is in the early stages, and I'm sure we'll all be hearing a lot more about it," was the closest I could come to noting the additional aspects I knew. He grunted his agreement, and we were about to say our goodbyes when our attention was drawn to two uniforms standing in the door to the Council chambers.

Norfolk County Sheriff Alan Ross had shown up in person with a deputy trailing along just behind him. A lean man of just over average height with a silver brush cut, his Pacific Northwest Native American heritage showed in the cast of his dark eyes and the shape of his features. He'd been in the County most of his life and had been promoted through the ranks of deputies; moreover, he had a smart way of being pleasant and authoritative at the same time. I knew and liked him from Public Safety Committee work, but what was he doing in Sheffield at seven forty-five in the evening?

The two men waited just inside the door for most of the meeting attendees to file out, then headed over to Dwight. Ross stood in front of him and said something I couldn't hear with the deputy to the side. The city manager looked dumbfounded, but all I heard from across the room was an emphatic "WHAT?"

Ross continued speaking softly, but directly, with a cadence that could have been a Miranda warning. Clearly, this was official, but he was avoiding a public scene by showing up at the end of the meeting, waiting for most everyone to leave, and leaving out the dramatics, including handcuffs. By now, Orkman had a strange mixture of anger, fear, and surprise on his face, but when the sheriff turned to stand on his other side and motioned forward, the city manager moved with them through the side door leading directly into the parking lot. As the door opened, I saw the flashing lights of a Sheriff's Department unit waiting. Then the door closed on the three of them, leaving George, me, and the few remaining people in the room with our mouths hanging open.

What the hell just happened? was about all I could think. Well, okay, what had just happened, obviously, was Dwight Orkman being arrested, or at least taken in for questioning. The county sheriff had to carry out the action because Orkman was our police chief's boss, but Abhay had to at least know about it, if not request it. The obvious assumption was that it was in connection with Greta's death, although that wasn't a given: Dwight had been hired in such a hurry that he might have any number of background problems we didn't know about. Gee, maybe he was behind on child support or had been involved in a drunk driving incident. One thing was certain: this was going to be the only thing talked about in Sheffield the following day.

But I had to move beyond that. I was one of probably very few people who knew that Dwight had an excellent motive for killing Greta as well as the opportunity, since I knew he had been moving around the Festival grounds during the fireworks that Saturday night. But how did all this fit together?

Sue Grafton's Kinsey Millhone would have put all her information on 3 × 5 index cards and shuffled them around until some sort of pattern showed up. If I tried that, I think I'd end up with scribbles, a chaos of card stock, and a lot of gaps. It was a fact that a lot of people had not liked Greta Sutton, that she had been a disastrous public official and an unpleasant human being. But was the investigation over? What should I do next?

It seemed like the logical next step was to talk with

someone with more information about the inner workings of City Hall these days than I had—not to mention that it would be fun to have lunch and a long talk with Kate Dennis—*after* I provided David with a blow-by-blow of dumbfounding events.

Chapter Fourteen

"Well, I guess that was inevitable," said a deadpan David when I had recounted the events of the meeting and its aftermath. I had come upon him sitting on one end of the living room couch, with Angus—as usual—taking up the other two-thirds while seeking a lap for his wiry head.

"Oh, come on, David. Can you say that you really expected Dwight to be arrested, right there at a public meeting?" Sometimes my husband takes his phlegmatic "nothing surprises me" attitude beyond the reasonable. I was still too excited to sit down and had been striding around the room while going through my story, waving my arms at emotional moments. "He's hardly the only suspect."

"Okay, maybe not the way it was done," he admitted. "But everything seemed to be pointed toward him, based on what you saw and heard. The mayor threatened him; she was holding his feet to the fire on this development thing; her activities were putting the City in an impossible financial situation and creating liability that would have dragged him down, too. If he didn't see any other way to save his job, maybe he thought getting rid of Greta was the only answer. Plus, there is the evidence of means and opportunity you provided. He definitely was there during the fireworks and could have been in the logging area before you saw him at the pavilion."

"I get that," I said. "But it seems a lot more plausible to just resign and get out of town than kill one of your employers for causing you trouble."

"You may think that, but keep in mind that you weren't stuck with Greta on your back all the time," David smiled.

I saw where he was going. "True. If I couldn't stand to be around her and her half-witted pronouncements for more than a few minutes, what would it have been like to have to meet with her for hours at a time? Let alone trying to counter her demands. I wonder how much opposition he put up."

"And how long it took him to give up trying," David said resignedly.

"If he does turn out to be guilty," I said morosely, "I wish he could just have been driven to drink instead. Greta Sutton is a horrible reason to spend the rest of your life in prison."

I called Kate the next morning to set up a lunch date. Luckily, we both were available the following day, so that part of the conversation went easily. But of course, we had to discuss the events of the night before, especially since Kate had already left the Council chambers when the sheriff came in. I described what I had seen, which just added some detail to what she had already learned.

"Good grief, how hard does this job have to get?" she moaned. "I mean, I'm really sorry about Dwight—if he's innocent—but how are we supposed to function without a mayor *or* a city manager?"

"Have you heard whether the County is still holding him?"

"No, no developments since last night. Felice, do you know anything about why they arrested him?"

"I know that Greta was giving him grief about that building you discussed last night, and I think he had both opportunity and motive." I gave her a quick summary of what I had told Chief Abhay.

"I can see that it's enough to get him brought in to answer some questions," she said, "but is it enough to get him charged with killing her?"

"No idea. As you know, there are unlikely to be any forensic results back from Portland yet."

"Well, I hope this gets cleared up one way or the other pretty soon," she said. "Our River Festival is due to start in two weeks, and all this bad feeling and uncertainty isn't doing its chances any good."

I had forgotten about the River Festival. It wasn't as large as the Summer Festival and hadn't been held as long, but its emphasis on Sheffield's maritime heritage made it more interesting to many. Vintage boats would be there from up and down the Pacific Coast, including Canada; events included great family and organization opportunities like a three-day boat-building contest; and there were always good shows by our local art community, who not surprisingly painted river scenes a lot. Because it involved fewer people from far out of town, Kate was right that it could be affected severely by a negative climate in the area.

"Kate, I've been sensing some really negative feelings around Sheffield, but you get more places than I do. What have you seen?"

She remained silent for a moment. "I haven't stopped to think about it, but I have to say I'm troubled," she mused. "I've talked with a couple of people lately—people who are active in the community—about running for Council or for mayor in November. Both turned me down flat, which surprised me, and they both said something to the effect of not wanting to deal with all of Sheffield's problems.

"And there's more. Where was I? Oh, yes, at the hobby store. I was picking up some thread. There were a bunch of women there, and you wouldn't believe the rumors I was hearing! About Greta being killed because she had stolen all of the City's money; then someone answered back and was pretty nasty; then a third woman just announced to everyone that all this is just par for the course because Sheffield is always going to be a pit. It was awful. They had been standing together like friends, but then they all marched off in different directions. It was like there was a big, black cloud hanging over the whole store."

"Yes. Social media has been about the same, but I was wondering about real life."

I couldn't help but think about the work Kate and others would have to do to repair the community's image of itself, but now was not the time to ask her whether she was planning to take it on.

We both agreed that we had a lot to talk about—I was ready to volunteer to keep something going during the Festival but didn't know what was needed—and ended the conversation. I was hoping for a more in-depth discussion when we were face-to-face.

My next call was to Chief Abhay. He might not want or be able to tell me much, but I needed to know whether he still needed my help.

"I understand you were in the Council chambers when

Dwight was picked up last night," was his opening after we had exchanged greetings.

"Yes. Bit of a shock there. He looked both surprised and angry."

"I wouldn't expect anything else."

"I'm assuming the County was there at your request," I ventured, and heard an assenting grunt in response. "Do you think there is enough evidence to charge him?"

"Not up to me. We don't have a lot of physical evidence, as you know, and don't have results back yet on what we did collect. Your statement showed that he had opportunity."

"And he apparently had some motive." While I knew that, strictly speaking, showing motive isn't a necessary element in a conviction, most juries expect to hear one.

"Well, that was part of the reason we wanted to talk with him. But it didn't hold up once the Sheriff started questioning him. We thought he was balking at that City property development that the mayor was pushing—we know from your statement that she threatened him about it. Turns out the venture capital company was paying Mr. Orkman a 'finder's fee' for moving the project forward."

"He was getting a *kickback*?" I was beyond appalled. Was there no end to the wrinkles associated with this thing?

"Not a kickback in the corruption sense, just a fee for finding the best city and property, supposedly. Hard to say where his responsibility ended, and it's probably contrary to his contract. But he apparently had about two hundred fifty thousand reasons for making that alternative energy center actually happen."

Holy crap. I was gobsmacked, as the Brits say (it's a great word; I wish American English had one to match it), and didn't contribute much more to the conversation with the chief than inarticulate mumbles. But working through what it meant kept my head spinning for the rest of the day and night.

Thankfully, figuring out whether Dwight's "finder's fee" was legal wasn't my problem, although being handed an amount of money that probably was a whole lot more than his annual salary didn't sound good. Chief Abhay hadn't asked me to keep the information confidential, so since the news about Dwight—and the fact that he had been released—was something that would impact Kate quite a bit, I expected to tell her at lunch.

"What is the Council going to do about Dwight?" was my first question once we were sitting together at a local Thai restaurant with the requisite beverages in front of us.

"Oh, man, I don't know," she said, dropping her forehead into her hand, her short, bobbed dark hair falling forward. "You don't fire someone because they were taken in for questioning—I have no idea whether he's actually guilty. And then there's that finder's fee thing. I'm almost positive it's against the law, but none of the councilors knows for sure, and we must get this right. I'm going to ask the City attorney for an opinion, but it will take a while to get it back.

"And I also don't know how the fee is going to affect how councilors feel about the energy center project. How can we trust that the information we're getting from Dwight is accurate if he came here specifically to push this project, and he's being paid more by the developers than we pay him as city manager?"

"So, you *may* have cause to fire Dwight—I think you probably will—but that doesn't mean you have to do it, either."

"No, that's true. We can't keep him as city manager if we

can't trust his judgment. But going through the process of hiring a replacement is something we really don't need right now. Assuming anyone would come to Sheffield, 'The Town Where They Murdered the Mayor,'" she said with her fingers in air quotes.

"The whole thing may be taken out of our hands, anyway," Kate went on. "What if he *is* guilty of Greta's murder? As far as I can tell, the police don't have any other real suspects."

"When we talked yesterday, you were worried about the River Festival," I prompted. "Has there been any issue with that?"

"Yeah. The whole thing is falling apart. I got a call this morning from one of the organizers: people who rented spaces are pulling their boats; vendors are cancelling, too. They're even having teams pull out of the boat-building contest. I'm not sure right now whether we can even hold a decent Festival."

"Wow. All this because of Greta's murder?"

"Well, the out-of-town response apparently is because of that, especially because it happened at a festival event. But the local people seem to be pulling out because of disputes with other people in Sheffield. Everywhere I go, I get asked constantly about how the case is going—as if I had information not available to everyone else—and then I get an earful about 'what probably happened' and complaints about how everybody else is behaving. Based on how people felt about Greta, and what was going on in City government, and the weather this summer, and their utility bills—you name it—it's manifesting in fights all over town."

"Fights?" I had to admit, I hadn't considered brawls breaking out.

"Well, verbal ones. People are saying things to other people that are going to cause rifts for years."

I shook my head and frowned. One of the things I had noticed about small-town life was the amazing ability of people to hold grudges. In a major metro, people had thicker skins: you either ignored a comment, made a quick rejoinder, or figured you probably wouldn't run into that person again, anyway. Also, people seemed to understand—at least in professional life—that you had to be tolerant because your current opponent might be needed as an ally in another situation or on another issue. Of course, there are other hazards in urban life, including the crazies who will take a gun out of a glove compartment and shoot you if you pass them on the highway. But you can't be prepared for everything.

In Sheffield, I had found that getting a large group together to collaborate on something was nearly impossible because certain people didn't talk to other people. If you asked why, most third parties didn't know, but "it might have been because of what X said to Y about Z." "Oh, when was this?"— thinking you must have missed a recent get-together.

"I think it was about ten years ago."

WHAT?

Okay, I'm digressing again. But it was an area of disappointment, given everything that could have been achieved if *all* the merchants, or *all* the artists, could have worked together. After a while, navigating the minefield of disagreements subdued the enthusiasm of even the most collaboratively minded soul. Believe me, I had tried.

This was the sort of divide I had been worried about since Greta died. Sheffield could suffer real damage as a community if people split into factions that couldn't get past their differences. Without the groups who worked together on projects of all kinds, a small town like Sheffield could degenerate into an inactive, unattractive dark hole, and quickly. I wondered whether Kate, or any community leader, had the authority or presence to bring people back together.

"So how does anyone fix this?" I asked her.

"I would say that the best way is to find out who killed Greta as soon as possible. But even that might not be enough," Kate mused. "Whoever it is, some people may try to defend him or her while others are screaming for blood. That won't help the situation."

"How do you defend the behavior of someone who murdered someone?" I said in disbelief.

"I know, but at this point, people are so entrenched in their opinions that they may try."

I was getting tired of ending lunches with great people on depressing notes.

After saying goodbye to Kate, I started home to cuddle with my husband and fight for the couch with our dog. I had an errand on Main Street on the way, so I found a parking spot. Not a good sign for the merchants, but helpful for customers— a parking space relatively close to your target store was the expectation, not the miracle it would be in a larger city. This time, the spot was right in front of my destination, a local pet store. My errand didn't take long, and both the owner and I managed to exchange greetings without talking about current events.

On the way out after picking up what I needed, I nearly ran into Rita Russell coming down the sidewalk. She didn't have a way of avoiding me this time and I didn't have a way of letting her do it, so I decided to make the most of the situation and exchange a few words.

"Hi, Rita!" When bowing to the inevitable, try to be civil.

"Felice," she grumbled reluctantly. "What do you want?"

"Just saying hello. I've been seeing George at Council meetings and a water group meeting the other night—had a good conversation with him about the water supply. But I haven't seen you since the Summer Festival. I enjoyed your playing."

She frowned at me. "Did you happen to notice there was a murder that night?"

"Well, of course," I looked back at her quizzically.

"Well then, why don't you just take your compliments and fuck off?" She turned as if to continue her progress down the street.

"Jeez, Rita. I've been having perfectly civil conversations with your husband—what's your problem?"

She turned back to me. "I don't have to talk to you. You people don't belong here; you didn't grow up here, you don't understand the way we do things here. Go away!"

I had heard this once too often, and she wasn't an appropriate person to say it to me again. "Rita, you didn't grow up here, either. What is it about 'the way we do things here' that I don't understand? Although I do have to admit, I'm not used to being in a place where City officials get murdered at local festivals. Is that what you meant?"

Rita started sputtering—there really was no other word for it—and it took her a few seconds to get her reply out. "Get the hell away from me," she finally almost shouted, and I was happy to let her walk away. I got to the car and sat for a minute, more than a little shaken. I don't handle that kind of rage well, unless it's part of a good, fair argument where both sides can shout. What was her problem? I hadn't thought of her as a close friend of the mayor, so I didn't think it was grief. *Could she be that shaken just by the fact of my being here?* It was a stupid idea, but since I also had never understood the basis for the rumors she and George had spread, it was the best I had right then.

Chapter Fifteen

David noticed my reticence when I arrived home, and I told him about the incident.

"I know Rita doesn't like me—I've never figured out exactly what she resents so much—but that was extreme. What have I done to her?"

There was more in that vein before I wound down, but David listened patiently. He did not, however, offer me a good answer. "We don't know what's going on with people," he finally suggested. "Maybe she had a fight with George. Maybe she's worried about money. Could be anything."

"But David, how can I be of use in helping Abhay if I don't even know why someone acts the way they do?

"I'm beginning to think I'm completely hopeless at this," I went on. "Half the time I'm worried that I'm upsetting people beyond redemption by asking them questions about a murder, and half the time I'm worried about making myself obvious to a possible killer. What do I know about carrying on an investigation?"

"Maybe you need to dress the part better," he said, looking down at the wildly embroidered espadrille shoes I was wearing.

I had put them on for my lunch with Kate, wanting the fun and cheer they promised. It was a bold gesture for the Oregon coast—you never knew when the temperature was going to drop to forty-five, the fog would roll in, and your light fabric shoes would get a soaking—but I couldn't resist them.

I held up one foot and tilted it back and forth, enjoying the sparkly bits mixed in with all the colors sewn onto the linen. "So, you think I need some brown oxfords and an old trench coat?" I knew he was changing the subject to make me feel better, but I didn't mind going with it.

"Yeah, and an old fedora to put with them. Then you need one of those offices with nothing in it but a big, old wooden desk."

"With a black Bakelite telephone."

"Maybe a filing cabinet."

"And a big window that looks down on the city street, with some gold lettering on it, backwards."

"No, the lettering is on the door."

"No, you have to have lettering on the window, too—it's advertising for all the people with problems needing investigating who may be walking down the street."

We laughed, having pretty much exhausted the subject. I wouldn't have expected David to have that many details of old gumshoe noir movies on hand—he generally refuses to watch anything that "isn't even in *color*"—but the man surprises me sometimes. And that's good.

It may have been August, but the breeze and the loss of the sun meant the evening was cool. It was after 10:00 p.m., finally dark even near the 45th parallel, and the streets of the small town were deserted, storefronts dark except for a pool of light two blocks south, where some diehards were still playing pool at a local tavern and pretending it was hot enough for another beer.

City Hall showed one light, from an office on the main floor in the front, although the shades over the windows were down. While the front door on Main Street was locked tight, the aluminum and glass version in back, off a small parking lot, showed a slight dent in its frame and a small slice of darkness where frame and door would have met when closed.

The corridor, too, was dark but gradually brightened closer to the office door. This, too, was partially open, as if the person inside was willing to talk but not anxious to hear all the noise that would have been coming from surrounding areas of City Hall during business hours. Soft light from a desk lamp set near the window—the source of illumination seen from the street—shone on fair hair bent over papers and a desk blotter.

Bent too far over, with a growing pool of blood next to the head that was deeply dark, soaking up what light reached it as it spread across the big desk. On the floor near the body of City Manager Dwight Orkman, as he sat in his important chair, was the bronze figure of a lumberman, off its longtime pedestal and decorated now with clear evidence of how the man had been killed. A darker shadow stood in the corner of the office, deep breaths now slowing, visually checking its contents before turning toward the door.

The shadow slipped down the corridor to the back and slid through the damaged door, pulling off a pair of leather gloves and pushing them into a pocket. After scanning the surroundings and the parking lot, it moved left to the side street, then right, walking calmly away from Main Street and the few remaining citizens enjoying their August night. About a block away, in front of dark homes, the figure halted its easy progress, slipped into a car, and drove off.

Chapter Sixteen

Another sunny summer morning, another neighborhood walk with a bouncy Scottish deerhound. We had just returned and I was sitting on the bench in our garden, enjoying the sun, deep blue sky and near-perfect temperature with the remains of my precious mug of coffee, when a Sheffield Police SUV rolled slowly down the street and parked quietly just before the driveway entrance.

Tom Abhay got out of the vehicle, his salt-and-pepper hair showing some glints in the sunshine. His walk toward me was heavier than usual and, although I gestured to the other half of the bench, he remained standing.

"Hi, Chief. What's up?"

His answering look was serious. "Felice, can we go inside? I need to talk with you again and I don't need to have your neighbors watching."

"Sure." I led the way under our arched portico and into the house. This time, when I gestured to a chair in the living room, he sat. Angus bounded up, always glad to meet another friend, and Tom gave him some welcome ear scritches before looking up at me.

"He's a nice dog."

"Yeah, he's great, as long as you don't need him to guard anything. The only threat he would be to a burglar is as a trip hazard in the dark." Abhay clearly needed to work up to whatever he wanted to discuss.

He chuckled, then sobered.

"Felice, I need to tell you that Dwight Orkman was found murdered early this morning in his office," he said steadily.

"*In City Hall?*" I blurted out, while I sat heavily and the blood drained from my face. For some idiotic reason, a killing within the civic headquarters of Sheffield seemed more obscene than one elsewhere.

"Yes. We've reorganized the Major Crime Team, since this is a new case."

"How was he killed?"

"I can't give you all the details and the medical examiner will have to rule, but it looks like blunt force trauma. His skull was crushed by a blow from a metal statue."

"Oh, my God. I just visited him there a few days ago. Wait a minute—was it that lumberman thing? I noticed that when I was there. I wondered whether it was his or had been in that office forever."

"Yeah, although we'd rather that didn't get around. That statue has a long history and some people would just be more upset."

"Aren't there cameras on Main Street? Could they show anything?"

"There are a couple, yes, but they mostly shoot down the street. We do have some coverage of City Hall, but it's mostly of the front façade. I have an officer going through those files from last night, but it was the back door that was jimmied open, so I'm not holding out a lot of hope in that direction."

"Which shows again that this is someone who knows the town. Damn."

"We think so, but the bar down the street was still open and there were people on Main Street during the evening. It would have been natural for anyone to look for a back entrance rather than risk being seen going in the front."

"Oh, right." I knew I wasn't raising anything with Tom that he and his colleagues hadn't already considered, but it helped my thought process to go through it and he didn't seem to mind.

"I assume the building is closed?" My thoughts turned to the difficulties in carrying on City business with such a tragedy.

"Yes, until we finish working there, and we'll probably keep his office closed for a while."

I nodded, unsure where to go from there. My head was whirling. If Dwight had been the prime suspect in Greta Sutton's murder, what did this mean? Was this someone's idea of payback?

"Felice," Abhay continued. "We won't know until the investigation is further along, but we have to consider that this is the same person who killed the mayor."

"Do you think that's more likely than someone retaliating against the person they thought killed Greta? It's only been a couple of days since he was taken in for questioning."

"That's possible, but it's hard to believe that there would be two bad guys, this bad, in Sheffield at the same time. I was at the scene this morning. Whoever did this . . . the killer was angry but determined, if you know what I mean. There wasn't any evidence of a fight or anything disturbed. It's like someone just came in, did what he or she came to do, and left again. I don't like the idea of someone like that in my city."

"I don't think the rest of us do, either, Tom," I said.

"Right." He waited a beat, then raised an index finger as he remembered something. "Oh, and there is one other development. Results from Greta Sutton's postmortem are back. She did suffer blunt force trauma, most likely from the choker chain we found. But the cause of death was definitely drowning."

"So, someone really put her head in a bag of water? That shows a lot of malice."

Even after two weeks of imagining it, I was appalled at the idea. If you're insane enough to act on wanting someone dead, a baseball bat works fine. Or a knife, or a gun, or poison if you're the sneaky type. To incapacitate someone, especially an older and weak woman who couldn't put up much of a fight, and then go to all the trouble of bringing a plastic bag, filling it with water, and putting her head in it while unconscious—who does that?

It raised questions in my unsentimental brain. "Chief, was the plastic bag found at the scene?"

"No. The killer was smart enough to think about forensic trace evidence. Finding one plastic bag, even if it's still in the community rather than the landfill by now, is impossible."

"Could any tests be run on the water in her lungs, or have I been watching too much television?"

"No, we can do that. The water wasn't treated, so it was probably from the river."

So, no help there; the river was adjacent to the field where she had been found. "Was there anything in Dwight's office that might tie the two crimes together?"

"Not really. Except that we think there's a possibility that both victims knew the killer. According to Patrick Sutton, he couldn't find Greta before the fireworks, but given her habits, he assumed she was talking with someone. We haven't found her phone, which had her calendar on it: according to Patrick and others, as mayor, she was busy enough to keep track of her appointments. Finding that might help us a lot—which is probably why it's missing."

"And that might be in a landfill by now, too," I mused. "Can I still help?"

"Frankly, Felice, right now I'd like you to stay out of things," Tom looked at me directly. "We have the MCT up for five more days, and I'm going to treat the two cases as connected so we can use the personnel to investigate both."

He continued to hold my eyes. "This guy is dangerous. There's some reason he or she thought that killing Greta wasn't enough, or maybe always planned to kill them both. Or maybe he didn't think Dwight being suspected was enough to keep him safe. I don't want you getting this guy's attention."

"I'm happy to stay out of things." I blinked and responded, trying to keep a touch of relief from my voice. After all, what did I know about criminal investigation? No training, no weapon (assuming I could use it if I had one), and no clue whether the next person I talked with might be the crazy one— that "determined" person who had killed two people for some unknown reason.

After Tom had left, I sat in a chair in the sunroom and stared out the window at the river in the distance. I was perfectly fine steering clear of the investigation, but I couldn't help running through everything I knew in my head, trying to turn it in different directions to see if it made sense. The police and other law enforcement types would be looking for evidence, but they also would be trained to look for the usual motives found for serious crimes. I was convinced that those wouldn't apply here.

I started thinking about what I knew. One person in a marriage gets killed, you look to the spouse. A lot of people in Sheffield had sympathy for Patrick Sutton, and he seemed—in his undemonstrative way—to be genuinely grieved for her loss. Plus, why on earth would he kill Dwight Orkman? Jealousy over how much time the city manager was spending with the mayor? The idea made me snort, apparently out loud, because our snoozing, sun-loving feline Roxana raised her head and looked at me wide-eyed.

"Sorry," I told her. "Just thinking."

She gave me the cat equivalent of frowning in annoyance and put her head back down.

Since the culprit was obviously not Dwight, my thoughts moved on to some of the other people I had been observing lately. My mind went through the list of councilors without inspiration—even Kate, but I didn't see her wanting the post of interim mayor all that much, and she was much too levelheaded.

There also was Carl Roetgen. He was said to be pretty upset with Greta's drive to annex his property, despite his longtime alliance with her, and probably would have seen it as a betrayal. He likely would be upset with Dwight for continuing the effort. So, unlike most people I knew about, he did have a motive against both. But murder?

Then there were the members of the Draper logging family. Some member of the clan may have had motive when Greta was angling for Festival gate money, but they were longtime Sheffielders who surely knew they could get that quashed through their connections around town. Killing the mayor was a bit harsh, and once the finance measure fell through, there certainly was no reason for them to go after Dwight. That seemed another dead end, as Abhay had already said.

And then again, there was all that anger directed at both victims. The means and timing of both crimes said, "The some*one* is one who knows them; the some*thing* is about the City," but the prior planning and ferocity said *personal.* I had to think further afield. There had to be something that tied this mess together—I just had to look for it without attracting unwanted attention. Because, in spite of the chief's telling me to stay out of it and my own doubts about my ability to find an answer, I felt a strong need to get the puzzle solved before any more harm was done to the community.

A lot of people would question my concern. Yes, two City leaders had been killed, but how was that a danger to the whole town?

I've mentioned (perhaps too often) that Sheffield is a small city: that poses certain risks. Five thousand people, most of whom are not active in the community beyond owning or renting a house, sending their kids to local schools, and occasionally patronizing a local store, are just barely enough to create a working structure. You expect the parents of school-age children to take part in the PTA or equivalent and in school-related activities—at least some of them. You expect older people to do much of the other volunteering because they have more time. In this case, that includes holding the local government positions beyond the professional staff. And business owners, most of whom are operating on thin margins in this era of online shopping, are also needed to support local activities like sponsoring teams or providing supplies for festivals. An arts community has the potential to provide depth, creativity, and beauty to local events as well as bringing art-loving visitors from outside. Unlike other towns on or near the Oregon coast, Sheffield could not rely on tourist dollars during non-raining months because we just didn't have the beach.

Now, along comes a shock, a tragedy like the violent loss of two City leaders, and the ripples radiate just like waves of an earthquake. Knock down any of the pillars holding up this structure—a loss of volunteers keeping nonprofits running that provide important services; a loss of visitors and local customers whose funds keep businesses' doors open—and you potentially cause disastrous, perhaps fatal, damage to the whole. Get people fearful, staying at home, angry with each other, not willing to cooperate on projects, not willing to participate in government—the results suggest themselves.

Having lived in several other places and seeing just how fragile Sheffield's infrastructure was—because we *did* see the same people all the time—I believed strongly that solving these killings was necessary to the future health of the whole community. Although that wasn't an opinion I wanted to share with too many people.

Chapter Seventeen

Given my musings, it seemed important to talk with Carl Roetgen, whom I hadn't seen since the Festival. He had appeared angry and frustrated when he talked about the mayor then, seeing her determination to annex his property as a personal betrayal. From my conversation with Dwight after Greta's death, Carl couldn't have expected a break from the City government even then. I wasn't sure a property dispute, especially a months-long process like an annexation, was a decent motive for murder; but then, I wasn't the cold and determined person murdering City officials. Carl had a slick and easygoing façade, but I didn't doubt he had a core of determination or he wouldn't have had the position he did in the community. I took a figurative deep breath and decided to see him.

The next morning, I headed to his business, away from the rest of downtown Sheffield but close to the river and the port, where the boats docked that needed his parts and services. A large building housed the marine engine cleaning and refurbishing activities and other processes that could be done away from a dry dock. Carl's office was in a separate small building with a distant view of the river. I was lucky: he was in.

"Felice," he said in surprise, rising to stand behind his desk as I walked in. I always appreciate such gestures, although sometimes I wonder if modern men do it as a defense mechanism, since they're often taller than women. But maybe that's my cynicism at work again. I know that isn't the motivation in the South, of course, having regularly visited: there, it's still a natural courtesy, and I have to remind myself to sit so that the average Southern man will do the same.

"What brings you here?"

I had wondered how to answer that question before coming. The excuses I had developed previously wouldn't work here, and now there was the news of Dwight's death. I had decided to be at least somewhat open about what I was doing and to appeal to Carl's vanity as a community leader.

"Carl, I appreciate your taking a few minutes to talk with me; I know you're busy," I began.

"No problem; what can I do for you?"

"I remembered our conversation at the Summer Festival and how tied in you are with City government; you've been here a lot longer than David and I have." *Never hurts to mention the hubby when talking with a man.* "I wanted to talk with you a bit about what's going on."

His chiseled face and blue eyes changed to a serious look. It was so perfect an instantly serious look, in fact, that I wondered how long he'd had to practice it in a mirror.

"It's a tragedy, of course. I don't know what's going on in this town that we could have two deaths like this."

"I agree; it's awful. And I'm concerned about what it may be doing to the community as a whole—I'm seeing factions and hearing grumbles pretty much everywhere I go." Which was true. David and I had attended the community theatre fundraiser a few days earlier, although we normally would not have gone. Rather than the normal Sheffield social event where everyone descended on the food, sat down at tables, and talked, the gathering had morphed into two rough groups at opposite sides of the room, each looking suspiciously at the other. Luckily, there had been no shouting or violence, but the tension had been thick. And that had been before Dwight's death. If the animosity got worse, things were going to be said or done that would launch feuds and not be forgiven for decades.

"Yes," Carl answered. "The police need to make some progress, especially now with Dwight killed, too."

"Well, that isn't easy for them. This isn't something that one detective and a small city force can handle along with everything else they deal with every day. You know that the Major Crime Team is only formed for a few days." He nodded.

"So . . . I'm trying to talk informally with community leaders to see if we can find a way through this." *Good, Felice— could you be any more vague?* "Do you remember anything strange happening on the Saturday night of the Summer Festival? Or last Thursday? These killings have to be connected."

"I don't think I can help you much with that," Carl said, looking at me sideways. "I was actually here that Saturday night—I don't go to the fireworks usually. I like to stay close to the yard in case kids or someone decides the Festival is a good chance to cause trouble."

In other words, you could have been anywhere, and we'll never know unless someone saw you somewhere other than here. No one generally described Carl as dumb, even those who didn't like him.

"As for Thursday," he continued slowly, "I couldn't have seen anyone downtown; I didn't have any reason to be there." He was eyeing me with increasing suspicion.

"Right. That makes sense." *Head another direction, Felice.*

"Carl, you knew Greta pretty well. Patrick Sutton told me she was excited before her death about a project—something she called her legacy to the City. Did she talk with you about that?"

"Oh, you mean that development on the City industrial property?"

I nodded.

"I had heard some rumors about out-of-town interest in that but nothing specific. Wasn't there a discussion about that at the last City Council meeting?"

"Yes, I was there. Turns out some company wants to develop an alternative energy center. Most of the councilors seem to be in favor of the idea. That wouldn't have any impact on your operations here, would it?"

"Not really. That property is farther up the river from the boat docks."

"What's your feeling about it?" I didn't think Greta's pet project could possibly provide a motive for murder for Carl, but I thought I'd better cover the bases.

He shrugged. "If it happens, great. It would be nice for Sheffield to have a center that could be a regional draw on energy issues. But to be honest, this kind of prospect has come up before without turning into reality."

"You don't think it's actually going to happen?"

"Let's just say it's a long way from an inquiry to an occupied building."

I nodded, keeping a close eye on his expression. Carl had a look of practiced wisdom at that moment—how much time *did* he spend in front of the mirror?—but not the smugness or hostility I would have expected if he opposed the project. It was time to move on.

"Could you give me your thoughts on what else is going on in City government lately? You keep close tabs on the issues, and you mentioned your property matter when we spoke during the Festival. I know you and Greta were friends"—*at least, before she betrayed the friendship for some tax revenue*—"did you deal with Dwight much? Do you know of anything on his plate that could have triggered such a violent reaction?"

He appeared to give my question some consideration before answering. "Frankly, Felice, I didn't have a lot of time for Dwight. Oh, I suppose he may have been a competent manager, but I didn't think he was the sort of strong leader Sheffield really needs. I would have liked to have seen more independent thinking from him. I think several City councilors felt the same way."

"I think you're right," was all I could think of saying while realizing Carl had not answered my question. "Was there any issue in particular?"

"Well, I told you about the proposed annexation of my property. I hadn't had a chance to really meet with him about it, but I didn't get the feeling that he was going to oppose Greta in front of the Planning Commission, even though he had to know that I would fight it."

Another nod. This was getting me nowhere. I decided to just wade in and see what sort of reaction I could get from him.

"Carl—who do you think is doing this? These are cold,

calculated murders by someone who is smart enough to act when no one else is around and to commit horrible killings without leaving much evidence. I don't know Sheffield well enough to get an idea of anyone living here who would fit that profile. Does anyone come to mind for you?

"I can't say I've given it a lot of thought"— *WHAT?*—"but no, I can't think of anyone. Most people around here go to work and live their lives, Felice. We leave the crazy people to Portland and Eugene." One corner of his mouth went up.

As a joke, it lacked a lot, but I offered the obligatory smile. In response, his face hardened, and his eyes glared at me.

"Now let me ask you, Felice. Why are you getting involved in something that should be left to the police? You said yourself—you're not that familiar with Sheffield—and you aren't an investigator. Why are you coming into my office, asking me a lot of loaded questions, and practically accusing me of murder?"

I made sure I was sitting up straight and took a moment to consider my answer. After all, I had no reason to be defensive or to get into a shouting match. But I was going to have to reveal my mission.

"Carl, I don't think I've accused you of anything. But as I said, I'm talking with a number of community leaders about what's going on." I lowered my voice and leaned forward a bit. "Between you and me, I've been asked to do it."

"Who by?" His voice was still raised.

"Chief Abhay."

He drew back abruptly, hackles almost visibly lowering. "Why would he ask you?"

"Well, think about it, Carl. I'm a relative newcomer without old ties to anyone here. I'm a lawyer. And Abhay doesn't have the resources to run around asking questions while trying to deal with the regular business of policing Sheffield."

He sat back, turning his eyes to the far wall of his office. "Ah, I get it. Okay."

"I'm sorry if I offended you—I wasn't trying to needle you. But it's hard to ask questions about murders without getting pointed."

He sat for a moment, then turned back to me, eyes hard again. "And you think I have a motive to murder both Greta and Dwight Orkman?"

"Not really—I know you've been upset about the possible property annexation, but you and I both know that that's a long and involved process. It isn't likely to happen if you really oppose it. But Greta's betrayal must have hurt." In Carl's world of influence based on personal contacts, it would have mattered more than usual.

"It did. I planned to talk with her, see if I couldn't make her see my position. But I didn't get the chance."

That seemed to be about the limit of a useful conversation, and after a few more minutes of exchanges, I left Carl's office. I wasn't sure how useful the information would be to Abhay, but I needed to report to him.

I don't know why, but I preferred to call the police chief from home rather than on a cell phone. So I made a few stops as planned after leaving Carl's business. That took me several miles from Sheffield.

As I've mentioned, we have some local, mostly specialized businesses, but the larger, big-box stores are in a shopping development about twenty miles north of town along the coast highway. I try to go there before giving up and choosing something online, if only to touch some actual goods or walk up and down and look at the latest décor trends I don't need to follow. I was walking down the main aisle of a big store full of such things when I spotted Councilor Anne Perez—short, thin, with cropped silver hair and a long face—perusing an assortment of bath towels.

I didn't know Anne Perez very well. I try not to make judgment calls about people before getting to know them, but I was aware that she had been the automatic second vote whenever our late mayor was building a quorum for her latest proposal. I freely admit that this bugged me. Don't get elected to a position, even a volunteer one helping to run a very small city, if you can't think independently.

I did know that she hardly ever seemed to smile and that the look on her face was sour, for lack of a better word. I also knew that she and Greta Sutton were about the same age, had been longtime friends, and both schoolteachers, so maybe they really did think that much alike. Although, it's a bit scary to contemplate that our children's teachers might all think in a pack as well. Never mind.

I hadn't had a chance to talk with her since her friend's death, so I thought I could at least offer condolences. I walked up the smaller aisle toward her and smiled a hello.

"Planning to interrogate me, too, Ms. Bowes?" was her immediate greeting as she turned to face me, long nose and chin outthrust.

"Uh—no, I'm not." I wasn't sure what aspect of that to react to first. The "Ms. Bowes" part probably startled me the most, as I don't think I had been greeted by my last name since moving to Sheffield. But the reference to my questions was a shock. If she had calculated that, I needed to make some points of my own back.

"Actually, I realized when I saw you that I hadn't had a chance to offer my condolences. I'm sorry you lost your friend."

Her chin retreated a bit. "I won't say thank you. I know how much you disliked Greta."

"We didn't get along on City issues, that's true. I didn't know her socially." *And was happy for that.*

"You don't know anything. You have no idea what a benefit she was to the town."

I was calling on whatever tact reserves I could muster. "I know you were one of her strong supporters."

"Yes, I was. And if some maniac hadn't *murdered* her, she would have done even more for Sheffield than she already had."

I really didn't want to get into what Greta had done for—or to—Sheffield with her; we would always disagree and it didn't matter now, anyway. I remained silent.

"And something else," said Anne, now standing stiffly. "My first thought when I learned she was dead was that you or that mouthy husband of yours had done it. I suppose, since Tom Abhay is having you ask questions of people all over town, that this is not the case."

Again, too much to answer, but I had to respond to the initial accusation. "Ms. Perez," I said almost as stiffly back, "neither my husband nor I am in the habit of violence toward anyone. Certainly not against an elderly woman, however misguided we think she might have been. And who said Chief Abhay asked me to do anything?"

"It's a small community," she responded, mouth tight. "Word always gets around.

"Anyway," she continued, "I have a pretty good idea of who wants to undermine everything Greta stood for. There have always been people in Sheffield who want to change things rather than appreciate them. They're going to have a fight on their hands. I—and the rest of Greta Sutton's friends— will see to that."

Great. Multiple sets of people with no idea who committed two violent murders, but it's enough to set them at war with each other.

"Anne," I tried, "I'm very worried about what's going on in the community. Shouldn't everyone be trying to pull together after events like this?"

She grimaced and stared at me. "You have no idea what you're doing. Leave it alone. Stay out of it and stop interfering."

She stalked past me, out of the aisle and into the middle of the store. All I could do was stare after her, my brain in turmoil. *Leave it alone?* She almost sounded as though she didn't care if the killer were found. I knew she was not a suspect, but I had a feeling Anne Perez was going to be up to her neck in any forthcoming community war.

And let's hope she doesn't run for mayor.

I did report everything to Abhay, including my conversation with Councilor Perez and her knowledge, or suspicion, of my activities. He didn't sound surprised, but he knew small towns better than I.

As it turned out, my report was more helpful than I had expected. Abhay took in the details of my meeting with Carl without comment until I told him about his ongoing efforts to meet with people about the property issue.

"Wait a minute, Felice," his voice barked through the

phone. "He said he hadn't met with Dwight yet?"

"That's what he told me. He didn't expect Dwight to fight Greta before the Planning Commission but was planning to meet with him just in case."

"He was lying to you, although I'm not sure why. City staff said he met with Dwight two days before the Council meeting where Dwight was arrested."

"That's weird. Why would he lie about something that easy to check? Carl's smarter than that."

"I don't know, but I think I'll find out. Thanks, Felice, although I do remember telling you to stop asking questions."

"I know, but the encounter with Anne Perez was by accident. The meeting—I talked with Carl during the Festival and wanted to follow up. I don't really think he had much of a motive, and he does know the city pretty well."

"And now you've pointed up an inconsistency that I'm going to look into. Be very careful, Felice."

I don't know whether it was Abhay's warning, the accumulation of stress from all the conversations I'd been having around town, or the chili I made for dinner, but I had a whopper of a dream that night. Nightmares are unusual for me, and those noteworthy enough to remember even more unusual, but I don't think I'll forget this one anytime soon.

Sometime during the night, whatever had been happening before during my dream state disintegrated, and suddenly I was in the City Hall Council chambers, which for some reason were hung all around the perimeter with floor-to-ceiling red velvet curtains. Where did those come from? A stage? The courtroom of the Supreme Court? I had been there a few times and the drama is impressive, but I never expected it to show up in a dream.

I was standing behind one of the curtains at the hall door and saw Patrick Sutton, Kate Dennis, and Suzanne Dryer all standing around a large wooden table in the center of the room. Suzanne was gesticulating; Kate had her hands up, palms outward, as if to soothe her, while Patrick watched them, with a not-very-nice smile on his face. I leaned in and suddenly, as you get in dreams, was able to hear their conversation.

"It was easy to kill that old woman."

"We took care of her, and no one knows."

"We finally got rid of her, but we still have to keep the secret."

Dreams tend to have truly forgettable dialogue, or maybe that's just mine. I think it's because your brain is digging up strong emotions—dreams don't seem to use the part of whatever cortex comes up with witty repartee. Anyway, there was more in this vein, very clandestine, and I was standing there becoming more and more amazed and frightened, when—you guessed it—one of them looked up, saw me behind the curtain, and said something to the others. Then they all stared at me. Suddenly, they all turned toward me and started walking—and where did the choker chains come from? Somehow, none of them seemed to have any trouble both holding and swinging a heavy, hooked chain. I turned to run, *of course* became tangled up in the curtain, and was flailing around, trying to avoid having my skull smashed, when I thankfully woke up, sweating and more than a little nauseated.

I straightened out the covers over me, turned to David— who of course had slept peacefully through the whole thing and continued to do so, blast him—and lay on my back, waiting for my breathing to slow down and my stomach to stop roiling. When the residual fear faded, I knew I wasn't going back to sleep immediately and started to think about what had just happened.

Where the hell had *that* come from? Why those three? Other than perhaps Patrick, none of the three was even a real suspect.

But was my brain trying to tell me something that I hadn't considered during normal operating hours? *Should* I be considering any of them more seriously than I had been?

I started evaluating what I remembered of each of them in terms of motive and opportunity.

Patrick Sutton might have had the usual spouse-related reasons for killing his wife: he had admitted to me that Greta hadn't been easy to live with and, almost, that he had resented her focus on City business to the detriment of their life together. Personally, I thought he was either a saint or a masochist to be married to her, but hey, I didn't know him well enough to know his quirks. Maybe he filled up the house with plastic frogs or constantly hummed off-key. If you don't think that's aggravating enough to warrant assault, try living with it.

In any case, while no one spoke of them as constantly fighting, they weren't known for living in each other's pockets, either. In all my dealings with Greta, I had never heard her mention Patrick except in passing, which is odd for a close married couple. Other couples we knew dropped each other's names all the time. Even as independent as David and I were in our thinking, we did refer to each other a fair amount, if only to check each other's schedules.

What all this boiled down to in my head is that the feelings between them just didn't seem strong enough to justify a violent, malicious killing. Patrick might have hidden depths, but he just didn't strike me as a likely multiple murderer, especially when he seemed to have no motive at all for killing Dwight.

However, while it's what everyone thinks about, motive is not an element of a murder case in court. We knew the means of both killings: in Greta's case, the choker, followed by the plastic bag of river water, and the vintage, and likely dusty, logger figurine in Dwight's. Patrick was fit and strong enough to have wielded them. What about opportunity?

Patrick had opportunity to kill Greta. I saw him looking for her just before the Summer Festival fireworks and walking toward the logging area where she died a short time later. He said he didn't go there; I don't know whether the police had been able to verify where he did go. And since I hadn't talked with him since Dwight's death, I had no idea whether he had an alibi for that time period. So—I needed to ask Tom Abhay whether he wanted me to talk with Patrick again and what else he might want me to learn about him.

Next was Suzanne Dryer. Fed up with Greta's demands for support, perhaps not liking where the city was headed given her family's long commitment to it? Weak. Suzanne said she was with her family during the fireworks and, while wiry, probably didn't have the upper body strength to accurately swing a choker or a heavy bronze figurine. I don't know why Suzanne showed up in my dream, but I just couldn't place her in the role of killer.

What if she wasn't alone?

Personally, I think having an accomplice is a dumb idea. If you're going to engage in illegal behavior, the last thing you should want is another criminal who knows what you've done. Not destined to be a trusting relationship, if you know what I mean.

But what if it were a family member? Suzanne had a husband, I knew: a sometime commercial fisherman named Steve with a reputation around town for less-than-hard work and a less-than-clean boat. Perhaps because he spent a fair amount of time drinking, then sleeping, on it.

Might the two of them have worked together to commit the murders? Again, I didn't know whether Suzanne—or Steve—had an alibi for the night Dwight was killed. Something else to ask Abhay, along with his take on a possible duo.

I'd better start a list. He probably wouldn't be happy to hear it, since he had asked me to stop interviewing people.

And to be fair, I had to examine why Kate Dennis had shown up in the dream. Kate was a friend and someone I respected a lot—but being smart meant she had the mental currency to plan and carry out both crimes.

Which made me stop and think. I had been focusing, as I think everyone had, on how nasty and violent these crimes were. But despite my saying to the chief that someone had to be dumb to commit murder near twenty thousand people, I realized suddenly he or she was not so dumb after all.

Greta was hit with a heavy chain, but it happened while there was a lot of distracting light and noise elsewhere and while there *were* so many other people all around, most of whom were not local. There was no way in heaven that a small police force, even supplemented with other resources, would be able to talk with everyone and perhaps find the one or two people who may have seen something happening in a completely different direction from where everyone else was looking.

Greta's murder didn't leave forensic traces, either.

Footprints? After dozens of guys in boots had been clomping around the hard ground all day? No fingerprints would be left on a rough chain, and the plastic bag had been removed and, no doubt, thrown away as one of thousands used and discarded during the Festival. The outdoor location also meant that any fibers or hairs would either have blown away or could be attributed to any number of people. Greta herself had come in contact with dozens of people while dressed in that turquoise outfit that day.

Dwight's murder seemed a bit riskier: killed in his office, on Main Street, at night. But the killer had known to use the back door, which wasn't visible unless you were in the parking lot that faced it. The only light had been one near Dwight's office window, meaning no, or only momentary, shadows would have been visible in the window while the crime was taking place. Nothing was brought in or taken out and, again, no fingerprints. I hadn't talked with Abhay about any hair or fibers that might have been found there, but chances were that any tests on those weren't finished yet. Something else for my list of questions.

So—back to the point. Kate was smart enough to have committed the crimes, although the style seemed very unlike her. *Rule that out, Felice—if we're talking about smart, she could have deliberately committed a crime in a manner that is unlike her.* Maybe. Abhay knew a lot more about this stuff than I did, and at three in the morning, I was probably overthinking it.

Kate had said that she and her husband were out of town for most of the day but had returned in time for the fireworks. She did have opportunity. I don't think she would have tried swinging heavy objects as a means of killing people, and I really didn't think it would have been comfortable for her. I didn't know where she had been on the night Dwight was killed, but she was likely in town, certainly knew the layout of City Hall, etc. She really disliked both Greta and Dwight, although I had never seen a hunger in her for taking over the mayor's job, and I had no idea what other motive there might be.

Despite my best efforts to be ruthlessly pragmatic, it just didn't play. I couldn't come up with a scenario in which Kate could be guilty. It was time to roll over and try to go back to sleep. Which I did, after responding to Angus' soft whining—you never know how your own stress communicates to your four-legged family members—by getting up to let him out into the cool, foliage-laden darkness of our back yard. I watched him do what he needed, then nose around for the sources of mysterious nighttime smells before I let him back in. I was smiling by then, which just made me appreciate yet again how our animals do us good.

Chapter Eighteen

I woke up at my usual time later that morning knowing that I had more work to do and more questions to ask. Amazingly enough, most of what I had considered during that unpleasant hour of nightmare and recovery had stuck with me. Rather than merely calling Chief Abhay, I decided to go sit in front of him and talk in some depth about the case.

Luckily, he was in and had time that morning, so I made the five-minute drive into downtown Sheffield and parked in front of the building housing the City's Public Safety Department. After identifying myself to the dispatcher also serving as the receptionist, I was allowed through the security door and pointed down the hall to the chief's office.

Abhay rose as I walked in and extended a hand. "Hi, Felice."

"Good morning, Chief," I smiled at him during the handshake and took a quick look around before sitting at the chair across his desk. The room was surprisingly institutional for a man whom I knew was confident and at home in his job—cream walls, gray carpet, two high windows with metal blinds, a biggish metal desk, and a couple of filing cabinets. The overall look was down to the City: the Sheffield budget didn't run to plush offices for department heads.

Despite his impressive résumé beyond the chief's job, Abhay had added only a few framed certificates on the walls; I didn't see any group photos, trophies, or other evidence of either his professional or personal life other than three framed photos on his desk, all facing away from me.

He was watching me look, a slight smile on his handsome face, so I thought I should cover my curiosity.

"What, no motorcycle trophies?"

He laughed lightly. "No, I keep those in a big glass case at home, right next to the Grammy and the Oscar. That's right, you haven't been here before, have you?"

"No. Guess there hasn't been a reason—you and I have been in meetings together, but always somewhere else." I refrained from the "I try not to spend a lot of time in police stations" comment that immediately came to mind.

He sat across from me. "What can I do for you?"

I sighed before diving in. "I've been spending a lot of time thinking about these killings—well, more than thinking, I've been having dreams about it."

His eyebrows went up. "You're here to talk with me about a dream?"

"No, I know better than to waste your time with that." *Damn, at my age you'd think I could keep from blushing.* "But this weird dream also has me thinking about things from a different angle, and I'd appreciate being able to talk things over with you. I know you're busy; I don't know how much time you're able to spend on the case."

"We're spending every available minute on it. Unfortunately, we've lost the Major Crime Team again—it's been five days since Dwight Orkman was killed. The various agencies will keep working on it as they can, but summer is when we're all kept pretty busy, anyway."

He leaned forward and his voice deepened. "Felice, I asked you to stop asking questions. This guy is nasty."

"And I have, really! But there is a lot of missing information out there, and some of it popped up in my head in the middle of the night. I know about alibis a lot of people have for Greta Sutton's death, but not for Dwight's, and the crimes themselves are looking different to me."

"In what way?"

"Chief—Tom—I've been focusing on how vicious the killings were. Have you also been thinking about how *smart* they were?"

The eyebrow went up again, and taking that as an invitation, I outlined my thinking from the night before.

"Greta's death strikes me as more premeditated than Dwight's, but both made the most of circumstances. And have you had any luck with forensic evidence?"

He pulled a stack of file folders from one corner of his desk, opened the top one, and went through the top two pages.

"No. No fingerprints from Dwight's office other than his and a couple of staff members' in places where they would naturally be. Nothing on the statue. City offices get cleaned once a week and his office had been done about three days before. There were a couple of hairs and fibers, but nothing that looked interesting, and we won't get the results back for some time."

He looked up. "Guy went in and out through the back door, didn't turn on lights so anyone would notice, didn't leave anything he might have brought or take anything out. Which tells us it wasn't a burglary—not that we thought it was, anyway. No one on Main Street noticed anything."

"That's what I mean. Both killings *look* risky: a death outdoors during a Festival, a death in someone's office right on Main Street. But both were intelligent. You're looking for someone who may be vicious and nasty but who has a brain. He managed both a premeditated crime and what looks like a more impulsive one without any apparent witnesses or a mistake we've discovered yet."

He nodded. "I guess we were heading in that direction but couldn't help thinking he had mostly been lucky. The normal run of criminal isn't known for brains."

"And we had already figured that this had something to do with City government; otherwise, why these two victims? That combination has to narrow the list of possible suspects, don't you think?"

"Yeah, it does. Not taking anything away from people in Sheffield, but I don't think a population of five thousand is going to net you too many that fit the criteria." He paused. "Frankly, Felice, if I didn't know better, my first bet would have been on you or David."

I started, blinking. Why does even an innocent person have a nano-moment of guilt when confronted by a police officer? Followed by a swirl of confusion. Even the police chief thought of us as suspects? What was it with this town?

"Um, if that's a sort of compliment, gee, thanks." I managed. "Thankfully, I believe that killing someone is a really stupid way of removing their influence from your life. I know David feels that way too, although he does sometimes announce that he's happy we don't own a gun."

Abhay's face went blank for a moment, then he threw his

head back and laughed out loud. "Yeah, I would keep guns away from your husband. He causes enough damage with his mouth."

I smiled, deciding not to delve into that issue any further. David sometimes makes a point of saying something outrageous; it's like throwing a verbal bomb into the middle of a conversation. He does it with a straight face, and some people can't tell if he's serious. He rarely is, but it has led to some shocked silences from people who don't know him well. It's given him something of a reputation for being outrageous, even if undeserved, and it's one of the many ways in which our approaches differ.

"Actually, that brings me around to some of the questions I had. Since this is likely City-related, do you have alibis for that group of people for Dwight's death?"

"We've talked with a lot of them, yes. Most of the councilors say they were at home. Kate Dennis and her husband were in Salem with family; we've checked that. Unfortunately, when you look at the pool of people who are familiar with City Hall, it's a wider group: staff, members of the Fire Department, even my officers. We don't work out of that building, but everyone knows about the back door."

"As do any number of Sheffielders who use that entrance to come in and pay their utility bills."

"Right. The public is supposed to use the front door, but a lot of people park in back and don't want to go around. We haven't tightened that up; it's a small town. Big-city security just doesn't work here, even if we could afford it."

"Have you talked with Patrick Sutton again?" Dumb dream or not, I thought it was worth checking out the random brain impulses I'd had the night before.

"Sure. He says he fell asleep on the couch before nine the night Dwight was killed. He said he's been doing that a lot since Greta died."

"And of course, he's alone in the house. So other than Kate, no one can alibi out of both murders by having a solid one for Dwight's."

"That's what it looks like. No real help."

"Well, I have to say I'm glad about Kate, anyway. She showed up in my dream, swinging a choker, and I felt almost sick."

He chuckled.

"Which brings me to another thought I had during my nightmare recovery period. Could these killings have been carried out by a pair?"

He nodded. "We've given that some thought, also. It's certainly possible, but we don't have any evidence for multiple people. In both killings, the victim was brought down by a single blow from a heavy object—that says one person. Could someone else have been around to help? Sure. Was a second person necessary to carry out the murder? Doesn't look like it."

"I was thinking about a second person to carry out the will of the first. For example, Suzanne doesn't have the upper body strength to swing the chain. But Steve does. If she hated the victims enough to start this, could he have been the muscle?"

Abhay shrugged. "Sure. I don't really see it in Suzanne's case—I've known her for a long time, and I don't think she had a real motive—but physically, sure, it could have happened that way."

"Okay. I don't have anyone in mind, but it popped into my head and I thought I should ask."

I hesitated before asking, "So, what's next?"

"To be honest with you, Felice," Tom said almost angrily, "all we can do is keep plugging away. We have to wait for lab results from Portland, and we have to worry about whether this guy has targeted someone else."

"And pragmatically," I said slowly, "that's a mixed question. On the one hand, you certainly don't want another murder scaring the town and creating another loss. On the other hand, maybe this guy's motive would be clearer if he did have another target."

The chief smiled grimly. "Now you're thinking like a detective, and that's a little scary. I don't want to lose anyone else, Felice. I wouldn't say I'd rather not catch this guy than have another murder, but it's close."

"And I don't see Sheffield recovering from this for a long time. Better if you do catch the killer, of course, but regardless, this is going to affect how outside people think of the city, probably be part of our reputation for years. And it will affect our dealings with each other.

"So—what can I do? If I'm thinking about this all the time, and dreaming about it, I need to do *something*. Do you need a murder board or anything?" I was referring to a big whiteboard with suspects' photos, arrows drawn between them, and facts listed. Something else from television—it was said jokingly, but I was feeling driven by all the information and questions in my head.

"Got one, thanks—but if you want to sketch this out for yourself and see what shows up, go ahead. But again, Felice, this is someone local. He or she has probably talked to you and may know that you were asking questions for me. Or he might think you're just being nosy. Either way, he probably knows you well enough to worry about what you might figure out. I don't want you to be a target. Keep your head down."

"Right. I wish we knew enough about the motive to know why Dwight was killed. To me, that's the key to the whole thing. But I'll stay away from everyone and play dumb. Thanks, Tom."

"I'm going to have a patrol car go past your house more often than usual starting tonight. I don't want to call attention to you, but this guy works at night and I think it's a good precaution."

"Okay. I'll tell David. Thanks again."

I wasn't shaken when I left the police building, but I couldn't help looking around to see if anyone was watching. *We must solve this thing,* went around in my mind over and over. I didn't like the idea of being afraid to live in my own community.

It must have shown in my face when I returned home because David took one look at me and asked, "What happened?"

I told him about the meeting with Abhay. "David, I think I've been pretty careful since I started talking with people, but what if this guy thinks I'm some sort of threat? Abhay says he's going to send a patrol car around the house at night."

David walked over and took me into his arms. "I won't remind you that I was worried about this. But you're going to have to be more careful until this guy is found. I don't want you going out at night, and we're going to be better at closing curtains and locking windows after dark."

I looked up into his face. "You know, this really pisses me off. Not only has this guy killed two people; not only is the whole town shaken up and the leadership left in tatters. Now he has people afraid to leave their homes at night.

"I haven't done anything to constitute a threat. It's like there's some sort of bogeyman out prowling at night. This is worse than a low-budget horror movie." I pulled away and stalked over to the living room windows, looking out at the clear sky, flowers, and towering firs of our neighborhood on a summer late morning.

"And it's getting worse," David said to my back. "The organizers of the River Festival put out a notice this morning. The Festival has been cancelled."

I whirled around. "WHAT? Oh, that just sucks. The River Festival is the best event of the summer! Why would they do that? It doesn't even have any events after dark."

"According to the announcement, vendors are nervous, and the organizers don't want to endanger anyone's safety."

"And I'll bet they're getting a sense that not many people will show up. The news of multiple murders in Sheffield has been out everywhere."

"Of course it has, and that's certainly going to have an impact on attendance. You can't exactly put out an announcement that 'you don't have to worry if you aren't a City leader,'" David said calmly.

"DAMN this guy." I folded my arms and stared at the carpet, then looked up as a thought occurred. "I wonder if this is part of the plan: not just to kill people he has a grudge against, but to unsettle the community enough to cause real damage. The River Festival is an important moneymaker for vendors and nonprofits who need the funds to get through the winter. Why would a local person do that?"

"I think you may be giving him too much credit, Felice. I know you said the killings are intelligent, but it would take a lot of planning and foreknowledge to know that his actions would cause this much disruption."

I sighed. "Maybe. In the meantime, the chief told me to go ahead and put up a board to lay out a theory of the case if I wanted. I have so much random data swirling in my head—I think I need to set it all down somewhere and draw a bunch of arrows, see if something shows up under the surface layers."

I didn't end up putting up any kind of board—let's face it, who wants something that ugly in a corner of their bedroom—but I did use up some paper. Yes, I had just spent time trying to organize all of this in my head after my rude awakening the night before, but it wouldn't all stick until it was written down somewhere I could find it again.

It was sort of a three-column arrangement: Person, Motive, Whereabouts. I started listing everyone I knew who might be connected to the crimes, then writing down any motive I could imagine. If there was something that withstood scrutiny (meaning, it wasn't completely laughable), I would continue with anything I knew about their whereabouts. And I left some room for random notes, 'cause you know, you'll probably need some commentary.

Greta Sutton had had several cronies in town, people I had never met or had run into once or twice at various events. I hadn't talked with any of them other than Anne Perez, didn't think they'd talk with me, and as far as I could tell, none of them had any motive for going after Dwight Orkman. Plus, most of them were elderly women. If any of them had decided that Greta had to go for some reason, she certainly would have chosen another means of killing her.

"You have to start somewhere, Felice, or you'll be going around in circles until your head explodes," I muttered to myself. I decided "Some Friend with an Unknown Grudge" had to be wiped from the list.

Greta had no children, so no vengeful offspring wanting what was in her will before she was willing to provide it. That left Patrick, the grieving widower.

"Patrick Sutton," therefore, topped my left-hand column.

When I turned to the center column, I was immediately stuck. What was Patrick's motive? Was Greta spending money they didn't have on electioneering or causes? Maybe lunches for people whose support she wanted? Was she spending too much time exercising her nonexistent mayoral authority and not enough at home, "caring for her man"? Patrick struck me as more enlightened than that. And why kill Dwight? The immediate temptation when looking for motive: sexual jealousy? Had our dearly departed mayor been engaging in nookie with the city manager?

"Yuck!" I said loudly into the quiet room. "No. Just no. Besides the creepiness of even imagining them together, there just wasn't that tone of intimacy between them when I overheard them that Saturday afternoon."

I realized I didn't know enough about Patrick to write anything reasonable. So, the first entry in my center column was a big question mark, followed by the notation, "Talk again to Patrick!"

Under Whereabouts, I entered the information about seeing Patrick heading toward the logging field shortly before the fireworks and his lack of alibi for Dwight's death. Not an auspicious beginning, but for the moment, Patrick Sutton was in the right place at the head of the list.

I decided to run down the list of councilors next. Kate Dennis was easy: she hadn't been seeking the post of mayor;

she *probably* hadn't known about the machinations over the alternative energy center, if she knew about it at all; but most importantly, Abhay had verified her alibi for at least one of the killings. I had to write down what I knew about her, but she was not a suspect.

Suzanne Dryer, possibly with husband Steve's help, was next. She had admitted to being fed up with Greta's duress on City votes, and her longtime Sheffielder sensibilities were offended by Greta's grabbing of City money for her pet projects. She was completely opposed to the City's taking money from the Summer Festival returns, but she hadn't known about the energy center—I was pretty certain of that from my talk with her—and supported it, anyway, once she learned about it. She might have decided Dwight had to go because of his continuing support of Greta's projects, but that seemed a bit far-fetched, even for someone who took the issues of a five thousand-person town more seriously than most. And she seemed to have a good alibi for Greta's death by sitting in a large family gathering during the fireworks. And as a side note, as much as I (and others) considered Steve something of a waste of space, he just didn't seem vicious enough to have carried out these killings, even with Suzanne's anger to back him up.

Dennis Waitly was next. I thought about him for a while and realized I was biased. He struck me as too smart to have used murder to accomplish a goal, even if he did have a temper that occasionally showed in public meetings; it was always a righteous temper and I had agreed with him. He had the same potential motives relating to Greta and Dwight's activities, which he may have considered illegal or merely distasteful. I knew him well enough to know that unethical behavior angered him. But Dennis was more the type to just shoot someone in public and turn himself in, if he were driven to ridding Sheffield of what he considered an evil presence. I hadn't talked with Abhay about whether Dennis had an alibi, but I assume the chief would have told me if Waitly was a viable suspect.

And more than anything, I knew that Dennis was deeply committed to Sheffield. He had served it in various capacities for years, including raising his children here. He would know how disruptive and harmful the killings would be to the town. I think that would have been enough to stay his hand even if he were tempted; the health of Sheffield meant more to him than speedily eliminating two officials who were harming it. Murder? No. Dennis would have chaired a recall committee instead.

I wrote a note to the side of Dennis' entry in my nifty little chart: "you are biased." And moved on.

Next on the lengthening list was George Russell. My conversation with him during the Water Resource Council meeting just emphasized his commitment to the environment: he, too, hadn't seemed to know about the alternative energy center but had shown support at Council meetings along with everyone else. I know he generally had gone along with Greta on previous issues, so he probably didn't have the anger that Suzanne or Dennis did about her activities or at Dwight for planning to follow through on her wishes. I knew George to be a bright guy and had wondered about his and Rita's baffling choice of spreading false rumors about David and me. And I thought again about my extremely hostile meeting with Rita some days before, then shrugged it off. Their dislike of us was immaterial to whether George might have killed two completely different people. George didn't seem to have a motive, and again, most importantly, he and Rita had the proverbial ironclad alibi that they had been on stage playing music during the Summer Festival fireworks.

I went through the remaining two councilors quickly; Abhay had said they had alibis for Greta's death. Then it was time to turn to other people who might have a connection to both victims.

Carl Roetgen headed that list. A friend and supporter of Mayor Sutton until she threatened his development plans—did his potential financial loss cancel out their friendship? He hadn't been at the fireworks and didn't have a solid alibi. He also seemed worried that the city manager was going to carry through with attempting to annex his development property, so he would have had the same motive to eliminate the continued threat without the obstacle of friendship. Annexation was not a quick or certain process—I wouldn't have thought he had much to worry about—but Carl didn't like being told "no."

He also was a fit man who certainly could physically have carried out both killings, and I had sensed a mean streak in him when crossed. He was a sharp guy who knew the habits of the town extremely well. I could picture him taking daring measures to carry out the killings when everyone was distracted in one case, or when downtown Sheffield was mostly deserted in the other. In fact, taking that kind of personal dare seemed to fit him well. Motive was the weakest point with Carl, but I kept him as a viable suspect on my list.

Moving into City Hall, I had to consider Pat Gregorio. My conversation with her had revealed her deep dislike of the mayor, and I had heard that she and other department heads weren't fond of Dwight, either. Having trash talked about you was infuriating, and Greta had had no business spreading lies about a highly capable, professional employee. Pat, too, was both smart and fit with a long history in Sheffield. But perhaps I was angrier on her behalf than she had been on her own. Her taking the radical actions of these killings didn't feel right—she was a numbers person, after all. I smiled while imagining her taking revenge by undermining their finances somehow. But I knew that was not a reason for removing her from a list of suspects. She stayed.

And that's where my imagination ran out. I knew I was missing people, but until I spoke with Abhay again, I had done about all I could do. It felt good to have written it all out, but I didn't know if I had come any closer to solving anything.

There had to be something else. My other lists, Issues and Events that might have triggered the killings, didn't add anything to the thought process. I needed more information—and had to wonder: how do cops ever know that they know everything they need to know to solve a case? Writers of crime fiction and detective series always seem to have the "regular police" stop too soon and go with simplistic answers. This is always proved to be wrong, of course, by the brilliant, deeper-thinking detective who sees the tiny clue that changes everything. Unlike Poirot or Father Brown, however, I didn't have a bibelot out of place on the mantelpiece or a chair moved out of position to tell me how things really happened.

I snorted at the thought and turned away from the antique desk at which I do most of my work. This startled the cat who had generously been helping me by reclining on top of the desk's high back. Alexander, our gray, aloof, and annoyingly smart cat, now gave me an emerald-eyed glare, demanding an explanation for the disturbance.

"I am not a detective," I explained to him, earning a sympathetic slow blink in response. "This doesn't make any sense. Either I am missing something I should see in all this mess in front of me, or there's something important still out there that's the key to the whole thing. I don't have the training for this, and I don't like feeling useless, especially when I've been asked to help!"

Another cat blink—cats are wonderful excuses for talking to yourself, you can always pretend they're listening. But this one knew that my paying attention to him might have positive consequences.

"All right, you. Thanks for the company—we'll go get you a treat."

Thus proving how smart he is. At the magic word, the pointed ears perked up, and we both left the desk to pursue more fulfilling pursuits.

The killer couldn't know that I had been focusing this hard on suspects and motives, but I had apparently nettled him or her enough to be worried, or just angry. Angus started whining at the front door the next morning—not his usual habit—and both cats were also nearby, tails swishing and noses pointed at the door. I was the first one downstairs to notice and waved them all back to check on what had caught their interest. Our front door includes a large, multi-textured glass panel, and there was a fuzzy shape visible through it, sitting on the front porch. When I went out to look, I saw that it was a cardboard box; when I lifted the loose top flap, I saw the gray-brown fur and naked tail of a large, dead rat.

Nausea instantly warred with intense anger. Nausea

because, well—a dead rat on my porch. The anger was twofold: at the person who had invaded our space with such malice, and, while I'm not more of a rat fan than the average person, because a living being was killed just so someone could be malicious. The arrogance of someone who could do that made me momentarily wish that person was standing in front of me, although I'm not sure what I would have done.

Luckily, one of David's many strengths—those things for which I love him greatly—is his willingness to deal with nasty things. I have no idea what sort of noises I made once I saw what was in the box, but it didn't take him long to be on the scene. He disposed of the box while I sat in the house, trying not to be sick and waiting to stop shaking. And noting two things: people didn't hesitate at the nasty and personal in small towns, and I apparently had already talked with the killer.

Chapter Nineteen

What did I know about what causes someone to go off the rails far enough to kill—twice? Like most of us, I couldn't think of anything that would cause me to do it. I can't imagine using deadly force against anyone, unless David or I were in imminent danger of our lives; then, perhaps, it would be a lot easier to pull a trigger or swing something heavy. Knives have always seemed too messy and risky to me—you have to get too close, and you might miss.

I decided to let all the information settle for a while and cast about for more, somehow without arousing any suspicion. Well, any *more* suspicion.

I hadn't spent much time with Becky lately—she had been even busier than we had, given the summer tourist traffic—so I called to see if she could fit me in for part of an afternoon. Surprisingly, she had a day off a couple of days later and asked if she could come to our house:

"It's a lot cleaner than mine, and you make good coffee."

"That's fine. We can soak up some rays in the sunroom. David wants me to stick closer for a while, anyway."

"How come?"

"Tell you when you get here."

By Friday afternoon at 2:00, Becky was ensconced in an armchair in our sunroom. The mid-August sun was just starting to work its way through the long, west-facing room with its large-paned windows, old Oriental carpet, and figured cotton couch. The cats had already wandered in for their naps, but since Becky wasn't sitting in any of their favorite spots, I figured we were good.

"You want to tell me why David wants you to stay home? That doesn't sound like him," she said after her first sip from a large mug of coffee.

"No, he doesn't try the paterfamilias stuff very often. Which is just as well."

I explained to Becky the gist of my recent conversation with Chief Abhay and David's concerns, and about the rat. "You know, Becky, I was being careful before, but since Dwight was killed, my rational self can't help thinking there might be some real danger here. I still haven't figured out why Dwight was murdered exactly, but there can't be any motive that would justify it. This guy must be nuts."

"I get the sense the killer is seriously pissed off about something," Becky agreed. "The guys at the firehouse are putting it more simply—they say it's someone who is tired of being screwed around by the City."

"That makes a kind of sense—but screwed around how, exactly? Do you know of anyone who has been treated badly enough to go after both the mayor and the city manager? I've written down all the issues I can think of, and nothing computes."

She sat for a minute and apparently decided to pass on a story.

"They don't think she necessarily did it, but the guys have been talking about a woman, Carla Graham, who has what she thinks is a large beef with the City. Her teenaged son was in a motorcycle crash with a Public Works truck about seven years ago. The accident was ruled his fault—there may have been some alcohol involved—but she's always blamed the City for his injuries."

I frowned. "How badly was he hurt? I've heard some wisps of talk about this, but it happened before David and I moved here."

"Pretty badly, although he's okay now. Mrs. Graham comes back whenever there's a change in City officials, asking again for damages beyond what was already paid. I don't think either Greta or Dwight paid much attention to her."

I considered for a minute, comparing what Becky had told me with what I knew of the facts of the murders. "A hurt child would certainly give rise to a lot of emotion, but why hurt these particular officials rather than other ones? And why not a longer-term City staff member, like Pat Gregorio."

"I'm not sure, but I can tell you that Carla Graham isn't doing well mentally. Her son left home a few months ago, and I don't think that's helped. The cops have been called out to her house a few times for noise and abusive language toward the neighbors."

"Sounds like maybe I should go talk with her."

"Weren't you just agreeing that you should stick close and *not* talk to people?"

"Well, maybe—but how else am I going to be able to judge whether she might be involved? It's an old event and it sounds like there's a lot of gossip surrounding it. And only she knows how she feels she was treated by Greta and Dwight."

"You're really considering going to the home of what might be a mentally unbalanced woman you've never met before and asking her questions to see if she's a violent murderer."

"You had to put it exactly that way. Wanna come?"

"I think I'd better."

We decided that going to Carla Graham's house and chancing her being home was a bit brighter than calling her first. The house was in one of several Sheffield neighborhoods of smallish family homes from the '50s and '60s. The street had seen better days, but some of the houses showed signs of recent renovation and had attractive small gardens. Most had fences, as most had had one or more owners with dogs over the years. The Graham house was white with shutters painted dark green on the two front windows flanking a small front porch. Concrete steps were also painted dark green, though the paint was worn through in spots. A sedan about eight years old was parked in an attached carport. In coastal Oregon's relatively mild climate, a lot of people went without garages, although a vehicle left outside during the wet months would soon sport a partial coat of fuzzy green moss, on its north side at least.

There was no wild barking after we rang the doorbell, which I took for a solid positive. Instead, sounds from a television halted suddenly, and there were audible footsteps approaching the door. When it opened, I was surprised to find my eyes facing the chest portion of a gray T-shirt and quickly raised my head. The unfriendly brown eyes looking back at me were coming from a gray-and-brown-haired, fiftyish woman who had to top six feet.

Well, there goes the idea that a pissed-off woman wouldn't have been able to commit these crimes. It was about all I had time to think.

"Who the hell are you and what do you want?"

"Mrs. Graham?"

"Yeah, I'm Carla Graham, which you would know if you had any real reason to be here."

I decided to ignore that bit, although it was a logical point. "My name is Felice Bowes, and this is Becky Stevenson. I haven't lived in Sheffield all that long, but I'm looking into some past incidents for Chief Abhay." Technically true: both murders had occurred in the past. I didn't have to specify how far back I was looking. "I wasn't here when your son was hurt, but I wanted to ask you a few questions about your case to see if something else could be done."

"Why the hell should they care about me and my boy now? I haven't had anything but a runaround from the City ever since it happened."

"We know you aren't happy with how things have gone, but the new leadership wanted me to come and talk with you. It has been some time, but there may be something that can be done to mend fences." I winced internally about what I was promising. *Note to self: call Kate Dennis and beg her to back me on this.* I didn't dare look back at Becky, although I knew I'd hear about this tactic later.

Carla's Graham's face relaxed a bit, but her look was still suspicious. "Like what?"

"Can we come in for a few minutes? We'd like to go over things a bit. I really don't know much about what happened, and I think it's important to hear that from you."

She opened the door a bit wider and turned for the interior. "Yeah, I can tell you. I can tell you how this stinking City has treated me and my boy."

I was feeling the shock from Becky on my back, and was a bit shocked myself that the approach had worked, but didn't hesitate to follow the tall woman back into the house.

The small entry led into a comfortably sized living room. My first impression was one of confusion: the basic layout of rug, sofa, and end tables was tidy, while a small tornado might have gone through another part of the room, where papers and a few dishes clustered around a large chair, with a small table beside it, facing the now-dark television. This, clearly, was where Carla spent most of her leisure time. Another wall held shelves filled with earlier photographs of a family of three and later ones of just Carla and a male child, presumably her son Timothy. The son alone, at every age from infant to late teens, was featured in even more photos. All of these were stiffly arranged and rigidly dust-free; I did not presume to touch any of them. I wouldn't have called it a shrine, but Timothy obviously was his mother's primary focus. There were no photos of her without him.

Carla saw me looking at the photos and gestured to them. "That's him. That's him before he got hurt and the City ruined his life." She gestured to the couch, and we sat, Carla taking her chair.

I wasn't sure where she planned to start her story, so thought I should try to guide the conversation a bit.

"Carla, I haven't heard too much about Timothy's accident and the events since—as I said, I wasn't living here then. What happened?"

"What happened was that a damn big truck ran into my son on his motorcycle during the winter seven years ago," Mrs. Graham said flatly. "It was one of those City trucks they use when they're fixing the streets, big and heavy. Came at him from the side in broad daylight and just about killed him."

"I'm so sorry. I know that he was injured pretty badly."

"His bike fell on him and broke his leg in two places; he had a couple of broken ribs and a concussion. We didn't know for a while if he was banged up inside, too, or if his brain had been hurt."

Becky spoke up. "Was he wearing a helmet? That certainly would have protected his head." We had discussed not challenging Mrs. Graham's position on the way over, so I knew Becky was just exercising her EMT knowledge to get more information.

"Of course, he was wearing a helmet," Carla growled. "God knows what would have happened to him if he hadn't been. But the accident wasn't the worst of it. We went to the City to get some help for him—it was their fault, wasn't it? But the City said they weren't responsible. Said they didn't owe us nothing. The damn city manager we had then protected his people in the Public Works Department; their report said it was my boy's own fault that he got hurt when he was hit by a big damn truck." Her eyes had narrowed as she spoke, and the last was said with fierce intensity. Not for the first time since entering the house, I felt the hair stand up on my neck, and I wasn't sure of our personal safety. I glanced at Becky.

She spoke again. "I remember when it happened. There was a fundraiser, wasn't there? Didn't the City help some, after all?"

Carla straightened in her chair and her eyes calmed. "Yeah . . . yeah. The people around here were good. The police department organized a couple events, dinners and things— our neighbors and other people pitched in and helped us out. That was good. I got no problem with Tom Abhay. I think the damn City was shamed into kicking in the ten thousand dollars they finally gave us."

I managed to keep my eyebrows down with difficulty. Becky had told me that the City was definitely not to blame for the accident, since Timothy had been under the influence and had run a stop sign, significantly above the speed limit, just as the Public Works truck was approaching from the side street. While ten thousand dollars wouldn't clear any major medical bills, it was a lot of money for a small city constantly watching the bottom line, and it could have been viewed as an admission of liability most City attorneys would not have approved. My lawyer brain kicked in, and I briefly wondered at the discussion that led to the action, well-meant as it must have been.

Carla was muttering, clearly working up her anger again.

"Eighteen years old and hurt so bad he can't keep his job. Now, he can't work logging or on a fishing boat—he doesn't trust his leg or his balance enough. What else you gonna get around here with a high school diploma?"

The anger blazed out of her. "He's left me! That's what's happened—he couldn't stay here, couldn't get work. And every time I've gone to one of those councilors, every time there's a new mayor or manager in the last seven years, I've had the same runaround. It's their fault my boy's gone. I'm all alone now, and it's their fault!"

Carla Graham had worked herself into a towering rage; her eyes were wild, and it sounded like a litany that had been repeated many times, the sort of internal egging on that can lead to disastrous action. Suddenly I understood why she might have chosen now to take the revenge she hadn't had since her son was hurt. I also understood that she was bigger and no doubt stronger than both Becky and me, maybe even together. The emotion of the meeting felt dangerous. I needed to diffuse that anger, if possible.

"Carla, I'm very sorry about what you're going through," I said quietly, hoping to catch her attention. "As I told you, I've been asked to look into what happened to see if things can't be made better. This is a small town, and whatever you think about the Council or the staff, no one wants bad feelings between the City and a citizen if they can help it."

I'd had a small brainstorm on the way over. I had no idea if it would work, but the basics appealed to me from a couple of angles, so I decided to give it a try.

"It doesn't sound like money is the issue here," *I really hope, because I can't offer you any,* "but Timothy's injuries are certainly remembered, and maybe we should pay tribute to him in some other way."

I looked at Becky, and she looked back, her face completely impassive. "You're on your own," her expression read.

Thanks a lot. I hope like hell this works.

"The anniversary of the accident is coming up in November, right?"

Carla nodded.

"What if the Council made a declaration—maybe stating the whole city's sadness at his injuries and perhaps naming that day this year Timothy Graham Day? I'll ask if maybe it could be put together with some information about traffic safety and the like. Turn it into a citywide event on the issue. Given our rain and the curving streets, that's always a good idea. Does that sound like something you and he might appreciate?"

I hoped she would go for it. Such an action could possibly mend fences, not only with Carla Graham but with others who might agree with her position, and the City could use its

223

authority to be thoughtful and even do some good without accepting any liability for the original accident.

She sat back again, her eyes staring to her right and her head tilted a bit.

"That won't bring him back to me," she finally said to us.

"No, I understand that."

"But it's nice. It doesn't fix what happened," her eyes swung to us again, "and it doesn't change the seven years those people have been assholes."

I smiled at her. "Maybe not, but these are mostly new people." *Knock it off, Felice—this is not someone to joke with.*

"Yeah. Okay. You get them to do that, and I'd appreciate it." The large head with its mane of graying hair swung back and forth between us, then to the photos on the spotless shelf.

I exhaled a long, internal breath. "All right. I didn't have the okay for this when we came, but I'll talk with Councilor Dennis—she's the acting mayor—and I think she and the Council will be happy to do it."

Becky and I stood up and started toward the front door.

"You should be hearing from the City when everything is official, and of course, you'll get an invitation to whatever is put together. Thanks again for seeing us."

"Yeah." She stood a moment. "Thanks."

We left the house and started down the path and out the gate in the chain-link fence toward the car.

"That woman is not a good example of mental health," Becky said quietly in my direction.

"That woman is potentially batshit crazy," I responded. "Now, I have to ask Abhay to find out if she could have committed two murders. Because I think she could have."

Chapter Twenty

I said goodbye to Becky at our driveway, since she had other places to be, and headed inside from the late afternoon light, still thinking over our encounter with Carla Graham. My first call, since it wasn't quite dinner time yet, was to Kate Dennis at her office. I glossed over the primary reason for my visit to the Graham house and Kate didn't push, bless her. She certainly was going to wonder what prompted it and I was going to have to explain at some point.

Better yet, once I outlined the conversation and my quasi-promise to the poor woman, Kate was supportive of the anniversary recognition idea we had put forward.

"You think she'll be happy with that?" was her response once I had laid it out. "She's been unhappy with every member of the City government for years."

"I don't think money is as important to her anymore as some acknowledgment of what happened. The City doesn't have to admit any blame, but using Timothy's accident to push traffic safety and making the resolution would give her the public statement she's been wanting. And it certainly wouldn't hurt the Council right now to make a good-faith gesture to soothe an unhappy citizen."

"Yeah, we need all the community togetherness we can generate right now. People seem to think it's our fault the River Festival was cancelled as well as everyone wondering if someone else is going to be killed.

"Do you want to come to a Council meeting and make the recommendation, Felice?"

"No! No. Much better coming from you, if you don't mind." I didn't need anyone else noticing that I was going around Sheffield talking with disgruntled people.

"Okay. Since I'm going to have this interim mayor job for a while, I've been trying to get up to speed on old issues, anyway. It would be good to have a positive solution to this one." She paused. "But one of these days, you're going to have to tell me how you ended up at her house."

The way she said it made hair prickle on the back of my neck. I was definitely getting too jumpy—this was Kate. "Not important right now. Really, Kate. I'll tell you later."

I also managed to catch Tom Abhay by phone before he left the cop shop.

"You have a fan in Carla Graham," was my attempt to head off his disapproval of my latest visit.

"Carla? That's nice," he said questioningly. "That woman's had a hard time."

I outlined Becky's and my visit that afternoon, along with the update of likely Council action in October to recognize her son's accident.

"Tom, I realize she's been angry for a long time. But her attitude seems to be worse right now because her son just left her to find work somewhere else." I breathed deeply before speaking again. "I was honestly worried about her mental state while we were talking with her. Do you think there's any chance that his leaving might have triggered violence against the people she blames for Timothy's accident?"

There was silence for a moment, then he sighed. "One, Felice, I'm glad you went with someone else. Two, I can't rule it out and I'll look into it. *I* will look into it; you stay out of it."

"Got it. No problem."

I was happy just then that I didn't really work for Tom Abhay, as I probably would have received a blistering reprimand if I had been one of his officers, and it would not have been fun. I ended the phone call quickly and went to look for a sure source of affection. Where was Angus, the yard-high cuddle, when you needed him? I spotted him, sound asleep on his bed on the living room floor, so I contented myself with a fond look and kept going.

When I went into the kitchen, David had his back to me as he loaded ice into a tall glass for a cold drink. He was dressed in a nice pair of slacks and a long-sleeved sport shirt, and I remembered that he had gone to a Sheffield Chamber of Commerce event over lunch, showcasing the various businesses around the community. I spent a pleasant moment admiring my husband's backside, then noticed that there were flyers on the counter from an area resort and a new clothing shop along with a cellophane bag full of trail mix.

"What's this?" I asked, holding it up.

He turned around. "Oh, yeah. Prescott's Funeral Home was handing those out. When I wandered by the booth, the guy went on a bit about avoiding cost increases and making 'early arrangements,' then handed me that bag of stuff."

I stared at the bag of nuts and raisins for a moment, then started laughing helplessly. David stared at me like I'd grown another head.

"Well," I responded to his look, "don't you think he's sending you a message?"

"Like what?"

I struggled to stop giggling. "You know—get healthy, go hiking, eat trail mix . . . and die anyway."

David's face remained completely impassive. "Felice, I think you need to start focusing on something other than murder."

He was probably right.

Our coastal August was not a time to miss because I was concentrating on nasty people, motives, and alibis. It was clear and warm these days with an almost impossibly deep blue sky, the smell of cedars and firs, just a bit of dust, and a hint of salt from the nearby Pacific. This was a precious time in Sheffield, the days we stored in our memories to bring out after the dark, gray wet closed in. Why couldn't all of this have happened in January, when the negative seemed more natural?

But, since all my whirling thoughts seemed predicated on the killings being tied to City issues, I needed to get better tied into those. It had been just over a week since the work session that ended in Dwight's arrest—and astoundingly, to his murder so shortly after—and the City Council was holding its last meeting of the month. It seemed imperative that I be there again to see what was on the agenda and try to get some sort of reading of those present. Somehow, *someone* had to show some emotion that could lead to the discovery of our local killer.

I added what I considered a business casual jacket to the top and pants I had worn for my time with Becky that afternoon and headed to City Hall that evening. Since it was a regular meeting, all the councilors were in their assigned spaces along the curving desk on the dais, the artwork gleaming behind them in the light that was focused on them for the cameras that recorded the sessions. The butt-killing audience chairs were back to empty except for a few of us. Interestingly, one of those present was Pat Gregorio, although a scan of the agenda didn't show a report from her.

There were no members of the public this time to take their five minutes of comment, even to express sympathy for the city manager's death. Granted, he hadn't lived here that long, but the dearth of citizens coming to express their regret didn't say good things about the community, especially given all the people who had felt compelled to be seen grieving after Greta died.

The two vacant chairs, one on the dais and one at the staff table, made the room look even more empty. I didn't know the official process for holding a meeting without the city manager, but it looked like the city attorney—a fortyish, pleasant man on retainer from a local firm who spent most of his time on land use issues—seemed to be trying to hold up the staff end of things. He was hanging on tightly to Dwight's usual three-ring binder and referred to it often as issues arose. That probably explained Pat's presence, as she certainly could answer any financial questions and would be a good source for answers from inside City Hall.

As a formal meeting—if proceedings in Sheffield could ever be considered formal—there was a more businesslike air tonight. There was a brief tribute to Dwight at the meeting's opening and condolences offered to his absent family, led by Kate and joined in by the rest of the Council, but no members of the public present to speak. The Council, with Kate in the central chair this time, then started clipping through standard agenda items like minutes and financial reports. The first matter that took any time was the introduction of a process to find an interim city manager.

"We've suffered another tragedy in Sheffield with the death of Dwight Orkman last week," Kate repeated, mostly to the cameras and any outside audience. "I've spoken with Chief Abhay, and we agreed that there was no need for him to make another police report at this meeting. I'm sure we're all aware that our officers, along with other agencies in the county and state, are doing all they can to solve these murders and bring Sheffield back to normal."

Her statement prompted sad or concerned expressions on the faces of the councilors and some staring at papers in front of them, but no one spoke up. I sensed a bit of fear as well; those who had thought much about the summer's events had to wonder if they were in danger of their own lives.

Kate asked for a moment of silence in remembrance of Dwight—it seemed to be the only act of respect he was going to get from Sheffield—before picking up a page of notes and moving on.

"I know the Council as a whole is very disappointed that the events we've suffered this summer have caused the cancellation of the River Festival, an important Sheffield celebration"—vigorous head-nodding and some angry looks—"and we're anxious that the life of the city isn't damaged further. If there is no opposition from my colleagues, I'd like to express our complete support for law enforcement in this matter on behalf of the Council. I'd also like to urge residents of Sheffield not to let these events impact their good relations with neighbors and other people in the city. Now more than ever, we all have to stand together as a community."

Good for you, Kate! She seemed to hit just the right note, as the agreement from the other councilors seemed to indicate. She asked if anyone else wanted to add to her statement, but surprisingly for people in elected office, no one did.

From there, a short discussion led to some agreement on possible candidates and a process for choosing an interim city manager, then a more permanent holder of the job. I didn't make any of the snarky comments that came into my head about the difficulty they might have in filling the position after the last holder was murdered. Internally, I figured that earned me a gold star for the evening. Maybe some ice cream? It was August, after all.

But the meeting wasn't over yet. With everything that had happened, I had almost forgotten the famous building that had Greta so excited. But it made sense that the Council had to deal with the mess that was left after the two deaths.

"Next," Kate sighed, "we have to discuss steps in the proposed development of City-owned property on the riverfront. I have spoken with the company that made the proposal for the alternative energy center, to inform its leadership of the deaths of Mayor Sutton and City Manager Orkman and to inquire about its continued interest in the property. The CEO of AllGen Partners says that it is still interested in moving forward, even with the delays that our current situation will cause."

Well, sure, went through my head. *They've already saved the big payment they were planning to make to Dwight, not to mention not having to deal with Greta and name the building after her.*

"Councilors seemed generally in favor of the project when

we last discussed it," Kate went on. "Heavens, was that just a week ago? It seems like six months ago," she sighed. "Are you still of the same mind about this? I don't propose that we make any formal decisions tonight, but I think we can direct our city attorney to begin negotiations with the company on next steps if that works for everyone."

It was a lot easier this time to see everyone's reactions, since they were ranged in front of me on the dais. The enthusiasm was tempered: it wasn't the first time everyone had heard the idea, and the project was still tinged by the deaths of its initial organizers.

Suzanne was the most eager, judging by the vigorous nod she gave Kate. Dennis Waitly also nodded and announced a quiet, "Yes, definitely." Pete Ichikawa nodded. George seemed lost in thought until Kate prompted him—he raised his head and also nodded. Anne Perez, who had offered me a hard stare when I arrived, announced, "Of course." There was no opposition, not that I was expecting any. Now that the Council had control of the issue and there was no more threat of behind-the-scenes dealing, it was hard to see a downside to an alternative energy center that would likely bring a lot of positive attention to Sheffield.

There was nothing else of note on the agenda and the meeting progressed quickly to its end in the strangely underpopulated room. The overall air was depressed, and if I was hoping for a magic answer to the question of the killer's motive, I didn't get it.

Which I reported to David when I returned home, slinging my soft leather purse onto the kitchen counter with an explosive sigh. "Nothing."

"What did you expect?" said my maddening husband.

"Did you really think the killer was one of the councilors and that he or she would give themselves away during a meeting?"

"There's always hope," I said inanely. "I guess I hoped that something would spark—something from the agenda or from something somebody said.

"David, I'm missing something. There's a big, black hole of something out there that has somebody really pissed off. It's inconceivable that an issue could be big enough to kill two people over and has something to do with the City but is invisible to the rest of us!"

"Well, keep in mind that those two people *are* dead," David said. "It could be that the issue died with them. The killer doesn't have to worry anymore about whatever it was, so you aren't going to get a lot of hints. As far as he's concerned, it's over."

"But there *isn't* anything like that. I've talked with Kate, I've talked with Pat Gregorio, even with Becky about public safety stuff. I've been going to meetings. There isn't anything going on around the City government that's raising emotions to that degree. Both Greta and Dwight had a lot to answer for, but the only thing they seemed to be conspiring over lately is that alternative energy center, and everyone's in favor of it. I'm completely stuck!"

"Then maybe you need to step back," responded David in a surprisingly loud voice, his blue eyes flashing. "You've done what Abhay asked you to do. You've done more than he asked and even stuck your nose in what I consider to be some dangerous places.

"I haven't said anything, I've made a concerted effort *not* to say anything that would interfere, but do you think I like you haring off and questioning people even after the chief of police tells you to stop? Do you think I *like* having to have patrol cars going by our house six times a night to make sure no one is hanging around who might want to kill us?"

David paused, his arm still in the air after pointing toward the street outside. I think he was as surprised as I was by his outburst. I had straightened, my normal reaction when feeling challenged, and was staring at him. I couldn't think of an answer.

"Felice," he continued in a calmer voice, "give it a rest. Give it up, preferably. You've done all you can do; Abhay couldn't ask for more. I think this case is going to be solved, if it's solved at all, by forensics and regular police work. The police will find somebody who saw something; they'll find a fiber or a fingerprint. Murder isn't a job for amateurs."

"I agree with you on that," I said with a sigh, even though I felt the sting of his comment and some corresponding anger. "And I am definitely an amateur. But David, it *must* be solved. I don't even want to think about the long-term damage to Sheffield if it isn't. The *mayor* is killed? The city manager is killed? And no one figures out who did it, or why? A lot more than the River Festival will be hurt if that's the outcome.

"This town has an inferiority complex as it is; people tend to believe in failure rather than success. How much worse will people in Sheffield feel about their community if two murders of city leaders just *happen*, and it looks like nothing is done about it?"

David didn't renew his argument; he had made his point. I wasn't the person who would solve this. I sat on our leather couch and dropped my head on the back, closing my eyes with a sigh. I was almost immediately surprised by a weight climbing onto my legs. I lifted my head and opened my eyes to meet the rich green gaze of Alexander, sitting so that his gray head came nearly to my chin. Noting that he had my attention, he proceeded to knead my legs before settling down and curling up with a gravelly purr.

I scratched his soft head in bemusement. If Alexander—the prince of "not my problem, aren't there treats?"—thought I needed comforting, I must have been putting out some truly upset vibes. David was right, I told myself. It was time to step back and try to resume normal operations.

Chapter Twenty-One

For the next several days, that's what I did. I worked in the garden, enjoying the continued sun and summer warmth. That's seventy-five degrees, contrary to how most people think of August. Most of America has wide swings between winter and summer temperatures—not the Oregon coast. Our range is generally between forty-five and seventy-five all year. Not exciting, barring the ninety-mile-per-hour winds and sheets of sideways rain in the winter, but it makes for a smaller wardrobe.

Inside, I worked on some hobby projects, made good use of summer produce in meals, and even canned some pears off the tree in our front yard. For an attorney whose history was limited to large cities with large grocery stores, and who formerly spent most of her spare time commuting, canning something was a real accomplishment. Don't worry, I at least knew enough to boil everything first.

Wandering around the house also led to the discovery of a large pile of neglected ironing. While ironing ranks right up there with bed-making as a futile exercise, I went after it, anyway.

I know, I know; no one irons anymore. But I have a strange taste for linens not made of polyester. I think it's the house's fault: since it's big and nearly a hundred years old, the seeds of an older, finer lifestyle get planted in your head, and you find yourself drinking tea in cups, with saucers, from vintage china teapots. On a tray. With a tea cloth that needs ironing. Never mind that we don't have the maid or housekeeper or whoever would have done all that laborious work in far-off decades.

Not that I didn't think about the murders, and the investigation, and the various people I had spoken with who may or may not be viable suspects. But I made a real effort to focus on other things. I didn't update my notes, or draw any diagrams with arrows pointing in various directions, or call Tom Abhay to ask questions with answers I wasn't really entitled to know.

Although he did call me. It was a short conversation and a disheartening one in some ways. He had spoken with Carla Graham, checked her story, and determined that she could not have committed Greta's murder. So that was one possible lead gone, although some minor good might result from the contact. And there was no good news on the forensic front: Portland labs didn't have much material from the case to work on and reported they wouldn't have any results for a couple more weeks.

Of course, Abhay was really calling to check that I was behaving like a good little civilian. At least I was able to claim truthfully that I was. I was making absolutely no noise that could be tied to the investigation.

In fact, the silence emanating from our house must have been intense, because Becky called me after about a week.

"What's new, Felice?"

"I canned pears. I am now officially a canner!"

"Uh . . . okay. Did you boil the jars first?"

"Yes! I boiled everything!"

"Right. Good." Becky knows how to do a lot of strange stuff, and is usually ready to jump into something she hasn't mastered yet after a minimum of study. And she never starts at beginner level. As a result, I can always count on her guidance when I try something new myself, which can be annoying if I haven't asked for it. On the other hand, she has convinced me to try activities I never would have done previously and coached me through them well enough to prevent disaster. Some have been more unusual than others. Someday I'll tell the story about the day I helped to shear a difficult, four-horned sheep with a pigeon on my head. But not right now.

Now, she continued, "Anything new on your investigation?"

"No. I'm leaving it alone. David convinced me that I am not the person to solve murders. And I was stuck, anyway." It sounded lame to my own ears, but Becky hadn't wanted me to continue, either.

No sound from her for a few beats; she was probably shocked into silence. She knows I don't give up goals easily.

"Probably for the best. But I have to admit I'm surprised."

"I know. Me, too, sort of. But I don't know what else I can do, and David was pretty upset about the possible danger. And like you said, Abhay told me to stop asking around."

Another beat of silence.

"So, you're canning."

"And ironing!"

"Felice, no one irons anymore. I don't think I've ironed

anything in the last twenty years."

"I have tea cloths. They look like papier-mâché clumps if you don't iron them."

"Uh-huh." Another beat of silence. "Just how bored are you?"

I sighed. "About to go out of my frigging mind, since you asked. Can we please go somewhere?"

She chuckled. "Sure. Want to take my god-dog for a walk down by the river?"

I haven't mentioned this before, but Becky and Angus really like each other. *Really* like each other. He runs to her with a huge grin on his face every time she comes to the house and lays on her feet if he gets the chance. It's a nice sign of affection, but kudos to Becky for actually enjoying a ninety-pound Scottish deerhound cutting off the circulation to her ankles. He stays with her when we go out of town and, being the noble soul he is, doesn't even pay attention to her canaries, who live in a large cage at one end of her living room. He'd rather just take up the length of her couch and put his head in her lap.

I looked at our couch now, where Angus was sprawled in a long, flat heap of midday nap. I knew it would take only two words to have him up on his tall legs, his flag of a tail whirling and his big grin wide, ready to go.

"Sounds like a great idea. We'll meet you in the parking lot for the waterfront park."

"See you in ten."

After hanging up, I leaned over the back of the couch, waited for Angus to sense my presence and open his eyes, and whispered the magic words, "Car ride." Then pulled back quickly, as all those legs propelled the rest of him off the furniture with one huge twist. Two more bounds had him across the room and in front of the hook where we hang his leash; did I mention that Scottish deerhounds are *big* dogs? The tail was going like a helicopter rotor and the smile showed all his teeth as he went into the Down Dog play bow that is his way of saying, "Please, please, please!" I could only grin at his excitement; it's fun to make your dog happy.

It seemed silly to drive the five minutes to the waterfront park, and the walk downhill would have been fine, but the steep climb back would have been hard on everyone. Plus, I didn't know how long Becky had to spare. So, we drove, pulling into the nearly empty parking lot at the park a few minutes later. I grabbed his leash and let the dog jump out of the back and waved to Becky, who was just getting out of her own car a few yards away.

We decided to walk the path along the river; the day was perfect for it. Not warm enough to bring out perspiration—in fact, in the last week of August, the breeze was cool, especially near the water, and I had put a long, lightweight cardigan over my short-sleeved shirt. It would be cool enough after the sun went down to need something even heavier. Meanwhile, the sunlight on the water was dazzling, the deep blue of the sky beautiful, and there were a few boats in the distance, where the river was darker and wider as it neared the ocean, still flanked by groves of tall conifers. We were just past the waterfront pavilion where Suzanne had been serving food during the Summer Festival when I saw some movement and heard splashing. The three of us hurried toward it.

We were rewarded by the sight of a pair of otters, rolling around in the water and doing their wonderful acrobatics. We stayed still, even the dog, although his ears were pricked up and his eyes were focused hard on the pair. I kept a strong hand on the leash—I didn't think he'd go charging into the water, but the otters were the same size as other sighthound prey, even if he hadn't seen any of these particular critters before.

The otters didn't seem to sense any danger, because they kept up their fun right in front of us even though they must have been aware of our presence. The three of us waited, almost breathless, until the pair of them finally dove and twisted their way across the channel to a small, brushy island and out of sight.

That sort of experience is one of the great things about where we live. You wouldn't see a pair of otters cavorting anywhere near the D.C. Beltway, except maybe in the National Zoo. Becky and I smiled at each other like a couple of six-year-olds, made the appropriate "Wow, that was *so* cool!" remarks, and resumed our walk, Angus happily trotting a few steps in front of us.

The waterfront path ends right in front of the large, open area ringed by trees that had hosted the logging show in July. It was green, sunny, and warmer with the protection of the trees, so we ventured across. I could even let Angus off the leash there: with the tree surround, I was confident he would bound around and enjoy himself without going far from me. I unhooked him and told him to stay close, then watched while he wandered off to sniff every square inch of this intriguing new place.

Becky wandered off in a different direction to check under some trees for indications of future mushrooms. This is one of those interesting country things she does, but an activity in which I have not joined her. Mushrooms sprout all over forests and wooded places in the fall, after the rains start. There are all different kinds: some are quite tasty, some even valuable. Some, of course, not so good for human consumption. Call me citified, but it just makes more sense to me to buy some nice mushrooms from a well-lit, dry store than to traipse around a forest with rain dripping off trees and down my neck and squelching into my shoes, looking through several years of mulch and dead stuff for fungal sprouts that may or may not be something I should eat. Becky is good at knowing what is safe and tasty, but in the final analysis, I'd rather be a city weenie.

Angus's inclination lay in the opposite direction from Becky's, and I realized I had been concentrating on the scenery and warm evergreen smells rather than watching him. I turned in a circle, searching for him, then headed in his last known direction. Like most of the sighthound family (Wolfhounds, Salukis, Borzois, Greyhounds, and those little Whippets, among others), deerhounds love to run, but not for long: after a couple of minutes of high speed, they need a long, recuperative nap. I wasn't too worried that I'd be able to find him, and sure enough, his wiry gray coat was visible through the lowest branches of a spreading fir just a few yards away at the edge of the clearing.

"Angus, what are you doing in there?" I said while ducking to investigate his shelter. He was curled up on a bed of needles under the branches and near the trunk, and he looked up to grin at me, obviously saying "Look at the great bed I found!" I knew I wouldn't be able to get him out of there from a distance, so I pushed through two interleaved branches to enter the shelter.

A glint of sun caught my eye—something shiny that wasn't natural to a bed of fir needles. I leaned down to pick it up, then frowned at my find, a cellophane wrapper with some purple lettering on it. It was obviously a piece of trash that had blown into the bottom branch of the tree at some point. I played Sherlock with it long enough to notice that it was fairly fresh, without the crumpling and fading that comes with exposure to long months of rain. I thus deduced it had not been lying there for years. I stuffed it into my sweater pocket so I could throw it away when we arrived somewhere with a trash can. Despite all the cleanup efforts, some residue from the Summer Festival had apparently evaded the volunteers. I muttered, "Blasted litterers," to myself, said something encouraging to the dog, and we both headed back out into the sun.

After twenty minutes more of the waterfront, Becky, Angus, and I headed for one of the two coffee depots near the park. I hadn't seen drive-through coffee places before moving to the Pacific Northwest and I don't know how widespread they are in other parts of the country. Here, you can count on at least one in every town of more than a thousand people; tiny buildings open from early morning to late afternoon with a drive-up window on each side. They mostly serve commuters and everyone else who utterly relies on their favored blend of that dark liquor of the gods: good, strong, locally roasted coffee.

We took our choices and started the walk back to the parking lot, sipping and talking. The park was almost deserted with only a solitary man walking about a hundred yards ahead of us. The otters were nowhere in sight when we reached the pavilion, and the lowering sun meant the breeze blowing off the bay was cooling fast. The shadows from nearby trees and our vehicles were substantially longer than they had been when we arrived. Becky looked at her watch.

"I have to go; I have to get home and feed the animals before my shift tonight."

"No problem. Thanks a lot, Becky—this has been a great break." I meant it. We hadn't talked about the killings, any other City business, or anything momentous. But I hadn't realized that my busywork in the house over the past week had been a form of hiding—a buried undercurrent of fear coloring all those domestic activities. I hadn't realized it until I emerged from my fortress, so to speak, walked around outside, and enjoyed the day.

She got into her car after a final leaning hug from Angus, and we waved her out of the parking lot. The dog jumped into the back of my vehicle and I closed the back hatch. I was headed around to the driver's door when I saw the man who had been ahead of us standing on the boardwalk in front of the parking spaces about twenty yards away. I recognized Patrick Sutton, remembered my decision to talk with him again, and walked in his direction after making sure Angus had fresh air in the car and had found his water bowl.

"Patrick, hello! I hadn't realized that was you walking ahead of us."

He glared at me while looking behind me to the dog's face, visible in the partially open window. "Felice. You come here a lot?"

"Not really," I replied, keeping my voice light while watching his mood. "I've been stuck in the house a bit lately, and it was a good opportunity to bring Angus somewhere different. Beautiful day, isn't it?"

"Yes." He looked around, breaking eye contact. Funny how a comment about the weather nearly always causes that reaction. It's as if we have to check before answering, even if we've been standing out in whatever the weather is for hours. His gaze came back to my face, and the glare came back into it.

"I hear you've been investigating for Abhay," he said shortly. "Anything you can pass on?"

I shouldn't have been repeatedly shocked when people asked: as Anne Perez had smugly said, "word gets around." Even city-bred me knows you can't keep secrets in a small town, and there had been that lovely rat on our porch. But this was the first time a real suspect had said anything to my face about what I had been doing, and I felt a jump inside that I hoped didn't show on my face.

"I wouldn't call it investigating," I said to Patrick as casually as I could. "I'm not a police officer and don't have the training for it. Abhay asked me early on to talk with some people"—I shrugged my shoulders to lessen the importance—"because he doesn't have the staff to do everything. But that was a while ago: I haven't been doing it since Dwight was killed." Not completely accurate, but Patrick was still under suspicion.

And he apparently wasn't finished with me. "And what did you find out? I assume that's why you were asking me questions at the dog park. I'm the husband; I have to be a suspect, right?"

"Patrick, if you'll recall, we just ran into each other at the dog park. I asked you some questions, yes, but it wasn't any kind of interrogation.

"And you probably were a suspect in Greta's death. I don't know, but spouses usually are. With Dwight's murder, I assume that changed." I was watching him carefully; I knew little about Patrick and didn't know what to expect.

"Then why am I still getting visits from Abhay?" He burst

out, angrier now.

My head went back and I let my surprise show. "Patrick, the chief doesn't tell me what he does; I'm just a regular civilian. Did you have a problem with Dwight?"

"I didn't like the amount of time Greta was spending with him," he growled. "Those last several weeks, she was almost bouncing around and she obviously had a secret, like I told you. She wouldn't tell me what it was, but I knew Dwight was in on it. I didn't know what to think!"

I silently blessed all the years I had spent learning how to control my reactions in meetings and negotiations. The idea of Patrick Sutton feeling jealous of what hatchet-faced, unpleasant Dwight Orkman might be doing with equally unpleasant, shapeless Greta—probably with her cat glasses on, even if nothing else . . . *No, Felice, don't even go there*—gave me an uneasy moment. But I remembered my impression when overhearing the two victims that Saturday. They hadn't seemed to be that kind of close.

"Did you ask Dwight about it?" was all I could think of to keep him talking.

"Yeah, I did. After Greta . . . was gone," he stammered, "I went to his office and asked what all the secret smiling had been about. He told me about this alternative energy center deal, about how Greta was going to get the developer to put her name on it and make it her legacy to the city. He said that's all there was." He stared out over the water.

"Did you believe him?"

Patrick's gaze came back to me. "Yeah, I guess I did. It sounded like her, anyway."

"I assume that's what you told Abhay."

"Yes, that's what I told him." Staring straight at me. "You

sure you aren't still *asking questions?*"

I remembered that Patrick was a retired teacher, as Greta had been. It wasn't a guarantee of intelligence, as we had seen with our late mayor, but it did show proof of education.

"Yes, I'm sure. I just wondered why you were still getting visits from the chief."

"What do you think, Felice? Do you think I killed two people by hitting them over the head? Do you think I stuck my wife's head in a plastic bag full of water and watched her drown? Do you think I have that kind of hatred in me?" His voice rose to a shout while his eyes glared into mine.

I stayed cool, although I was shaking inside. "I don't know, Patrick. But it isn't my job to find out. I hope things are better for you soon."

It took a lot of my courage to turn my back on him and walk to my car, where Angus was whining softly, his nose still out the window. I got into the car, talking to him quietly, started the car, and drove out of the parking lot.

Chapter Twenty-Two

Another conversation with Patrick Sutton that really hadn't netted me anything. Part of that stemmed from my lack of standing: I didn't have the authority or, let's face it, the guts to stand toe-to-toe with a suspect and challenge his alibi or his statement. I didn't even know what was in his statements, since I had never been privy to the official case file. I was shaken by the encounter, but that didn't say anything about Patrick's guilt.

I thought over the conversation to see if there was anything to pass on to Chief Abhay and finally decided on a message outlining what Patrick said about his jealousy of Dwight in the weeks before Greta's death. Abhay probably already knew whether Patrick had been to see the city manager before Orkman, too, was killed. If there had been words between them, or if Patrick had not been satisfied with Dwight's answers as he claimed, other people in City Hall would certainly have heard an argument. I'd spent time in that building. Despite good plaster walls and heavy wooden doors, voices traveled.

Message sent, I concentrated on putting something

together for dinner. David came down from his office and we caught up on our respective days. I'm still amazed how two people who are not working full-time can manage to hardly see each other over the course of an entire day. In some ways, our evenings were remarkably similar to the high-stress East Coast days: catching up on people we have seen, conversations, events from an entire day of not being together. The difference, of course, is that now, we don't have to race through everything, prepare for the next day, and throw ourselves into bed so that we can drag ourselves out of it to face the whole grind again. Speaking for myself, of course—David is one of those irritating morning people who almost bounces out of bed and can answer complicated questions at 7:00 a.m. Even my work colleagues had known better than to approach me without caution before about ten o'clock.

Those days were over, thankfully, and we could take our time. We were sitting in the living room after dinner, Angus taking up half the couch so that David was forced into a chair across the room, both of us reading, when a low rumble came from the street outside. When it was accompanied by a grind of gears and the squeak of air brakes, we looked up at each other.

"Truck," David said shortly.

Rather than answering, I got up and headed across the room to the front door, opening it to look out into the cool dark and the street lit by a single streetlight. Sure enough, our nearby residential intersection was dwarfed by a huge semi, its seventy-five feet of cab and trailer inching slowly past, its height completely blocking the normal view of the house across the street.

Time for another short explanation. Sheffield has a truck

route that goes through the back side of town. It's meant to be a substitute route for the traffic to and from large industries and businesses, such as Carl's marine repair operation, but in the State's eagerness to get large trucks off the state highway, it naturally failed to mark the alternate route adequately. The truck route ran about two hundred yards away from our house, but occasionally, especially at night, trucks made an odd turn and had to toil up our hill. If they kept going, they would get stuck in a grid of narrow residential streets with tight turns and no opportunities to turn around, so we always tried to stop them and get them headed back in the right direction if we could.

It seemed clear that this driver had figured out his mistake, since the truck had stopped, but I made my way across the front yard to the door of his cab and waved until I had his attention.

The window went down and the face of a thin, middle-aged man wearing a trucking logo ball cap appeared dimly, looking down at me. I couldn't see his eyes very well, but the light from the streetlight glinted on about a day's worth of gray whiskers.

"Wrong turn. Shouldn't have made that right up the hill, right?"

"You got it," I concurred. "Do you need any help turning around? You really shouldn't go any farther this way. There isn't a route that will get you back to the truck road and the streets are really narrow."

He looked around. "I think I can do it, but a little help might be good, thanks." He sighed. "Why do I always seem to end up in Sheffield after dark?"

I chuckled. "Do you come here often?"

"Not really. The last time was about a month ago, and I didn't get here until it was dark then, either. Although that was worse because you guys had some kind of big festival going on. I had to go through town to make my delivery and the streets were all blocked off. Finally got there, but it was too late to leave, so I ended up spending the night in the truck."

"Oh, right—that must have been our Summer Festival." I decided not to mention the murder committed that night. "I hope you had a chance to enjoy it, at least."

"Yeah, it was all right. I started walking around some, had a bite to eat, and then stood by that music stage to watch the fireworks. You guys have great fireworks."

"Yes, we're pretty proud of those. Did you like the music group?"

"Don't know—there was no one around and they were playing canned stuff while I was there. I took off once the fireworks were over to get away from the crowds."

"Ah." I stood riveted in place. Luckily, the dark hid what felt like the complete draining of color from my face, while my fingers and toes were tingling. *They were playing canned stuff?*

"So—you didn't see anyone on stage?"

"Not then. Hey, do you mind giving me a wave while I back up into this side street? Make sure I don't run into a pole or something in the dark?"

"No, not at all. Um, do you have a card? I don't want to take up your time, but something happened that night and our people might want to talk with you quickly. Just to hear your story." Hell, I didn't know whether truckers had cards, but I figured he had a business, and I had to get his contact info.

"Yeah, actually I do. I do some regional runs, so my wife told me I should get some made rather than making people write down the phone number." He turned back into the cab, then turned toward me again holding that magic rectangle of white card stock.

"Thanks a lot . . ." I could barely make out the biggest print on the card, "Gary. I appreciate it, and you won't get a hassle."

"No problem." He was finished talking. The window went back up and the truck shifted into reverse as I walked several yards to get out of the way.

It took a few minutes for Gary and his semi to carefully back into a side street, then move forward again to go back past our house and down the hill toward the truck route. He waved a salute as he drove past; I waved back, holding his card and wondering at small miracles. I looked up at the bright stars of a clear Northwest late-summer night, trying to assimilate this new bit of data.

They were playing canned stuff. If this was true, then the Russells' solid alibi had evaporated like mist. If they weren't on stage . . . it was the biggest break anyone had had in this awful mess in all the weeks since Greta's murder. It wasn't much, but I had to follow up. I shook my head and headed back into the house to call Abhay. If he was asleep, too bad. He wouldn't mind being awakened for this.

If he was annoyed, he hid it well and asked for a meeting at the Public Safety building the following morning. Despite stretched nerves and a jangling brain, I managed a few hours' sleep, then was surprised when David insisted on coming to the meeting.

"The two of you are going to be discussing how to use this. You're going to want a piece of it, no matter how dumb that is, and if you're in, I'm in. I don't want you walking into some potentially dangerous situation alone."

I bridled a bit at the "dumb" inference, but if he expected an argument, he wasn't going to get one.

"That's probably a good idea, if only because it means I don't have to tell you everything later." I smiled a sweet smile at him that he should have guessed promised retaliation. David means well when he does this, but after all our years together, he should know how I *hate* being patronized.

"Really, David, I don't know how Abhay will want to handle this. I don't think there is enough evidence to arrest George or Rita just because a passing trucker says they weren't on stage during the fireworks. I don't know of any motive they might have had for the killings to begin with. All George would have to do during questioning is stick to his story or say that they left for five minutes for a bathroom break, and we'd still have nothing."

David nodded. "You don't have much. Given your research, how good a lead do you think this is?"

I closed my eyes and thought for a moment. "I can't tell you why—maybe just because it's the first glimmer of light—but this clicks for me. It's because of the lie; why say they were on stage if they were just taking a break or something? I think he did it, either by himself with Rita covering, or the two of them together. George is a smart guy, but I think there's a temper under there. Maybe Greta humiliated him somehow, maybe there was something in the works that threatened his environmental principles . . . I don't know."

I opened my eyes and looked at my husband. "But it suddenly makes sense that George Russell very nastily killed two people who got in his way."

Chapter Twenty-Three

I knew it would take more than my gut feeling to convince Tom Abhay, and so it went. On the other hand, we both knew this was the first solid lead—or evidence of outright lying—that the case had had since Carl's oversight about meeting with Dwight.

I gave him Gary's card so that he could follow up on the details, but what the trucker had told me the night before was enough to warrant questioning George Russell again. After going over everything one more time, including the lack of forensic evidence against George (or anyone), the chief indicated that the councilor would be brought into the station.

A warning bell went off in my brain, and I've learned not to ignore those.

"Tom, excuse me if I'm overstepping, but is that really what you want to do? I'm concerned that George could just sit there across the table from you, insist he and Rita were playing, and not budge. He's smart enough to know there isn't much against him and he doesn't strike me as the type that would blunder into a confession. Is there another approach that might jar him more effectively?"

Abhay's famous eyebrow went up again. "That's what I have, Felice—I can't exactly take him for coffee and ask casually if he killed two people this summer."

"No, the headline 'Murder Suspect Trashes Café' wouldn't go over too well. I'm just wondering. George spoke to me civilly at that water group meeting, even though I don't think he likes David or me. He went on for quite a while. Do you think I would have any chance of shocking him into telling me more? With you and other officers within earshot, of course. Despite my husband's opinion, I'm not an idiot."

"I didn't say you were an idiot," David grumbled from his seat next to me. "I said I didn't want you taking part in anything alone that might be dangerous."

"Mmm," seemed to be my best response, because 1) he was right, and 2) this wasn't the time or place to discuss it any further. I kept to the subject.

"Tom, I'm showing my ignorance here. Do people really do that TV stuff, wearing a wire and going to a meeting with bad guys? Because that would seem to be an option."

Abhay smiled. It was a little patronizing, but he was entitled.

"Let's not rush into this, okay? You have an idea that Russell is the killer. We don't have any real evidence against him. On the other hand, from what I know of the man and what I sense from him, he could be our guy."

"So, what we're looking for is more information and as much of a read as we can get from him," I mused. "Is there any other way of getting something more—real evidence that would be usable by a prosecutor?"

I tilted my head and thought for a second before continuing. "What could you find in a search of his house? Not a murder weapon: the choker used on Greta was left at the scene. So was the statue used to kill Dwight. The plastic bag"— I shuddered; that part of Greta's murder had always seemed gratuitously nasty—"is a nonstarter. Would any of his clothes likely have blood on them?"

"Possibly. Blunt force trauma wounds can put blood on the perpetrator; it depends on the circumstances. If he's smart, he's disposed of what he was wearing just in case.

"But Felice, we're getting ahead of ourselves. I don't have enough to get a warrant to search his house, whether there's anything there to find or not. Is talking with him while wearing a wire something you really think you can do? You now think you have a reason to be afraid of him; can you act like you aren't while you're interviewing him?"

I looked at David, then back at the chief. "I think I could cover up nervousness by acting angry. I could tell him that one of my neighbors saw him dropping that box with the dead rat on our porch and ask him what the hell he was doing. He'll be so busy trying not to say, 'That's not true, no one saw me doing it,' that maybe he'll slip up on something else."

Abhay stared at me for a moment, then burst out laughing. David just sat and looked at me, bemused; but then again, he's more accustomed to the stuff I say.

"Believe it or not," Abhay finally said, still smiling, "I've used that trick before, and you'd be surprised how often it works."

"Yes, but George Russell isn't an idiot. It was just a thought." I sighed. "The other issue is what I'm trying to work toward if we have this conversation. I have to get him to expose his motive, and I've wracked my brain for weeks trying to figure out why Greta and Dwight were killed."

"I think we're all agreed that it has to be something City-related," David stated, looking at both Abhay and me. "Felice has interviewed a lot of people in the best position to know what that might be. Don't you keep coming back to the energy center proposed for that City land?"

"Yes. None of Greta's other pet projects seems to have anyone upset enough to kill her, and even if it were, the motive disappears for Dwight. Except for that center. The only problem is everyone seems to like it. I mean, what's not to like about a center researching alternative energy solutions that means a nice building on your property, some good jobs, and regional, if not national, attention for Sheffield?"

"Not to mention money and the possibility of additional businesses," David added.

"Okay, we're getting off-track here again," put in Abhay. I wondered at his patience in dealing with gabby civilians. "Whatever his motive, I don't see you, Felice, getting far in a conversation with George Russell. If we want to pursue him as a suspect, I think we need a different direction."

That shut everyone up for at least a minute.

David finally broke the silence. "What I keep coming back to, Tom—what would be your normal course of action? Say you had the resources of a couple of additional people."

"Again, the normal channels probably wouldn't work," said Abhay with a frown. "Checking his financial records isn't likely to net us anything, even if we could get a warrant for them. Same thing with his phone records. This isn't like a drug ring or even a murder-for-hire situation.

"If I had the manpower, I'd probably have someone follow him for a couple of days. But again, I don't know what that would net us. If he's the killer, I don't think he's working with anyone outside. And we have no idea if he's planning to kill again."

My head shot up. "Kate!"

Abhay looked at me. "Kate Dennis?"

"Yes! She's the acting mayor, and she and the rest of the Council told the City attorney to move forward with discussions on the energy center at the last Council meeting. Do you think she's in danger?"

"I don't know. But I had a word with her a few days ago. She hasn't had any nasty incidents like the one you experienced. I told her to be careful and not to go anywhere alone."

I breathed a large sigh of relief. "Wow, I'm so glad you did that. This seemed to be more about the former leadership, but I should have thought of it."

Abhay gave me a look. "That's my job, Felice."

"Right, yes, of course. Sorry. But she's a friend, and I didn't think to worry about her."

I thought about all the times in recent weeks I talked to or met with Kate and how important her friendship was to me. And then, my thoughts flashed to other local women I considered friends, and then to those who weren't. And one in particular.

"Rita," I breathed. I looked up at David and Tom Abhay with a growing light of certainty.

"Rita Russell?" This time, it was David who repeated the name.

I nodded and kept nodding, my eyes focused downward to help me think. "Rita is the weak link in all of this."

I told the chief about my recent meeting with Rita on the street and her irrational behavior.

"I didn't understand it at the time; I just put it down to her general dislike of me and some stress that became directed at me. But what if that stress comes from being involved in two murders? Even if she's fully supportive of what George is doing, that can't be easy.

"And Rita always makes a big deal of how she's tied to the community. She has to see how the killings this summer have torn up Sheffield."

"Yes, she's been here for years, although I don't think she grew up here. She's been active as a musician as long as I've been here," Abhay continued.

"She takes a lot of pride in being part of the community," added David. "Of course, that's usually in the context of telling us that we aren't."

"If I can get Rita to blow up at me again the way she did last time, she might reveal something," I offered to both Tom and David. "I seem to be an irritated nerve for her. Well, let's poke at it."

The two men looked at each other. David shrugged. "Okay, that doesn't sound quite as dangerous as provoking George Russell. But I want it in a public place."

Abhay nodded. "Yeah. I think she can be safe enough. Let's talk some more about how to make this work."

Chapter Twenty-Four

As it happened, it was Kate Dennis who gave me the information I needed. I felt terribly guilty over not thinking to warn her of possible danger—yes, I know, not really my job, but that doesn't help with guilt. I called her that afternoon to find out how she was coping.

"I'm okay. The interim mayor stuff isn't taking as much time as I worried it might, although finding an interim city manager is turning out to be a headache. Most candidates move around before the school year starts, so we're running late." Amazingly, it was already nearing the end of August. "I may have to look for someone who's willing to come out of retirement for a while."

"Sorry you're having so much trouble. Is anyone saying anything about not wanting to come to Sheffield particularly?"

"Not in so many words, but there is some hesitation over the phone when I mention where the position is. The sudden end of the previous job holder is definitely a factor."

I made a rueful noise. "Um, Kate—you are being careful, aren't you?"

"Not you, too!" She laughed. "Chief Abhay told me that I shouldn't go anywhere alone."

"He's right. Think about it, Kate. The people who were killed were City leaders. It's almost certain they were killed because of some City issue. Now, you're the leader, and we don't know that you aren't in danger, too."

She waited a beat before answering. "Well, I've been the acting mayor for a month. And I can't think of anything I've done, or any issue I've promoted, that the Council didn't agree to do. I certainly haven't stuck my neck out for anything; I didn't think that would be appropriate."

"Yes, but you're being rational; I don't know that the killer is. Please be careful." I didn't want to tell her about the suspicion about the Russells or about the dead rat on our porch. But now, I needed a way to get the conversation around to Rita without it looking like I was on the same topic.

"Yeah, yeah. Okay."

"Kate—about the cancellation of the River Festival."

"Aaargh," came back over the phone. "I can't tell you how many phone calls ALL the councilors, and City Hall, have fielded because of that. It wasn't our decision—the organizers called that all by themselves—but you'd think we had announced that the city was closing for the year. People are furious, they're afraid; we're even being asked about whether there is going to be a Halloween parade or a Christmas tree!"

"Wow, I hadn't realized that."

"And what they're saying to us is always just the tip of the iceberg of what's being said amongst themselves. The rumor machine in this place is awful. The latest thing I was asked the other day was whether it's true that half the City staff has resigned because they're afraid of being killed."

"Oh, good grief. *Has* anyone resigned?"

"No. But if they keep hearing all this talk when they go anywhere, it might start happening, and then we'd be in a real world of hurt."

It was true. Professional staff is the backbone of every local government; they're the people who actually keep things running. Elected leaders come and go; even professsional managers stay in their positions only an average of about five years. You can do without them in a pinch if everyone stays on target, but once knowledgeable staff members leave—experienced people like Pat Gregorio or Tom Abhay; a Public Works director who knows where all the potholes are; or a fire chief who knows which houses are empty and run-down firetraps—processes start to fall apart and services suffer. That would be Kate's, and the Council's, biggest fear, since staff had been cut to the bone to keep the City solvent and it was difficult to get good, experienced people to commit to a small town. Not being able to fill important staff positions would almost certainly drive the city into further decline because of the harm to the infrastructure.

It was one more bad consequence of the summer's awful events that the rumor was circulating. But in the meantime, I had to get back on subject.

"I was thinking about the music acts, especially, for the River Festival. I was wondering about whether anyone had considered a concert in September."

I winced inwardly at the untruth. *You are going to have a lot of apologizing to do when this is over, kiddo.* But Abhay hadn't told me that I could pass on our suspicions yet, and who knew how all of this would turn out? I mentally pledged Kate a large lemon drop cocktail—okay, maybe two—when I could recount the events later, assuming it all went okay. *Don't go there, Felice.*

I kept going. "I don't know many of the musicians, but I do know George and Rita. I thought maybe I could talk to Rita, see if there is any interest in a sort of makeup concert. Do you know where I might find her during the day? I don't want to bug them at home, and as you know, I might not be welcome if I tried."

Kate didn't seem to notice that I hadn't mentioned contacting Rita by phone or other means, or maybe she bought the idea that a personal approach would be more effective. As I expected—Kate had surprising knowledge about a lot of people around town—she could help.

"Rita teaches in Portland sometimes, but when she's in town, she usually hangs at L'Abstrait."

This was not a surprise, and I should have thought of it. L'Abstrait was a two-story café near the bluff that was a favorite hangout for those who (let's say tactfully) lived an alternative lifestyle along the coast. The service was terrible, but the food was decent, there was a lot of locally produced art all over the walls, and there was a near-constant stream of music, poetry readings, personal expression, and whatever else that took place on a downstairs stage. Having been lucky enough to see some world-class theatre and music during my life, "interesting" was about the best I could say about some of the offerings. However, we'd had some enjoyable evenings there with friends and in larger groups, and I had very much enjoyed the one amateur performance in which I had participated. Some creatives adored the place and spent a lot of time at its square, heavy wooden tables.

"Kate, I owe you," I said now, "more than you know."

"You want to tell me what's really going on?"

Oops.

"Ouch. I am *so* sorry. I was thinking multiple cocktails when this is over, really I was. But I can't tell you."

"I'll hold you to the cocktails. And I'll keep quiet. But I hope Chief Abhay is sticking close to you, too."

I took several deep breaths while getting ready the next morning, planning to hit the café before lunch. Luckily, the weather was cool enough for a long cardigan over my patterned shirt and pants, so I could make use of an old public speaking trick. While I'm not nervous in front of large audiences, my hands shake for the first minute or thereabouts, so I generally wear a jacket with pockets. Stick one hand in a pocket and gesture with the other: you look comfortable, even casual, and no one can see your hands shaking.

They were shaking plenty as I parked the car on the street near L'Abstrait—the place didn't have a parking lot. I looked around but didn't see Tom Abhay, any other officer, or a marked car. I figured he was either well-concealed or would be there shortly—we really didn't expect physical violence in a public place, even if Rita was irrational these days. We had decided against any sort of microphone.

The restaurant had a wooded courtyard in front, obscuring most of its two-story wood frame, with a path leading to the central front door. Once inside, I climbed the stairs and went to the second-floor bar for coffee. Rita was there, all right, sitting at a table overlooking the main floor with an empty coffee cup in front of her. I picked up my own full mug— another deep breath, a hopefully neutral look pasted on my face—and I walked over to her table and stood opposite her seat to get her attention. I planned to congratulate myself on my courage later.

"Hi, Rita. Can I get you some coffee?"

"I didn't invite you over here," she snarled after looking up and seeing me. Rita wasn't looking her best. Her long hair was tangled, there were heavy shadows under her dark eyes, and her T-shirt and jeans looked carelessly thrown on. Her usual long silver earrings were missing as well; I don't think I had ever seen her without a pair. Something was throwing Rita Russell off her game, and I was fairly sure I knew what it was.

Still shaking a bit inside—I really wasn't looking forward to this confrontation—I knew it was imperative that I look calm and in control. So, I stood my ground, tilted my head, lifted an eyebrow, and merely repeated, "Can I get you some coffee?"

"I don't want any fucking coffee from you," she growled, staring at the table.

This is good—she isn't screaming directly at me. This is practically an invitation!

I took it as such and sat down across from her, picking up my mug and taking a sip as she raised her head and snarled at me.

"What the hell are you doing? I said I didn't invite you here. Go away!"

"Well"—I started (*okay, Felice, make this good*)—"I'm by myself, you're by yourself, and there isn't anyone else here I know. So I thought I could have a conversation with you."

"Well, I don't want to have a conversation with you. Fuck off and leave me alone!"

"If you want to be left alone, I'm surprised you're here

rather than at home," I offered, hoping for an opening. "George told me about how beautiful the setting of your house is, right over the river. It sounds lovely."

"I don't want to be at ho—" she shot back before stopping suddenly, looking at me again and narrowing her eyes. "What the hell do you want?"

"Like I said, just a conversation." I shrugged my shoulders. "I don't know why we haven't stayed friends, Rita—we may disagree on things, but I have a lot of friends like that." I was tempted to delve a bit more into this, but now was not the time. I didn't want to distract her from what was really eating at her. "How are you doing?"

"It's none of your fucking business how I'm doing!" The exclamation was almost a whine. "How many times do I have to tell you, just go *away!*"

A large part of me wanted to do just that. Rita was a big woman and, in this emotional state, unpredictable. There was a certain amount of physical fear. But another part knew I was on the right track. I sat silently, sipping my coffee and looking at her calmly, then looking around the restaurant, then back to her face. I could feel the tension building. After a minute or two, it was time.

"It's really eating at you, isn't it, Rita?" I kept my eyes on hers as her head shot up and she stared at me. I leaned in and spoke softly.

"What is it now, about five weeks? That's a long time to have to dwell on something, relive it over and over."

"What the hell are you talking about?" Her voice was a whisper, but her eyes held fear.

I continued softly. "I wouldn't have thought it was an easy thing to do"—who knew if that were true; I could easily see Rita

Russell with a large, blunt instrument in her hand—"watching your own husband slamming someone in the head, someone you knew. Helping him drown her? What was the point in that, by the way?"

She reared back, sitting up straight; I could tell she was desperately trying not to glance around to see who might be listening. "You bitch! Who the hell do you think you are? I don't know what you're talking about!"

"Sure, you do. You and George killed Greta Sutton. I don't know exactly why yet, but I know you killed her. And then you killed Dwight Orkman."

Rita was in full denial mode, but I could tell from her eyes that she was lying. "You don't know anything, you crazy bitch. How dare you accuse us? How dare you—" she was spluttering, trying to find the right words, I could tell, to make this go away. She stopped talking and a mean look came onto her face.

"Have you been spreading this story? You repeat this to anyone, I mean *anyone,* and you and that bastard husband of yours will be sorry."

"Oh, right. We don't belong here. We don't know anything about Sheffield. Yada yada." I put as much knowledge and authority into my face as I could muster. "You know what, Rita? I am really stinking sick of hearing that—from you or anyone else.

"And you know what else?" I waited until I knew I had her full attention. "Abhay knows."

I watched her dark face go gray and nodded. "That's right. The cops know. You think I'd be stupid enough to come talk to you like this if they didn't?"

I leaned back, enjoying being able to finally confront her while feeling slightly sick at the same time. "The dead rat on our front porch was unpleasant, sure. But I would strongly recommend that you and your husband stay far away from me and mine. The cops *know* you're guilty of two premeditated murders, and they're watching every move either one of you makes. You stay away from me."

Rita was sitting absolutely still, seemingly frozen, and staring past me. I pushed back from the table and set my now-empty mug, none too gently, on the table. "And something else. I have to think that most people in this town would rather have David and me around than a couple of vicious killers. Just a thought."

I forced myself to turn my back on her and walk away, knees shaking, across the room, down the stairs, and out the front door of the café, without looking back.

I was somewhat surprised, not to mention relieved, to see Abhay leaning against his vehicle parked next to mine on the street about half a block from the café entrance. I walked up to him, but a smile was a bit beyond what I could manage.

"You look pale, Felice. How did it go?"

"Well, thanks for being here, to begin with. Confrontations with people I know have killed other people aren't my strong suit." I took a deep breath and blew it out, trying to stabilize, then looked up at him.

"They did it, Tom. I let her know that you know, and that woman is scared. She was already on the edge—can you imagine the average person having to live with that for weeks? Now, she's not only upset, she is really scared."

"But she didn't confess to anything."

"No. I might be the right person to scare her, but I'm not the person to whom she might have confessed anything—especially since I think she feels a real need to protect George, even though I think she's disgusted by what they've done."

I smiled weakly. "Dime-store psychology, but that's the read I took from her. The big question now is: what will they do next?"

"Do you think they'll come after you and David?" Abhay's arms were crossed and his look was serious.

"I don't know. Do you think so? You know a lot more about criminals than I do."

He chuckled. "How does David put up with such a wiseass?"

"Habit, I guess. He likes my cooking and I fix his spelling. Really, Tom, what do you think happens now?"

"Let's go back to the station and talk about it—get David there, too. I don't know if they'll turn on you, but I think we need to be prepared for it."

Chapter Twenty-Five

Abhay and I followed each other's cars on the way back to the Public Safety headquarters. I had called David from the car and he met us there.

Once inside and around a table in a small conference room, Abhay sat thinking while I related my meeting with Rita to David. He listened carefully before turning to the Chief and asking, "Well, do we need to start packing?"

Abhay looked at him squarely. "It's an option."

I looked at the two of them with amazement. "No, it isn't! Beyond the logistics of packing up two people, two cats, and a deerhound, where on earth would we go? I can't think of anywhere that would take us. And I *don't* want to leave my house empty for anyone who might get the bright idea of vandalizing it."

I turned to Abhay. "How has the situation changed since yesterday? Has my conversation with Rita just now moved the case along at all?"

"Yes and no. I think you've put the fear of God into Rita Russell, and she'll certainly pass on your conversation to George. If that prompts them to take action, we'll probably have a reason to arrest both of them—him, at least."

Great. George Russell shows up to hit us with a blunt object or burn down our house, and THAT provides probable cause. This was not the sort of help I really wanted to give the police.

"On the other hand, we don't have any more evidence than we did, and we don't have a confession," Abhay continued. "Even if he doesn't take any action, hopefully your conversation has shaken him enough that I might get somewhere if I bring him in for questioning."

Frustrated, I leaned back from the table and stuck my hands in my cardigan pockets. There was a rustle from one side as my hand encountered something, and I pulled out a shiny piece of cellophane with purple printing on it. It took me a moment to remember why I had it: this was the sweater I had worn to walk with Becky and Angus along the river, and this was the piece of Summer Festival detritus I had seen and picked up, meaning to throw it away later in the walk. I looked at it some more, read the lettering in purple print, and had another of those "blood draining from the head" moments I'd last had while talking to Gary the semi driver.

"Oh, my God," I breathed, breaking into the conversation Abhay was continuing with David. "I do not believe it."

"What?" asked David, staring down at the piece of cellophane in my hand. "What's that?"

I held the shiny wrapper up before the two men. "It isn't much, but how about a small piece of physical evidence?"

"What," Abhay stared at it. "That?"

"Yes, this." I took a breath before starting in. "I don't think it will convict anyone, but I found this wrapper under a tree on the logging grounds during a walk a few days ago. I picked it up to throw it away and just stuck it in my pocket.

"I noticed at the time that it hadn't been there long—see how shiny it still is? This hasn't been rained on—and I just figured it was probably from the Summer Festival. It wasn't until just now that I remembered where I had seen something like it.

"This"—and I held it up high so they could see the lettering—"is the wrapper off a package of kale crackers. They're dark green; I can't imagine how bad they taste, but I can guarantee there wasn't any vendor at the Summer Festival who was selling them. Which means someone brought them. And the last time I saw a package of them was in the hand of George Russell."

I quickly described my conversation with George during the Water Resource Council meeting some weeks before and my wondering at his taste in snacks.

"And you're sure these are the same thing," Abhay said doubtfully.

"Absolutely the same package—and I've never seen them anywhere else. He must get them from a health food store or co-op, not a local market."

Abhay opened a drawer in his desk, took out a pair of tweezers and a plastic bag, and took the wrapper from me with the tweezers, placing the wrapper carefully in the bag before sealing it and writing something on it.

"You realize that this could have belonged to anyone and that, even if George did bring the package, even if his fingerprints are still on it along with yours"—I winced, but how could I have known?—"it doesn't prove anything except that he was on the logging grounds."

"I know. He had a reason to be there, and it could have blown from anywhere; he lives here, so it may have been dropped since the Festival. But it's real. It's tangible. Can you use it?"

He looked at the bag and its contents for a moment. "Yeah. Yeah, I think I can. If nothing else, it's a decent reason to bring him in again and try to convince him that we know he's guilty and it isn't worth holding out any longer."

David and I spent the rest of that day and all the next in that "agony of suspense" you read about but rarely feel. It was a bit like continually sensing some small insect crawling on your arms and legs even though you know there isn't anything there. We couldn't settle: moving from room to room and task to task, playing with the pets, reading something or watching the television, then putting it down or turning it off when we realized we weren't paying attention. We periodically looked out of various windows but saw nothing unusual. David finally disappeared into his office upstairs, his official location for puttering or just online surfing. I left him to it, then got the bright idea of baking something as a way of passing a couple of hours.

I have no recollection of what it was or whether it turned out decently: either success or a total flop is a definite possibility when I bake, since I don't do it often. David, when handed an example, just says, "Oh, *thank you*," and eats it, bless him.

One thing we did not do was go out. Angus got a short walk through the neighborhood, which is enough for a sighthound on a slow day, and we watched every time we let him into the fenced side yard to take care of business. We had no idea what sort of retaliation my recent activities might bring, if any, but we decided there was no need to tempt anyone by showing our faces around town.

Abhay finally called the following afternoon, about forty-eight hours since our meeting in his office. I ran to the phone in the kitchen when it rang, but David appeared in the room just as I picked it up. I angled the phone so he could hear all of the conversation.

"I thought I should let you know," Abhay said after basic greetings, "we've tested the wrapper here in the department and did get some partial prints off the cellophane. Along with yours, we identified those of George Russell."

I nodded to David. I hadn't thought it likely that anyone else would have brought those kale crackers to the logging grounds. All this did was confirm what I had suspected. I didn't ask why the police had Russell's prints to make the comparison: he could have had an arrest sometime in the past; they could have taken some elimination prints after Greta's death, although that seemed unlikely; he might even have joined some union or other that required identification prints. Now was not the time to inquire. Tom had had an officer take mine, as much as that bothered my privacy-minded attitude, because we knew they would be on the cellophane.

Abhay continued, "As we talked about, it isn't enough for an arrest, let alone a conviction; we already know that George was in the area all day on the Saturday of the Summer Festival. But finding the wrapper at the murder scene, with his prints, is enough to bring him in and try to shake him a bit.

"I know George some, and I think stressing the harm being done to the community is a decent approach to see if he'll confess. We can't work on him about the evidence we have."

"Not that you need any help from me," I responded when he fell silent, "but I agree with you. George is a community leader, and his position as a City councilor creates an assumption that he cares about Sheffield and its future. I think most people believe that about him. These crimes have certainly hurt it; he has to have seen that this summer."

"You've talked with him, Felice," Abhay surprised me by asking. "Is there any other approach you would suggest?"

This felt like a huge compliment from someone who had been dealing with difficult people for decades, at levels much higher than his current position or any I'd had. I stifled the momentary warm, fuzzy feeling to concentrate on his question.

"There is the environmental angle," I finally said. "You know how much he cares about that. We've come to the conclusion that this is all about the energy center. George indicated his support for it, but what if he's concerned about its environmental impact or something? The most earnest conversation I've had with him was when he was talking about the beauty of the water his house overlooks, and the City property is visible from there."

"I'd hate to think two people are dead because of a NIMBY issue," Abhay said with disgust. "But yeah, I may bring that up if other lines of questioning don't work.

"I'll call you two back when I have more." He hung up, and David and I were left to pace some more. Over the next few hours, we talked through every detail of the events of the past five weeks: the killings, the responses from people all over Sheffield, the Council meetings, the disagreements, the rumors we'd heard. We didn't come up with anything new. We could only hope that our part in the drama was over and that the professionals would get what they needed to bring the case to an end.

Chapter Twenty-Six

It was shortly after lunch the following day when we heard from Tom Abhay again. I had slept in that morning, apparently tired from all the mental activity of the previous day, since I certainly hadn't done much on the physical side. Angus was happy to get a longer walk that morning with David. The reality of George Russell being questioned certainly didn't remove all risk to us or ours, but you can't stay cooped up like a fugitive forever; it feels cowardly. Plus, we assumed that Rita was smart enough not to try anything while George was at the police station, even if my warning had not been enough to deter her otherwise.

I was sitting at the computer, checking on developments with former colleagues in my professional field, when the phone rang. This time, David answered one of the many landline extensions around the house – we have the line so we don't have to carry mobiles everywhere — and brought it into the room with my desk, where I had picked up another.

We exchanged the usual greetings, then Abhay stated flatly, "We had to let him go."

Silence on our end. It wasn't a huge surprise, but we had

hoped . . . the chief continued with details.

"It went pretty much as we all expected, and I sent him home a couple of hours ago. But there were some interesting developments. I'd like to talk it over with you some, but not on the phone. How would you feel about sitting in a cop car and drinking coffee?"

David and I looked at each other. He had been in on the recent meetings, so he might want to hear this. He shook his head as I looked at him.

"You go. You're the one with all the details of this in your head."

I smiled into the phone as I responded to Abhay. "I'll come. You do realize you're fulfilling all the stereotypes of cops on television, right?"

"Yeah, sure. But I don't do donuts," Abhay responded. "I'll be there in fifteen minutes."

True to his word, Abhay arrived in his marked SUV decked out in antennas and light bars. I was watching for him, so I shouted a goodbye to David, grabbed my big leather bag, and went out the front door to get into the oversized vehicle sitting by the curb on the side street.

He named one of the local drive-thru coffee outlets, which was fine with me, so we made our way through town toward the business. While there weren't that many people on the street, I couldn't help the realization that sitting in the front seat of a cop car with the chief made my part in this truly public, however it might have been talked about before. *Oh, well—if the case is solved, I don't really care whether my approval rating goes down a bit more.* Why I thought I would be castigated for helping to identify a killer, I wasn't sure, but that was the sort of energy that was seeping around the city.

We each ordered and received our preferred beverages, and Abhay drove the vehicle to the parking lot of the waterfront park, the same area where Becky and I had parked for our walk days before. Once there, he turned off the engine after opening windows—the breeze, as usual, was lovely and about fifteen degrees cooler than the overall temperature. We turned toward each other, as far as the heavily equipped front compartment would permit: there were radios, a screen, and various boxes of tech taking up a lot of space. I don't think anyone ever rides in a police vehicle for comfort.

"Like I said on the phone," Abhay began, "we had to let George Russell go this morning. We didn't have enough to hold him, and he certainly didn't confess to either killing."

"We knew he was smart. I wouldn't have changed my story, either."

"I could tell he was shaken a bit when I produced that cracker wrapper. I told him it had his fingerprints on it and told him where it was found, although I didn't tell him you had found it. I told him we knew he had been on the logging grounds where Mayor Sutton was killed.

"He tried to shake it off, and he found the weakness in the evidence pretty quickly. He admitted that the wrapper was his; the crackers are apparently from a health food store in Eugene and he eats them pretty regularly. Of course, with the fingerprints, he couldn't claim the wrapper belonged to someone else eating kale chips. I don't know how he stands those things, myself.

"And he jumped on the fact that it only proved he had been here at the park, and that was no secret; he and Rita played on and off all day that Saturday. When I told him about our witness, he blustered through it: he claimed he and Rita hadn't left the bandstand during the fireworks and our witness was just mistaken. I could tell he was prepared for that. They had to have known that someone might have noticed and decided in advance how to deal with it. You can't guarantee that every person in that crowd was only watching the fireworks."

Abhay stopped to take a deep sip from his coffee cup. I reviewed what he had said, went through the notes in my head, and asked him, "Were you able to confirm any connection to the energy center?"

Tom shifted in his seat and his face brightened a bit.

"Yeah, we had a bit of a breakthrough there. When he wouldn't crack based on the evidence, I shifted around to motive and told him we were pretty sure the killings were linked to a City issue. The more we found out about Greta Sutton and Dwight Orkman's dealings on that proposed energy center, I said, the more hinky it looked. He was on record in Council meetings as being in favor of the development, but I pressed him on whether that was true and whether he really thought it would be good for the city.

"Felice, I think he's been waiting for a chance to let loose on that, because it didn't take much to get him to start talking about it. He went on for a bit about the need for alternative energy, but when I brought him back to the City property, he got red in the face. What was this company really going to do with the property? How did anybody know that their motives were pure—that sort of thing."

"So, he didn't trust the proposal."

"That's the way he put it, but I think it had more to do with what building a facility would do to his own backyard. He went on a rant about water purity and wildlife, then went back to saying he didn't trust a company who would come to Sheffield for a project like this. He actually said that the project is suspect just because it was proposed for Sheffield."

I sighed. "There's that Eeyore attitude again. I have never understood that about Sheffield, but never mind."

"I knew there was something else behind what he was saying," Abhay continued, "but I couldn't get him to admit it. I had to change course again because we'd gotten all we were going to get on the motive.

"So I went back to trying to break his story. I told him we know that he and Rita left the bandstand during the fireworks; we know that the two of them killed Greta Sutton; and when Dwight Orkman made it clear that he was going to pursue the energy center after Greta's death and it came out that he had brought the project to town himself, we know that he went to his office and bludgeoned the city manager. Whatever trace he left in Dwight's office, we'll get from the lab in Portland, and then we'll have him for both murders."

I shook my head. "He killed two people—*they* killed two people—and for nothing. The energy center is going forward anyway."

"Yeah, I mentioned that. 'You're a leader of this community,' I told him, 'and you have to have seen the damage that's been caused by these killings.' I told him to consider the good of the city and confess so this can be over with and we can try to get back to normal. It didn't get me anywhere, but I think he took it in.

"We didn't get anything else useful after that, so I finally let him go about ten this morning."

We sat in silence as I processed everything that Abhay had told me. He was no doubt a skilled interrogator—he had pushed on every issue his department's investigation had raised, regardless of any small help from David and me. But he was up against a clever and intelligent suspect who knew the limited value of each small bit of evidence that had been collected and, also, what was not present. No forensic evidence that could not be explained away—even something that might arise from Dwight's office could probably be claimed as there from a previous visit. No DNA that was not equally dismissible. No one had come forward with a story of seeing George or Rita around City Hall the night of Dwight's death, and Gary the semi driver's testimony was an instance of "he said, she said" if George continued to deny it.

Still, it looked as though some cracks were appearing. George's avid environmentalism seemed to be in conflict with a standard "not in my back yard" response to a development within sight of his house. Maybe that warranted some additional pressure, as the rant on water issues Abhay mentioned indicated that George's usual rationality was not at one hundred percent.

I was about to start this discussion with Abhay—he had been sipping his coffee and looking down the river while I sat in thought—when the radio between us spoke.

"Dispatch to one-oh-three."

Abhay quickly put down his coffee cup, picked up the mic, and spoke into it.

"One-oh-three. What's up?" From which I deduced that this must be his vehicle number.

"Citizen report of D-B, 335 West Frontage Road."

Abhay glanced over to me before answering again. "Any continuing activity? Is there a reported perpetrator?"

"Negative. No reports of perpetrator or continued activity. Will you respond, Chief?"

"One-oh-three responding. I'm about a mile away now."

Abhay put down the mic and quickly turned to me. "Felice, normal protocol calls for me to put you out of the vehicle while I respond to a call. But it doesn't sound like there's any danger and I don't have a way of getting you home, so I'll take you with me. But promise me you'll do whatever I tell you."

"Of course."

Abhay put the SUV in gear, switched on lights but no siren, and headed out of the parking lot. He turned left on the street, heading away from Sheffield's business district, across the bridge over the river, along a lesser riverfront road that wound its way to the oceanfront bluffs where Sheffield ended a mile or so away. We didn't go that far, turning left again after only a hundred yards onto a small street and heading downhill, driving along a range of houses whose backs must face the estuary itself. I had not been on this street before but now envied those who lived here for their view, especially this time of year. During winter, the vista, other than trees, would be mostly gray in all directions, and they would have to fight the all-pervading damp more than those of us living higher, but it might be worth it.

The chief pulled into a gravel driveway that formed a circle in front of a two-story, square frame house that looked about fifty years old. It had the natural, deep brown of unpainted shingles with window frames painted a rust red and a front porch running along the full length of the side facing us, held up by square columns. The front door, oddly to me, was white. That was about all I had time to notice before Abhay pulled the vehicle off to the side, facing away from the house, and killed the engine.

"Stay outside. I'll be back when I know more."

"Of course," I said again. He was working, and I could tell he knew more than I did about what he was going to see inside; staying out of the way was the best thing I could do.

Abhay automatically checked his equipment as he got out of the vehicle and headed toward the house. I opened the passenger door and stepped out, but stayed on the far side of the SUV; I seemed to have a need to stay attached to it rather than straying around the front yard. My focus was all on the police chief and the front door he was going through—I didn't even look around as I normally would.

There was apparent silence for two or three minutes. The chief finally came out of the front door, looked toward his vehicle, saw me, and nodded his head before speaking into the radio mic on his shoulder. I took that as permission to come onto the front porch and walked across the gravel toward him. When I got there, I couldn't help noticing the sadness that emanated from him.

"Have you seen a dead body before, Felice?"

I nodded, wondering why he would consider having me see this one. "I saw a few while I was a reporter, years ago. Traffic accidents and fire victims, mostly. Not enjoyable, but I'm okay."

He nodded, turning to precede me back into the house.

I had an impression of a hallway with a cotton runner on the wood floor and a staircase to our left, running upwards back in our direction. We passed the bottom step, then went through a doorway into a large living room with windows facing the river.

The Russells'—for that's whose house I realized this must be—love of music was evident; two guitars were mounted on a wall, and recordings in various formats were stacked on shelves along with a lot of audio equipment. My peripheral vision also took in doorways to other rooms to our right and behind us, but I was focused on the cluster of living room furniture in front of us and what was sitting there.

George Russell's days of playing his beloved R&B were over. His body was slumped in a corner of a couch facing the windows, his long, graying tail of hair hanging over the arm. I didn't see any signs of violence, thank heaven—I had told Abhay the truth of my experience, but that was a long time ago and I'd had no connection to the victims. Instead, there was a prescription pill bottle on the dark wood coffee table in front of the couch and a single piece of folded printer paper with Abhay's name written on it.

Tom walked over to the table, pulling on a latex glove as he went. He picked up the bottle with that hand and looked at the label.

"It's an opioid, and the prescription is recent, so it looks like there were a lot of pills left. I think he had a back problem that caused him some pain." He tilted the bottle, which was clearly empty, then pulled a plastic bag from his back pocket and put the bottle into it, placing the bag back on the table. He was reaching for the folded piece of paper when there was a noise from a doorway to our left.

Rita Russell must have been the person who called the police, but I hadn't known she was in the house until she rushed into the living room, shouting something unintelligible and crying. She stopped in front of Abhay and her husband's body on the couch but immediately turned and saw me. Her face was mottled and ugly as she shrieked at me.

"You BITCH! What are you doing here? Get away from my husband, get OUT of my HOUSE! Don't you see he's dead, my husband is dead! You killed him, you fucking bitch, you and you"—pointing to Abhay—"and this town—you made him do this. Get OUT!"

I was paralyzed, dumbfounded. I think I tried to say something stupid like, "I'm so sorry for your loss," but I realized I could be of no help at all and turned to go out, to defuse the situation as best I could.

I wasn't fast enough. Rita grabbed something off an end table—I think it was a carved onyx bull but only saw for sure that it was something hard and heavy and about eight inches long—and rushed toward me, arm raised. I turned sideways and thrust one arm upward in defense while, like an idiot, holding the other in front of me in a fist (*what are you going to do, Felice, hope she runs into it and knocks herself out?*), waiting for the blow to fall.

Just before she reached me, her forward motion stopped suddenly as Abhay grabbed her from behind around the waist. He brought down the arm with the weapon, which fell to the floor at my feet, then took Rita to her knees while reaching for her other arm. He looked at me and motioned "Out" with his head while reaching behind him for his handcuffs, and I hurried to follow his instruction, turning toward the doorway to the hall, still dazed.

He called after me. "I've already called for another officer and an ambulance, Felice; send them in when they get here."

I turned back to him, nodded dumbly, then headed through the doorway and out of the house.

It was a shaky few minutes leaning back against the driver's side of the police SUV, taking deep breaths and repeatedly going over the events of the last few minutes in my head. I couldn't stand to get inside the vehicle; I needed sky above me and breeze on my face.

This time, I took the opportunity to look around. No wonder George had been so adamant about protecting his little bit of the environment; the location was idyllic. From where the vehicle was parked, I could just see around the corner of the house toward the river. The water is always moving as it passes Sheffield because of the tides; now it was deep, rippling past the house and sparkling in the midafternoon sunlight. There was birdsong in the trees and a couple of water birds swooping over the estuary, looking for an afternoon meal. The end-of-August air was clear—the sky that deep, slightly indigo blue I've only seen in the Pacific Northwest. Looking farther, I could see the empty area of the City-owned property just up the river.

The light wind was cool, even during the warmest part of the day; that, plus the merest hint of color on the hills beyond the estuary and a few miles inland, reminded me that summer warmth was gradually moving toward autumn and the inevitable beginning of the long rainy season. Other plants in the house's front yard confirmed it: the only blooms came from a patch of dahlias in front of one side of the porch. Other summer flowers were finished.

Nearer the house was a stand of tall conifers along with some alders: I could see how their shadows would move around the building as each day progressed. The place smelled of cedar and slightly salty water, sun and dust, since there now hadn't been any rain in months. The restfulness of it all healed my shakes, and I was calm again when another patrol car showed up along with an ambulance running lights but no siren. Happily, Becky was not in the crew that descended from that vehicle and headed inside.

I waited several minutes more—they all had a lot of sad work to do—then saw Tom Abhay come out of the house again. He crossed the gravel to me and joined me in leaning against the SUV, pulling a folded piece of paper out of his breast pocket.

"I should probably treat this as evidence, but—" he said, then handed it to me. "I think you should see it."

Like his other actions, George Russell's suicide had been thoughtful and planned, however dramatic. The note had been drafted on a computer and printed.

Chief Abhay,

Your interrogation of me was more successful than you knew. I have tried my best to salvage what I love, but I know now that I will not succeed. When I compare the magnitude of my actions with their likely outcome, I find that I have no alternative but to atone in a manner commensurate with what I have done.

Despite my earlier belief in her, Greta Sutton's actions as mayor proved that her self-interest would always come before environmental concerns. Do I believe in alternative energy research? Of course. Will I stand for my river, my ospreys, my local ecosystem being destroyed so that she can have a building with her miserable name on it? I will not and did not. I removed her, letting her taste some of the river she was endangering. Dwight Orkman proved to be a miserable puppet, even worse than she because he brought damage to my community in exchange for money and a job he did not deserve. I feel no remorse for removing him.

But this project is not going away. No one knows what harm it will cause, but it moves forward regardless.

You warned me that my actions were hurting Sheffield. I

have sought to save Sheffield from the folly of its leaders and from questionable "progress." I have been unsuccessful, but I will not remain to watch the devastation.

The letter was signed "George Steven Russell" in ink at the bottom of the page.

I have never been the kind of woman who collapses in a puddle as the result of an emotional event, and I have been judged cold because of it. Now, all I could think of was the waste and tragedy, and even stupidity, of what had happened today and what had been going on for weeks. I was deeply saddened but almost angry at the same time.

"Why didn't he just *say* something?" I nearly shouted. "He must have found out about the building before the rest of the councilors; why didn't he tell them about it, tell them about his misgivings and his concerns about the river? George was respected; people would have listened to him."

I stared out past the house, at the river, not really seeing it.

"We're already starting to forget the hold that Greta Sutton had over other councilors," Abhay responded. "He knew how determined she could be. He may have decided that it was hopeless to try to fight her in the normal way."

"Yes—but two murders, suicide, leaving his wife alone to face her own charges. I assume there will be charges against Rita?"

He nodded. "Not up to me, but it's likely. I think he was trying to protect her when I questioned him, but they had to have been working together. We know they were both gone from the music stage at the same time. I think she helped him drown Greta Sutton, and she probably drove the car when he went to City Hall to kill Dwight."

All I could do was shake my head, my eyes falling to the

gravel driveway at our feet.

"This is all so awful. So absolutely, bloody *stupid.*" I looked up and into Tom Abhay's tired face. "And you have a lot more work to do before you're finished with it. I'm sorry—I should be out of your way. Is it okay if I call David to come and get me?"

"I'd appreciate it. We may need a short statement tomorrow; I'll let you know. And Felice," he said, calling my attention away from fumbling for my cell phone and back up to his face, "thank you for your help."

I frowned—nothing effective I could possibly say—and nodded. Then we both turned away to do the next thing.

Epilogue

It was six weeks later, and both Kate Dennis and Becky Stevenson were at my house, enjoying an autumn afternoon's mild warmth in our sunroom. We had managed to find a mutual empty spot in our schedules to get together for—what else—coffee. However, the precepts of a higher quality of life, seemingly absorbed from the walls of our hundred-year-old lumber baron's house, required that I offer cups and saucers, tea if anyone wanted it, and a choice of tea bread or cookies, at least one of them baked by my own hands. These were arranged on plates on a tray, as well as I could manage it, but I stopped short of paper doilies: those have never made much sense to me.

Apparently, my house had rubbed off on Kate and Becky, too, because both had felt the necessity of showing up with additional baked goods. Now we had a veritable feast in front of us that all of us felt too guilty to eat. At least at first.

David felt no such compunction when he stuck his head through the French doors into the room where we were sitting and talking. He took one look at the laden table in front of the couch and announced with joy, "Goodies!" He grabbed a plate and loaded it up.

He did take a moment to glance at me and saw my look. But I wasn't going to embarrass him in front of guests, even good friends, to remind him of his decision to lose ten pounds, stated only the night before. He looked at his plate, back at us, said, "Great to see everybody! I'll come back later," and departed the scene. David likes good conversation; I knew he would be back after the plate was empty.

I had brought Angus's bed into the sunroom so he could enjoy the company and the afternoon sun. He was curled up, happily napping after receiving all the love and admiration he felt he deserved from the visitors. Our cats were more desirous of privacy, so after the feline equivalent of a frown when they looked into their favorite room and saw all the people, they had removed themselves upstairs. They were probably occupying the top of the bed, sound asleep.

The three of us had been wondering at the weather. The sunny days had persisted even to today, the fifteenth of October, at least a couple of weeks beyond the usual.

"The ground is bone-dry," I said to the group. "We've been watering our lawn and the garden plants to keep them from going brown."

Most people along the coast just let their lawns go brown during the summer and trusted their trees and shrubs to get their water from deep below the surface. Usually, that was enough to last through the dry months. But not this year.

"I have seen some clouds off to the west, over the ocean," countered Becky. "But nothing has come close yet. It's too bad there haven't been some events scheduled these last few weeks—the weather has been perfect."

We all thought about the events that had not occurred this

summer and the reasons why. But there had been enough talk about that since the end of July, and no one wanted to bring it up again.

Finally, I ventured, "I hesitate to say it, but things feel almost . . . normal again, if there is such a state." I looked at Kate.

"Normal operations, yes," she responded, "but not like they were before. We've lost four businesses from the city—they just couldn't make it through the summer with the events cancelled and no one coming into town. Some nonprofits have had to cut down on services as well."

I shook my head. Several people had lost their jobs, and many more trying to live on "not enough" wouldn't be able to get the local services they needed. It pulled the overall quality of life in Sheffield down a bit more. That was the reality of a town on the knife-edge between healthy community and deterioration.

"What about the election next month?" Becky asked. "Did you finally find enough candidates?"

"Yes. I have another two years in my councilor term, but it was like pulling teeth to get people to run for mayor and the other open spots."

Kate had decided against running for mayor herself but would remain as interim mayor—she had been voted into that position by the Council—through the end of the year. Whoever won the position in November would be sworn in in January. Anne Perez and Pete Ichikawa, shaken by the summer's events, had decided not to run for reelection.

"Thank heaven Dennis stepped up for mayor—and we managed to convince enough people on committees and boards who have some City experience to fill up the slate.

There won't be any competition for seats, but at least we won't have vacancies."

I had been happy to hear about Dennis Waitly's decision to move up to the top spot. He was sensible, he knew how to run an effective meeting to get things done, and he had deep roots in the community. It was good of him, too, because he knew there would be more work than usual to get Sheffield healthy again. His job would be made even more difficult by having to deal with several inexperienced councilors. Assuming Dennis won his race – Sheffield had seen some strange write-in results in the past — only Kate and Suzanne would be coming back to join him on the dais, and there would be new people in the other four seats.

"Dennis will be good," Becky spoke up. "Have you talked with him about the job yet?"

"Oh, yes," Kate nodded, "although there wasn't much to pass on that he didn't know. We've been sticking to basics until we have a new city manager and can get a real handle on the budget. Pat Gregorio, as usual, has been a lifesaver, but she says it may take years to mend the damage that Greta did."

There was another silence as we all considered what might be ahead. We could only hope that Sheffield residents would back the City government as it did what was necessary.

I got up to turn on some lights, as the afternoon seemed to be turning toward evening. The conversation turned to other subjects, the pile of goodies on plates was reduced a bit more, and Becky had us all laughing at one of her recent aborted ambulance calls. Then Kate looked out of one of the big sunroom windows and exclaimed.

"Where did *that* come from?"

We all looked out and our mouths dropped open in shock.

Somehow, while we were talking, the fading light had turned to solid gray. The cloud cover coming from the Pacific was absolute, with more moving east and getting thicker. The wind had picked up, too, lashing the tops of the Douglas firs and cedars near our house and around the neighborhood. As we looked outside, leaves from a nearby maple went tearing across our front lawn and the plastic lid from someone's trash can rolled up the street.

"Time to go," announced Becky, getting up and reaching for her jacket. Kate did the same, and they put them on as they headed toward the front door. Naturally, the light jackets they had brought, perfect for the late-summer day, were now completely inadequate. As I opened the front door, we all shuddered at a temperature a good twenty degrees lower than it had been. And on cue, the skies opened and the first heavy sheets of water came pouring down.

Becky and Kate shouted their goodbyes as they ran for their cars. I waved from under the large portico of our front porch and watched them drive off, drops splashing off the tops of their vehicles, bouncing off the pavement, and already starting to run down the street.

I stood, arms wrapped around myself, and looked at the collage of deep gray sky, silver drops, and almost-glowing neon green of vegetation, then sent my view downhill to a pewter river whipped to whitecaps by the gusting wind.

The long and eventful summer was over. The rains were here.

Acknowledgments

This book is the product of much experience and some hard-won knowledge, but it could not have been written without the willingly shared expertise of several people and the kindness and patience of others.

To Maj. Gen. David Enyeart, Oregon National Guard (ret.), for early and extremely helpful information on local police procedure in coastal Oregon.

To talented artist Becky Miller, for her insightful cover painting as well as great comments on the manuscript. More than once!

To Chris Haizlip, Larry Lehnerz and others who read passages, scenes and whole drafts as we went along. I appreciate your time, attention and recommendations, without which this would be a more-flawed book.

To my mother, Diane Mace, who helped in many ways. Even if she only made it to Chapter Six.

To Nick Courtright, editor *extraordinaire* Alexis Kale—whose coping skills are amazing—and others at Atmosphere Press, for their choice of this book and all the help and encouragement they have provided. I won't go all Sally Field on you, but your support is incredibly gratifying to a fiction newbie.

And to the residents of a certain area of coastal Oregon, who made the whole thing possible.

About Atmosphere Press

Atmosphere Press is an independent, full-service publisher for excellent books in all genres and for all audiences. Learn more about what we do at atmospherepress.com.

We encourage you to check out some of Atmosphere's latest releases, which are available at Amazon.com and via order from your local bookstore:

Saints and Martyrs: A Novel, by Aaron Roe

When I Am Ashes, a novel by Amber Rose

The Recoleta Stories, by Bryon Esmond Butler

Voodoo Hideaway, a novel by Vance Cariaga

Hart Street and Main, a novel by Tabitha Sprunger

The Weed Lady, a novel by Shea R. Embry

A Book of Life, a novel by David Ellis

It Was Called a Home, a novel by Brian Nisun

Grace, a novel by Nancy Allen

Shifted, a novel by KristaLyn A. Vetovich

HOW TO SAY "MURDER"
IN GAELIC

Chapter One

There are actually several ways to say "murder" in Gaelic.
I looked it up, later; it was one of those weird things you do
when your brain is casting around for a distraction from the
horrible.

I found Roberta Murphy's body. It was a beautiful Sunday
morning, the beginning of the last day of the Norfolk County
Festival of the Gaels. I was a volunteer and wasn't needed until
later but had decided to head to the fairgrounds early to check
on something; I didn't expect to see many people around. I
headed for the concrete block building being used by the Celtic
Association as a headquarters-slash-office well before eight
o'clock, an ungodly hour for a confirmed night owl. It was
locked up tight, but I had my husband's key; as a Board
member, he rated that, at least. Going through the steel door, I
had my eyes on another door halfway across the room, but the
sight on the floor was enough to stop my forward progress
instantly.

"Well, she'll certainly be remembered for this," isn't the
most charitable thought to have about a murder victim. On the

other hand, it isn't everyone who's found with a large Scottish claymore through the middle of her torso. In the twenty-first century. On the coast of Oregon, USA.

CPSIA information can be obtained
at www.ICGtesting.com
Printed in the USA
FSHW010719140721
83199FS